Craig, *Irish Times* Books of the Year

'McGill proves once again she is a masterful story-teller . . . historical fiction at its absolute best' *Lady*

'A novel to haunt you' *Sunday Mirror*

'Hard to put down, this atmospheric book will stay with you long after the final, heart-rendering denouement' *Belfast Telegraph*

'*The Watch House* is beautiful and lyrical, tender and fierce; one of those rare novels, with the power to break you clean in two . . . Bernie McGill writes with such lightness of touch and tremendous heart . . . this is storytelling at its best' Guinevere Glasfurd, author of *The Words in My Hand*

'Displays the surest instinct for human nature in all its complexity and fascination . . . endlessly intriguing and exhilarating' *Dublin Review of Books*

'An evocative novel that's brimming with suspense . . . [it] reels you in and keeps a grip on you until the very end' *The Incubator*

# THE WATCH HOUSE

BERNIE McGILL

First published in Great Britain in 2017 by Tinder Press
An imprint of HEADLINE PUBLISHING GROUP

First published in paperback in 2018 by Tinder Press
An imprint of HEADLINE PUBLISHING GROUP

1



Cataloguing in Publication Data is available from the British Library

ISBN 978 1 4722 3958 7

Typeset in Caslon by Avon DataSet Ltd, Bidford-on-Avon, Warwickshire

Printed and bound in Great Britain by Clays Ltd, St Ives plc

Headline's policy is to use papers that are natural, renewable and recyclable products and made from wood grown in well-managed forests and other controlled sources. The logging and manufacturing processes are expected to conform to the environmental regulations of the country of origin.

HEADLINE PUBLISHING GROUP
An Hachette UK Company
Carmelite House
50 Victoria Embankment
London EC4Y 0DZ

www.tinderpress.co.uk
www.headline.co.uk
www.hachette.co.uk

For Sarah

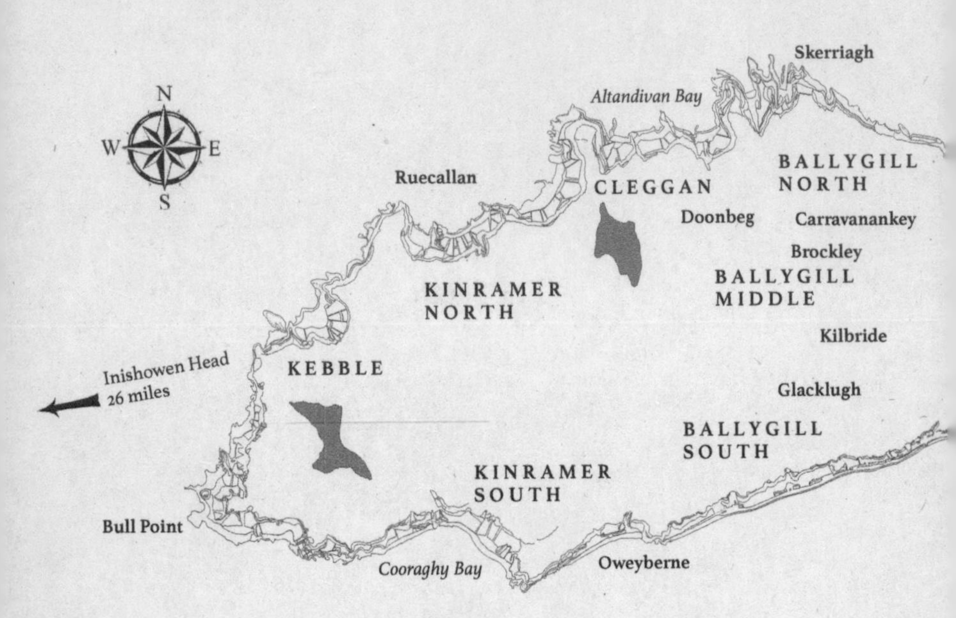


Rathlin Island

Rathlin Sound

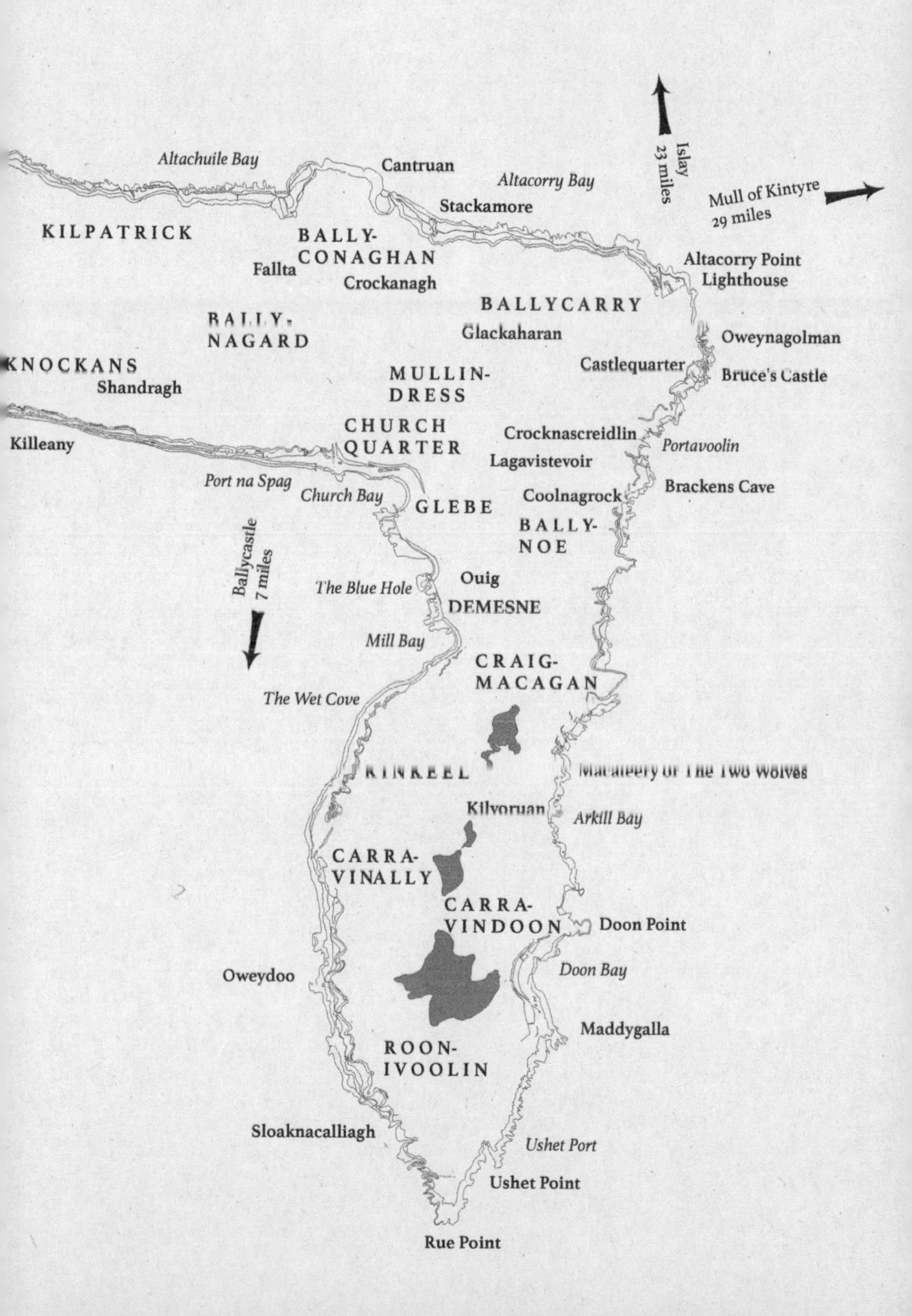
Altachuile Bay
Cantruan
Altacorry Bay
Islay
23 miles
Mull of Kintyre
29 miles
Stackamore
KILPATRICK
BALLY-
CONAGHAN
Fallta
Crockanagh
Altacorry Point
Lighthouse
BALLYCARRY
BALLY-
NAGARD
Glackaharan
Oweynagolman
KNOCKANS
Shandragh
MULLIN-
DRESS
Castlequarter
Bruce's Castle
CHURCH
QUARTER
Killeany
Crocknascreidlin
Portavoolin
Lagavistevoir
Port na Spag
Church Bay
GLEBE
Coolnagrock
Brackens Cave
BALLY-
NOE
Ballycastle
7 miles
The Blue Hole
Ouig
DEMESNE
Mill Bay
CRAIG-
MACAGAN
The Wet Cove
KINKEEL
Kilvoruan
Arkill Bay
CARRA-
VINALLY
CARRA-
VINDOON
Doon Point
Oweydoo
Doon Bay
Maddygalla
ROON-
IVOOLIN
Sloaknacalliagh
Ushet Port
Ushet Point
Rue Point

# Ginny McQuaid

## Rathlin Island, April 1899

The face of her, grey as flint, lying there in the iron bed.

Such a lot of blood to birth one measly thing. Grainne Weir said she'd never seen so much. 'But Nuala Byrne is young and strong, she'll get over it. Let her sleep. It's the best tonic for her. We'll give the child panada till she comes round.'

'You'll take a drop, Grainne? It's been a long haul. You'll have a wee drop for your trouble?'

The way it came out, the veil still round its face. I'd never seen the like of it and nor had the handywoman. Speechless, the pair of us, till she thought to wipe that thing off its face with a scrap of muslin like you would a cobweb off a windowpane. The yell it let out when its face appeared, fit to raise the dead. And Nuala Byrne in the bed moaning, only half sensible to what was going on.

'What a thing,' said Grainne Weir, after a sup, 'for an islander to be born in the caul. A child born like that, it can never be drowned,' she said, quiet. Putting curious notions into my head.

Nuala Byrne thinks that my oul eyes see nothing, that I didn't know what was going on the time she was up at the watch house. I had my suspicions, sure enough. And then, 'There'll be another mouth to feed in the spring,' said she, innocent as you like, rising from the fire, and our Ned the Tailor looking like she'd slapped him across the face, before he came round and smiled his big childish smile over at me like he'd done something right after all. And her, blowing the breath out her nose like the bellows in the forge pushing out air, like she'd gotten away with it, like she'd fooled us all. She might have fooled the Tailor with her story-making, with her telling of it the way she'd like us to believe it and not the way it was. Our Ned's a good man but he's an awful gam. God knows where he'd be without me. Nearly six years between us, I've always had the care of him. For all I know he believes he's begotten a child by rubbing his chin on her face. But I'm not fooled. Every morning since she's stepped over that threshold I've checked the sheets in the bed in the upper room and they've been as dry as if they'd just been shook out off the hedge. If there was to be another mouth to feed, I knew that mouth wasn't the Tailor's doing and I'd a fair idea whose doing it was.

And as for this blind runt with the blood at its ears and its sprout of black hair, swaddle it up with its mewling mouth closed, bind tight its wriggling fists and heels. Let Nuala Byrne believe it didn't thrive. She's that far gone with the pains and the blood-letting she knows no sense. Grainne Weir is too stewed with drink to remember anything other than what I tell her to remember and the Tailor, still on Islay, will believe anything I say: 'The child was sickly. Nuala wasn't fit to nurse it. That can happen with a first. The priest was off the island, you were away. Grainne Weir was wrung out working with her and the two days of her hollering. I buried it in the killeen over at Kilbride myself, in the unhallowed ground, before I left for the Fair. Nuala's healthy and strong. She'll get over it. There'll be other babies. You'll see.'

Kilbride is too far for me to walk but there are other ways to do. Thread a thick length of twine through the eye of the cracked loom stone that's been propping open the lower room door these fourteen months and more. Wrap the twine round the bundle, a good tight knot. Slip it into the basket under the fine linen napkins that the glenswomen go mad for at the Easter Fair. Tuck a piece of sail around it to keep the splash water out. April morning early, the warble of a skylark rising out of the barley rigs over by Coolnagrock, singing the same question over and over, bright, insistent, not a lullaby. The basket heavy and rocking with the weight of the bundle and of the stone as I walk up the road from Portavoolin to meet Dougal coming from Ballycarry on the cart, leaving Grainne Weir and Nuala Byrne sleeping, the pair of them like babies in the crib.

Climb up into the cart, grip the side tight.

'Walk, Susie,' says Dougal, believing what I tell him, knowing nothing of what I'm carrying, his big soft heart breaking for the Tailor and for Nuala with the sore sad news of it all. 'You should have sent for me,' he says, rubbing his hand over his great stubbled chin.

'There was no work in it for a man.'

'I could have buried the child,' he says. 'I would have done it with a heart and a half. It was too far for you to walk.'

'There are times when you get the strength from somewhere you didn't know you had,' I say to him. 'It was an important thing to do.' And Dougal nods, and I know from the set of his mouth that he's biting the flesh on the inside of his cheek the way his big soft father used to do to stop the tears from spilling. There's too much of the Duffins in my cousin Dougal, not enough of my aunt, who was sharp McQuaid through and through. He's no match for the cunning of a woman. The cart rattles over the white stones all the way down to Church Bay.

On the pier a commotion: three islanders, foorins from the upper end, trying to boat a cow. They have the beast coped over on a scattering of straw and they are going at it hell for leather, binding its legs, lowering it down with ropes into Jimmy Boyle's boat where it lies looking up at us like a dog curled on the hearth. Nobody pays heed to an oul' woman in a shawl with a basket full of linen for the Fair, and if there is a peep out of the basket, how would you hear it with all the roaring and bellowing of the beast? Push the napkins tight in round it, swaddle it up well. Who will buy this bonny bundle? Hah! No need to worry. It'll never make it as far as the mainland. A small thing makes a small splash in the swirl of Slough-na-Mara south of the Rue, where the eddy will swallow a thing and never throw it up again. No bastard child under my roof taking the McQuaid name. We'll keep this quiet. We'll get a son for the Tailor yet, his name on a piece of island soil. I've drowned many an unwanted kitling in the Lough in a sack with the mouth tied tight. One more'll make no difference.

## Nuala Byrne

### Rathlin Island, February 1898

Ash Wednesday, and every brow on the island is marked by the sign of the cross. Forty days of fasting and abstinence ahead of us, which is just as well, maybe, since I think there's many a head still throbbing from Saturday's celebrations. Me and the Tailor are four days wed.

We had a fine day. Dorothy made me a dress the like of which was never seen on the island before. A mauve skirt with a white bodice, an inset of Carrickmacross lace, a design in it of a four-leaf clover, a hat with a veil down over my face. The day she took my measurements she sat back on her heels in her little parlour above the shop in Ballycastle. 'Nuala Byrne you're a wonder,' she said up at me. 'I've never known a woman so balanced in her shape.' I love my cousin Dorothy, but she would be the first to say that in appearance she takes after her father's side, is built as lean as a brush shaft, looks like she'd snap in two if you bent her. She has fine, mousy brown hair and a small thin mouth. 'All the looks in the family slid to the one side,' Granny used to say, 'and you were on the lucky side, Nuala.' If that's true then all the skill slid to the other. Dorothy could turn her hand to anything. I would like to have been a dressmaker, I think. It'd be a fine thing to have a trade. But I never had the hands for it. I was always better at cooking, mixing up potions, helping Granda Frank with his cures.

'It's too good,' I told Dorothy then, eyeing the outfit. 'I'll never wear it again. It's a shocking waste of material for just the one day.'

'You'll need something to remember it by, and the bodice has a good long tail on it. It'll double as a christening robe when the time comes,' she said, winking at me. 'That's if the Tailor has any juice left in him.'

Dorothy Reilly, the things she comes out with. To look at her you'd think she never once had a stray thought, but she has a glint in her eye. I never let on I heard her.

She came over on the boat last Friday, laden down with garments for me, fitted me out with a trousseau, wouldn't take a penny for it. Lace-edged chemises and knickerbockers, a flannel petticoat trimmed with pink ribbon. And she had something else for me – a book called *Married Love*. I was to lie quietly in the dark on my wedding night, it advised, and await my husband's arrival. I was to desist from moving around too much until the act of consummation was complete. I would experience some discomfort, perhaps, but this was to be borne quietly. I thought Dorothy was going to burst, she laughed that much. It occurred to me that at the time I had accepted the Tailor's proposal, I hadn't given this area of the deal much thought.

'Do you really think it can be all that bad?' I asked Dorothy.

'You'll be fit to tell me soon enough,' she said, and off she went laughing again.

I didn't relish the idea of it. The Tailor is not a young man; he is nearly thirty years my senior. He is thin and slight, with skinny legs and a high hairline, and heavy-lidded eyes and a nose like a peregrine. He has thick white sideburns and a beard bordering his chin, and a poor show of straggly hair on his head. I think perhaps he was handsome once, though well before my time. Still, I've yet to hear anyone say an unkind word about him. He is not a cruel man, I think, and, as the whole island knows, we didn't marry for love.

Dorothy was insistent that everything was to be done according to tradition, so as not to bring bad luck on us. She headed out on Saturday morning and came back with a handful of snowdrops and maidenhair fern, wrapped them in lace paper and ribbons, made posies for the pair of us. The men called to the house. I was to walk ahead, she said, with Dougal, the Tailor's cousin and his best man; she would walk behind with the Tailor, and my uncle, Dorothy's father, behind them. There was frost on the ground when we set out. We were an odd procession on the road; Dorothy in Granny's old shawl, me in Dorothy's good plaid coat, such was the cold. 'Something borrowed,' she said as she held it for me to slip my arms into the sleeves.

As we passed the road up through Ballyconaghan, the warble of a clutch of Brent geese caused us all to stop and look up, and to follow them with our eyes as they passed over us. 'They'll be on their way to Newfoundland, to where your people are,' said Dougal, 'to tell them the news,' and a tear came into my eye for my absent family. Dougal saw it and lowered his head, regretting his foolery, and we walked on quiet to the chapel.

Father Diamond read our vows and we pledged our troth: to have and to hold, till death would us part, as the Holy Church had ordained. Those were solemn words. I felt the full weight of them, standing there in my bridal dress with the light from the stained-glass windows falling on to the tiled floor in green and red and gold. When it came time for the blessing of the ring, the Tailor slipped the loop of the door key from his pocket. There was nothing new in that; I'd witnessed it done a dozen times or more. There are few people on the island who can pay for a wedding band. But as I felt the metal, chill in the cold air, slide on to my finger, binding me to the Tailor, to the island, I found myself wondering how my days would change, what life in the Tailor's house would mean for me.

On the way back from the chapel, we walked through Church Quarter so as not to retrace our steps, past the school and the Pound House and the Big Garden and back along the low road to Portavoolin for the wedding breakfast. All the boats in the harbour had their flags up to mark the occasion. Dougal was ahead of us at the bend in the road with a bottle of whiskey to toast our health, and when we'd all had a sup of it he dashed the bottle against the stone gate post with the drop still in it. 'May your offspring be numerous,' he shouted, as is the tradition, but the bottle bounced off into the grass and didn't break, and he had to pick it up and fling it down a second time to smash it. When we got to the door, Ginny, the Tailor's sister, was waiting there on the threshold to hand me the tongs of the fire. I thought it odd at the time since the house is a new one and the fire has never been hers to hand over.

'I brought a hot coal from Church Quarter,' she said to the Tailor. 'It's the same fire we've always had.'

'We?' I thought to myself at the time, what does she mean by 'we'? But the Tailor looked delighted at this, turned and smiled at me, then stood back to let me cross the threshold first.

We had a great party: roast chicken and tipsy cake and custard and then the bridecake was broken over my head. When it was all cleared away we danced a dozen reels, Cal Stewart on the fiddle, Kiltie Clarke on the dulcimer, one of the young Harrisons beating out a rhythm on the bodhrán. The Tailor couldn't be persuaded to take to the floor, pleading aching bones from a draught he'd caught out in the punt, but both Dougal and Mr Kernohan from the Light marched me up and down till the new floor was well trodden in and Jamesie, the Tailor's other cousin, swung me till my head spun. Dorothy saw that everything was done as it should be. When I threw the stocking stuffed with oatcake it was her that got hit on the head. 'You're next,' I shouted at her, but Dorothy laughed at me. She has no notion of marrying. She told me as much the day I went to see her, to tell her I was for taking the Tailor. She's far too settled as she is.

Dougal had brought my things in the cart from Crockanagh on Thursday past and we'd unloaded them into the cottage. I don't have much of any value: a few pots and baskets and earthenware jars, blue plates from the dresser, a patchwork quilt Granny made, the crib I'd slept in as a child myself. 'Where do you want it?' Dougal said, carrying the cradle in and the question hung in the room like smoke that's been blown back down the chimney. I shifted it into the corner behind a hanging frame, covered it up with the quilt.

Saturday night, when the door had closed after the weddingers, when everyone had left apart from Ginny, and quiet descended on the house, the Tailor stepped over the floor to me, took my face in his age-spotted hands, leaned over and scraped the rough of his beard across my cheek. Then he looked over to Ginny, as if to say, 'Is that right?' and she nodded and smiled her old black-toothed smile at him, like he was a child taking his first steps. She walked over and opened up the settle bed and stepped into it and lay down, bleary-eyed with whiskey, under an old coat of the Tailor's. I lay down on the bed in the room behind the fire and the Tailor lay down in his combinations beside me. He smelled of the chalk he uses to mark the cloth and of poitin and of pipe tobacco, and of soot from the fire. I had the sash open. I like to feel the air, no matter what the weather's doing. I was lying on my back, looking up at the timbers, at the place where they meet the lathes under the new thatch, waiting for a word from him.

'Nuala,' he said, 'are you awake?'

'I am,' I said.

'There's a shocking draught coming in that window.' So I got up to close it and slipped back into bed and it was no time before I heard him snoring and grunting and before the grunts and snores of his sister began to answer him from the other room. The pair of them kept it up for hours till I began to wish they would choke on their own breath. I hit him a dunder in the small of his back with my knee and he let out a snort so loud he woke himself. Then he got up to use the chamber pot, except one of the weddingers had put Epsom salts in it for a joke and the whole thing fizzed out and up and over the top of the commode and he let a curse out of him and at the finish-up I had to get up and take the pot out to the midden to empty it.

A clear, cold night, the sky full of stars, the beam of light from Altacorry reaching out over the sea. The place was silent, apart from the ripple of the water. I could have been the only person awake on the whole island. On my way back from the midden, I stopped a moment to look down towards the Sound: Fair Head and Torr rising dark to the south, to the east, the lights of Sanda and Kintyre, and there, down by the shingled shore, a lone figure standing still, picked out each time the light passed over. I didn't go down and I didn't call out to them, whoever it was. I stood silent by the door, counting the seconds between each sweep of the beam: ten in the dark, fifty in the light, and still the figure stood there, with its back to the land, looking out over the Moyle, the light brushing over us both.

Then I heard a rustle from behind me and Ginny's voice: 'What are you doing standing out there in the dark with the door lying open? It'd founder you,' she said. So I stepped back in, to the glow of the embers in the grate and closed the door against them. In the morning the room reeked of the Tailor's breath and of his body. He got up and plootered out, bow-legged into the yard with the white hair still standing on him. When I looked out through the sash, the shore was empty.

I thought at first it might have been the Miller I saw. The Tailor's house is built on the founds of the old mill; the sea to the north of Portavoolin is where the Miller's four sons were lost. They were coming back from Islay with a new millstone in the boat when the current caught up with them. Their father was waiting for them by the headland, shouted and waved at them to turn the helm, witnessed the boat go down. They say his arm froze in that position, that he suffered a stroke on that very spot, that they buried him with the arm still twisted. The people say you can still see him nights, standing above at Altacorry, shouting to try and save his sons, waving his twisted arm. Those stories don't bother me, but I don't think it was the Miller I saw, I think it was a girl. Something about the turn of the head, the fineness of the figure, something familiar in the slope of the shoulders, the straightness of the back. I think I saw her one time before. I think I saw her in the Tailor's house.

That evening, in October last, a month or so after Granny passed away, the Tailor turned up at my door in Crockanagh in his good brown three piece tweed and cap. I don't remember him coming much to the house before, except once or twice when he was looking for Granda Frank to cure a sty in his eye. Granda was the cobbler on the island, but he had the cure as well, so the islanders used to come to him to have their feet measured when they had a bit of money, and to have their ills cured at the same time. He passed the cure to me, taught me how to mash up the herbs and mutter the prayers under my breath the way he used to, and after he died, I carried on, and gave the people the same directions that he had. They'd leave me with a can of cream or a shoulder of turf for payment and go on about their business.

I wasn't long in the door in front of the Tailor. I'd been to the mill at the Kil Avenue for a bag of oaten meal, had the sheepskin rim out on the table, ready to sieve it through. He came into the floor where I was standing and he said, 'How're you, Nuala Byrne?' and I said, 'I'm grand, Tailor McQuaid. How're you, yourself?' Hardly anyone uses the Tailor's given name; even Ginny rarely calls him Ned. But then he did a strange thing. He lifted the tail of his jacket and moved over close to me. 'What ails you, Tailor?' I said to him, growing nervous that he wanted me to lay my hands on some part of him. But it wasn't the cure that the Tailor was after. 'Feel the heft of that,' he said, passing me the tail of his coat. 'Our Ginny wove it into a fine herringbone and I cut it to fit myself. Six shillings a yard if you were buying it in the town.' So I reached over and felt it, what else was I to do, and I said, 'That's a grand jacket, Tailor, will you take the weight off your feet?' He sat down on the stool by the fire and just as quick rose up again. 'They say you're for America,' he said, 'now that your grandmother's gone, God rest her.'

'Newfoundland,' I said to him. 'As soon as I can go.'

'That would be a terrible loss to the island,' he said, 'a fine girl like yourself.'

It'd been a while since anyone had called me a girl. I opened my mouth to answer him when he started up again. 'I have a strong house near finished at Portavoolin,' he said, 'in good stone from the old tumbled mill. Will you come and have a look at it?'

I eyed him like he was away in the head, wondering did he think I could cure damp in stone as well as in bones and I said to him as kindly as I could, 'What would I be looking at a house for?'

He licked his thin lips and then twisted the cap in his hands and looked down at the floor. He said, 'I got the lease of it from old Benson the time the rents came down a while back. I've done nothing with it these years, only tie the punt up there, but I thought, maybe, if you liked it, you'd take it – and me into the bargain.'

You could have knocked me down with the draught from the chimney. He seemed half terrified, like I might take a swipe at him with the bag of oaten meal. His Adam's apple bobbed up and down in the craw of his throat while he waited for me to answer him. I was thinking what a good story this would make to tell Dorothy, or Mammy when I got over to Newfoundland, but then I thought of the bravery of his coming to me like that, and I thought I could spare him an hour of kindness. So I said, 'I will, then. I'll have a look at it.' And I went with him.

It was a short enough walk over to the well and through Glackaharan to the road down to Portavoolin. The Tailor talked to me the whole cut of the way about what a great house he had. I hadn't been down that way in years; I'd no call to be. Portavoolin is a lonely spot on the shore on the east side of the island. The path down to it goes nowhere else. But it was a pleasant enough evening, the sky just purpling, the cold of the winter not yet taken hold, rabbits scattering to the east and west of us as we walked down the loanen, the strip of green grass running like a chaperone between us.

Nearer the sea the path steepened and dipped down alongside the millrace. I could see the roof of the house below, the new yellow thatch lashed tight with strong rope, the whitewashed stones anchoring them at the eaves. The cottage faces the shore, is well sheltered behind by a clump of alders, a yard set with cobbles at the front, a shingle path that leads down to the old pier. A new red-painted half-door opened directly into the kitchen, a big open chimney inside. An empty dresser stood to the right, a fine deal table in the middle of the room; against the wall to the left, a newly varnished settle bed with the hinges and latch well oiled, above it a good wall clock in a teak frame on the whitewashed wall advertising Goulding's manures. I looked up through the lathes in the roof to the thatch above. 'The timbers,' said the Tailor, 'were salvaged off the *Girvan* the time it went down off the upper end with the cargo of whiskey on board.'

I nodded and smiled. Granda used to tell the story. 'The time the pigs were drunk for weeks,' I said.

There was a good-sized room behind the fire, another at the lower end, no furniture in either. The second room had high shelves and pegs that I took to be meant for the Tailor's work. But when we came back into the big room, there was a change in the air, a movement over by the fire and there, down on her hunkers, running a poker through the empty grate, looking like she owned the place, was a girl I'd never seen on the island before.

I turned to the Tailor and looked at him for some word of introduction or explanation, but he smiled his wide smile at me and said, 'What do you think?' and made no sign of having seen her or having noticed anything strange. I knew enough by then to make no mention of her. The dead don't usually show themselves to me, though I hear them often. This one was silent.

I nodded to the Tailor. 'It's a fine house you have,' I said, and I walked to the window on the pretence of looking out, and then turned back to examine the girl. She was dressed like a fisherman, or a farmer, with her head uncovered like mine. She looked younger than me, twenty or thereabouts, her dark hair brushed off her face, pinned into a roll at the back of her neck. Sun-darkened skin, blue eyes the shape of plum-stones, dark eyebrows, a serious face, intent on the dead fire, staring into it, a face, I thought, not given much to mirth.

The Tailor followed my gaze. 'I had the hearth laid in the old style,' he said. 'Dougal made a good job of it, I think?' I nodded at Dougal's work, a crescent of black and white pebbles laid into the floor, the girl still crouched there, not heeding either of us. 'Does it please you?' asked the Tailor.

I was about to answer him when there was a rattle at the latch and in walked Ginny. She looked me up and down the way you would a heifer going to market and nodded her old hairy chin. Then she reached out and took me by the two hands. 'A great strong lass,' she said, 'indeed, with good cold hands for the butter-making and the baking,' and she smiled at the Tailor with her two black teeth. Neither of them made any mention of the girl and when I turned my head back to the fire she was gone.

'I'll have a think about it,' I told the Tailor that day when I left him and Ginny in the cottage, with no real notion of thinking about it at all, but I felt a pity of him, soft-spoken as he is, and I walked back up to Crockanagh wondering about the girl. There is only one door in and out of the Tailor's house and Ginny was standing in front of it. I know for certain the girl didn't use it.

I was still very young when I first started hearing things that other people didn't hear. It must have been soon after my family left for America. My mother and father and my two brothers took the boat over twenty years ago, out to my father's people who had themselves left in the forties when times were so bad. I was too small and too sickly then to go, plagued with asthma, so they left me with my mother's people, with the promise to send the passage when I was old enough to travel on. They settled in Pembroke, Maine, where the men found work in the steel factory but after it closed, they moved north into Canada to an island that healed their homesickness for a while, to the fisheries in St John's in Newfoundland. They did well there until six years ago when a fire that had started in a stable in the east end swept through the town and destroyed their house, along with three-quarters of the city. By then, Granda and Granny were the ones that needed help so I stayed on the island where I was needed.

At first I confused the voices I heard with living voices and I'd answer someone who wasn't really there, or who was only there in my head. Granny and Granda would look at me strangely and say, 'Who are you talking to, Nuala dear?' I took to carrying my raggy doll everywhere, said I was only talking to her. I had enough wit even then to know not to tell them the truth. They'd have carted me off to the priest to drive the devil out. I heard Granny and Granda one night by the fire, whispering, when they thought I was asleep in the loft. I loved to lie and hear them talk, my hand on the heat of the chimney breast, the smell of turf smoke in my nose, my little quilt pulled up to my chin. Granda's wooden lasts all hung about in pairs from the hooks in the rafters like they'd grown there; I remember them casting strange flickering shadows on the rough white walls in the firelight. 'Every foot on the island is hanging from our roof,' Granda used to say. Sometimes when I fell asleep I'd dream about them, that they all took off walking about the island at night, looking for their owners, knocking on cabin doors.

'She's a strange child,' Granny said, 'like one that's passed this way before.' In the yard at school, Nancy Gilmore nicknamed me Cock Robin, said I always had my ear cocked, listening for worms in the ground, and everybody laughed at me and pointed and chanted the name over and over. I stared at her until a voice came into my head and the voice was a man's that said, 'Come on out into the byre, child, and give me a hand with the cow.' So I said that to her, low, so no one else could hear and the colour all slid off her face of a sudden the way you see a cloud sometimes slipping over the side of Knocklayde on an otherwise sun-bright day. She said, 'How did you . . . ?' but she didn't finish it and backed away from me. I don't know whose voice it was, but it meant something to her for she never spoke two words to me again and no one called me Cock Robin after. I don't know what she said about me to the rest of them. So long as they let me be, I didn't much care.

I got used to them, the noisy dead, and with practice found a way to drown them out with other sounds, and now they're as much a part of my hearing as the screegh of the shearwater overhead or the jabble of the ebb. They're at their noisiest at night when the living are quiet, when there's a better chance of them being heard. I never hear my own people, though. I was afraid of that but I don't. I think I only hear the lonely, or the vengeful, or the aggrieved. I like to think my own people are at peace.

Dorothy wasn't pleased about Granda passing me the cure. 'That'll be you tormented now,' she said, 'with the whole island coming the way they did with Granda Frank, beating a path to the door with their aches and pains.' But everyone that came brought something and I was glad of it after Granda and then Granny had gone. I'd no other way of feeding myself. When the people came, I'd listen to what ailed them and I'd press my hand into theirs and I'd try and hear what the voices had to say and if one of the voices lifted clearer than the others and spoke words of comfort, then without knowing who was speaking, I'd use those words back to them again and the sufferer's heart would ease. Listening's a gift too. There's not many has it. Sometimes I think that's what Granda taught me and not the cure at all.

Dorothy was sent over in the summers, to keep me company. Many's the night's dancing we've had in the kelp house on the island, swirling round the floor, our skirts flying to 'Shoe the Donkey' or 'The Haymaker's Jig'. The men couldn't houl' foot to us. But they didn't come to me looking for love. I've seen them give a glance or two in my direction. There was the odd bit of grappling at the bottom of the steps coming out, maybe, after the dancing, in the dark of the lane. But the truth is, they've been wary of me since our school-days, since Nancy Gilmore said whatever it was she said about me. The cure makes them warier still. There're those on the island that think an ailment leaves a stain, that it can't really be cured, but is passed on to the healer. They think I'm full of all their ills, like I've eaten them. Even Dorothy asked me once if I wasn't afraid of that. I was looking forward to getting out of here and going to Newfoundland, to a place where nobody knew a thing about me.

The day after the Tailor's offer, I went to the post office and there was a letter with the orange Newfoundland stamp on it, the face of the Princess of Wales in her pearls and her beautifully curled hair. Cissy Turner handed it over the counter to me. 'That'll be your passage coming now,' she said. 'It'll be no time till you're away.' Cissy knows everyone's business, or thinks she does.

I took the letter from her and put it in my apron pocket. 'I'll open it at home,' I said, which wasn't what she wanted to hear, and then, as I was turning out of the shop, I said to her: 'The Miller, up at Portavoolin, did he have a daughter at any time?'

'The Miller?' said Cissy. 'Not that I ever heard of. Just the four sons that were lost.'

'And his wife, when she died, was she a young woman?'

Cissy shook her head. 'She outlived him by a good lock of years. Why do you ask?'

'No reason,' I said to her, 'just a notion I had.'

I took the letter home and opened it by the fire in the cottage in Crockanagh, but it wasn't the letter I wanted at all. I'd sent a sorry tale to my mother and she was sending one back again. She was heartbroken, she wrote, at the news of Granny Cat's passing, and so soon after Granda, too. Though it was many a long year since they'd left the island, she had always dreamed of seeing her mother and father again and now that dream was gone. Things weren't so good in Newfoundland, she wrote. They'd been putting a brave face on it in their letters home, but the truth was, they'd never really recovered from the fire. In short, there was no money for a passage, and no prospect of it. She was sorry, she said.

I looked around at the cabin I was born in and that

never would be mine, at the dirt floor I'd tramped over for nearly thirty years, at the lank bit of lace curtain that dipped on the length of twine at the window, at the black soot from the chimney that joined the white dust from the walls, and formed a grey layer that settled on everything no matter how much I dusted and swept. No amount of curing under this roof, for a handful of eggs one day or a pat of butter the next, was going to earn me a passage to Newfoundland. And then I thought about the Tailor and the Tailor's new house. I thought that I'd never heard him raise his voice, that his hands were fine, that his fingernails were short and clean. I was thinking there could be worse companions. I thought of what it would be like to sit on a stool by the fire in the evening with the Tailor for company and the wind howling outside, and a good strong roof over my head and not have to worry about where Benson's rent was coming from. I thought of what it would be like not to have to scrimp and save. I had done my duty by my mother's people. I had stayed to tend to them into their old age. I had done the work that by right my mother should have done herself. I owed her nothing more. I took the letter she'd written me and I threw it on the fire and I watched it blacken and smoke and curl. I would have liked to have burned the news that was in it. I would have liked not to have read it at all, but having read it, I was unromantic about my options. I walked down to Church Quarter, to where the weavers' houses stood, and knocked on the Tailor's door.

'You'll not go?' he said on the threshold, his thin eyebrows lifting.

I shook my head. 'I've decided to stay.' The Tailor smiled his wide smile. 'I haven't much in the way of a portion,' I told him.

'Haven't you a cow?' he said. 'Many's the one came with less.' And so the match was made. The Tailor undertook to get the licence. We set the date for the last Saturday before the start of Lent.

The morning of the Apple Fair, crisp and bright, I crossed to Ballycastle on the mail boat and walked up to the Diamond to tell Dorothy about the Tailor's offer. She was with a customer, a black-haired lady with a basket on her arm, tall as me, who smiled shyly as she left. Fair Day is busy for her, but Dorothy always has time for me. She got Sadie, the neighbour's girl, to mind the shop for a half-hour and the two of us settled into the window in her upstairs parlour with a pot of tea and a plate of soda bread between us. The Diamond was packed with carts and cattle up the street as far as Mooney's. I knew she wouldn't take the news well about the Tailor, so I brought her a pot of gooseberry jam. The situation needed sweetening.

'That was Mrs Corcoran in the shop,' said Dorothy. 'Her husband's doing all the work in the chapel. Did you see the way she does her hair? That must be the style in Belfast.' Mrs Corcoran was crossing the road outside, her shiny black hair piled high on her head, the curls falling down round her face. 'And there's Dougal – was he on the boat with you? God love the creature, he's running errands for everyone on the island, as usual. Remind me to give you a barnbrack to take back for his mother. I hear she hasn't been well.' I watched Dougal stop to let Mrs Corcoran pass, his thick pink lips and round apple cheeks, his belly hanging over the waist of his britches, and I wondered, not for the first time, why it was that Dorothy always seemed to have time for him. I listened to Dorothy chatter for a while and then there was nothing for it but to come out with it.

I crossed my hands in my lap. 'I've heard from my mother,' I said.

'Well?' said Dorothy.

I looked at my hands. 'There's no money for a passage.'

Dorothy sighed. 'Ach, Nuala,' she said. 'I'd give it to you gladly if I had it, though it makes my heart sore to think of you going. And Daddy's sent them everything he could to get them lodgings after the fire.'

'I know that, Dorothy. I wouldn't ask it of either of you. You've done more than was your due.'

'What will you do now, do you think?'

I waited until she took another mouthful of soda bread and jam, then I took my chance. 'The Tailor has made me an offer,' I said, 'and I'm going to take him.'

She stopped chewing and stared at me, wide-eyed. After a moment, she swallowed the bread: 'Ned McQuaid, the Tailor from Church Quarter?'

'The same.'

'Nuala,' she said, 'tell me you're codding.'

'I'm not. He has a great house built out at Portavoolin with three rooms. He took me to see it and I've given him my word.'

'Jesus, Mary and Joseph,' she said, 'there must be thirty years between you.'

'Near enough,' I said.

'Ach, Nuala, no. He's a wee runt of a man. If you're

not going to Newfoundland, there's plenty of good stout fellas about, you could have your pick.'

'There's not too many of them with a decent house in the bargain.'

'What about Clem Duggan?'

'Sure he's never bothered with me.'

'You never give him any encouragement, Nuala. You look at the men like you'd take the head off them if one of them looked the road you're on.'

'Clem Duggan hasn't a good new house. His mother and father are both still living and they've no word of dying, either of them.'

'Randal Smith. He has a house.'

'He hasn't two straight eyes in his head. He spends every penny at Jem Sorley's still. I met him on the road the other morning, the old pratie sack britches hanging off him by a length of twine. The place is falling down round him.'

'Ach, Nuala, there's somebody for you.'

'They don't trust me, Dorothy. They think there's something odd about me.'

'There is something odd when you're talking about taking that old galoot the Tailor, a young woman like you.'

'I'm not young, Dorothy, that's the difficulty. I've

waited half my life for that letter from Newfoundland and now it's never going to come. Old maids is what we are, whether you like to admit it or not.'

Then, 'What about Dougal?' she said, and looked at me, a challenge, and I had to stuff my mouth with soda bread to stop myself from laughing. Dougal is a big kind soul, he'd do anything you asked him, but even an old man like the Tailor is a more marriageable prospect than him. Dougal with his back bent and his big chin jutting out in front of him, marching to some tune that only he can hear.

'You can take Dougal, if you want him,' I told her. 'I won't get a better offer than the Tailor. It's all right for you with your good warm work and a roof over your head and your father still here to mind you. I'm fed up scraping and grasping for the rent on that pitiful parcel of ground. Old Benson can have it back and welcome. I'll take the Tailor and be glad of him.'

'Have you written to your mother yet?'

'She has no say in it. I'm my own woman now. I'll make my own decisions.'

Dorothy supped her basin of tea and looked out the window. 'Is there anything I can say to turn you?' she said, and I shook my head. Dorothy sighed. 'Then the least I can do is make you look decent on your wedding day.'

'Thank you, Dorothy. You're a true friend.'

I left Dorothy in the shop mulling over the news and slipped out the side door into Clare Street and up to the chapel to light a candle. It was cool and dark inside and quiet. There was a ladder propped against the wall in the side chapel where the candelabra stood, heaps of small tiles on the floor, a man in overalls with his back to me. When I got closer, I could see that he was working on the mosaic, that there was a drawing on the wall into which he was setting tiles: the Madonna and child, her hair and body veiled in blue, a gold halo above her head. Her eyes were downcast, her mouth downturned, her nose long and straight. She looked sad, and tired. She was holding the blessed infant loosely, without energy. He looked like he was trying to escape from her. The man, Mr Corcoran, turned and nodded at my step, then bent back to his work. I did not have great hopes for my union with the Tailor, but I said a brief prayer that it would be a happy one and that one day I might know what it was to feel the weight of a child on my knee. A child would be a blessing to have, I thought, someone of my own to love.

* * *

I hoped that Ginny's sleeping in the settle bed was an arrangement for the one night, but the day after the wedding it was clear she wasn't for shifting. Dougal and Jamesie and some of the other men began carting the Tailor's things up from Church Quarter. I wondered at them putting his fine oak-topped work table and sewing machine and stool by the window in the kitchen. 'I need plenty of light to work,' he said. The bolts of cloth and pattern books and spools of cotton they piled on the shelves in the lower room. Then the next thing I knew, what was coming in through the door only Ginny's dismantled loom, and there she was up directing them as to how to install it in the room at the lower end. Dougal dropped the loom stone on the cobbles carrying it in. It cracked but didn't break. 'It'll not do,' said Ginny, 'the threads'll tangle in it. We'll have to get another one. This one'll do for stopping the door.' And it was then I realised she wasn't going anywhere. This was to be her house too.

I took the Tailor aside. 'You didn't tell me,' I said to him, 'that Ginny was part of the bargain.'

He looked at me with startled eyes. 'Sure, I couldn't leave Ginny on her own,' he said. 'She's looked after me my whole life. And isn't there plenty of room for all of us?'

'Will you come in to them, Tailor,' shouted Ginny, 'before Dougal has the whole thing smashed to bits?' And he took off into the lower room after her and left me standing on my own.

It had taken them two days to set up the loom and as soon as they had it finished, Ginny settled herself on the wooden seat with her back to the open door and the heat of the kitchen and began threading yarn through the eyeholes of the heddles. And in no time at all the thud of the reed on the fell of the cloth and the creak of the turning of the take-up roll have become the steady rhythm of the Tailor's house. It is hard and heavy work, but Ginny has been doing it for so long it is like a dance to her. The shuttle shoots across the warp, her feet on the pedals tap out the beat to which everything else keeps time. And I can't help but think as I look at her back, watching her work, her right hand on the wood of the picking stick, yanking the cords, her left hand on the batten to press the yarn, that she is like the puppeteer I saw one time at the Lammas Fair, making the little wooden stringed puppets dance to every flick of her wrist.

## Nuala

## June 1898

Ginny has the toothache. She only has the two black teeth in her head that I can see and both of them are giving her bother. She blames the spinning, years of pulling linen thread through her teeth to dampen it. There's hardly a spinster on the island over thirty that has a tooth left in her head. She has me up at Mullindress gathering yarrow to ease the pain in her jaw. She has put a stop to the people coming to the Tailor's house, looking for the cure. She says curing is a gift for a single woman and has no place in a married woman's house. It's an odd thing for Ginny not to want to profit from something I have to offer. I think in my heart she's a bit afraid of the power it gives me, though she's not against me using it to cure what ails her. She can stop the people from coming but she can't reach her hand inside my head. She can't prevent me from hearing what I hear and seeing what I see. I go to anyone that asks for my help and I do what I can for them. If Ginny knows it she doesn't say.

It's a relief to get out of the house, away from her gumming and shooting dulse into the grate, the red juice running down the sheugh of her chin. She's as sharp as a blade of arrow grass, is Ginny. I can't move two steps but she's asking me where I'm going, giving me some task of her own to do while I'm about it. But there's a good view from Mullindress down over the harbour, and I have my own reasons for coming down. Jamesie Duffin took the boat to Ballycastle this morning early to pick up the strangers. If I bide my time, I'll get a look at them when they come in. The priest has told us about them. They are Marconi's men, come to catapult their words out over the sea.

I was coming out of the chapel a couple of weeks ago when I was last over in Ballycastle and Miss Glackin, the priest's housekeeper, stepped out and waved me into the parochial house kitchen. She's an island woman, she's always after news, but this time she had news for me.

'Come in, Nuala Byrne, till you see,' she said. 'Only Father Diamond has gone and bought himself a gramophone and he's giving a demonstration.' I stepped into the parlour where the priest was playing master of ceremonies. The mosaic man, John Corcoran, was there with his wife. His overalls were all caked with white putty and lime, but I could see that he had washed his hands and that one of them, the left, was cupped under his wife's elbow, as if to steer her away, to protect her, from the boom of Father Diamond's voice.

'Welcome, Nuala Byrne,' shouted Father Diamond. 'Come in, come in, come in.' Father Diamond is a big, red-faced man who looks more suited to life as a publican than to that of a parish priest. He's been looking after us on the island ever since our own priest left. He has a very definite twinkle in his eye. I nodded to the Corcoran couple and stepped forward. The parlour is not a comfortable room. It is long and narrow with a dark wooden floor and a rug in red and blue that does nothing to lift it. The gramophone sat on a polished wooden table under the window, its big black horn sticking out like a trumpet into the room, a metal handle jutting out like a thraw hook underneath. Father Diamond picked up a black rubber disc with a hole in the middle and with great ceremony laid it down on the machine. He turned the handle like you would to twist a straw rope and released a little brake and then set the metal arm down on top of the disc. There was a sound like the keel of a boat scraping over stones and then a crackle like when tinder catches and, despite ourselves, me and the two Corcorans jumped near out of our skins. Father Diamond laughed his big loud laugh and Miss Glackin grinned and then there was the sound of piano music coming out of the machine. I looked to the corner of the room, to where the piano sat, lid down, stool empty, but of course the sound was not coming from there. I'd never heard music like it before in my life.

'Ragtime!' declared the priest. 'It's the newest thing – from America.'

'Ragtime?' said John Corcoran, and his wife looked at him with wide eyes. 'Is that what they're calling it?' And Miss Glackin nodded her head, now an authority on all things musical.

'What an extraordinary thing it is,' I said.

'Extraordinary is the word,' said Father Diamond, 'and getting more extraordinary by the minute. You haven't heard the latest, Nuala. A letter, from the Wireless Telegraphy and Signalling Company, expressing an interest in the use of the church spire as a site for their latest experiments.'

'I hope you gave them short shrift, Father?' said Miss Glackin, her face pinched. 'You won't want them traipsing about here, clambering all over the chapel roof.'

'And send them to the Protestants?' said Father Diamond, winking at me. 'I told them they were very welcome to try the spire if they wished. If they're going to be sending signals to the island, we must do what we can to ensure that it's Catholic signals they're sending.'

Miss Glackin looked mollified at this answer and Mrs Corcoran smiled at me, a beautiful smile, and looked down again at the gramophone, and I was trying to think who it was she reminded me of and then I had it: the Madonna in the mosaic in the side-chapel. And I smiled to myself at the thought that John Corcoran had given the image his own wife's face.

I turned to the priest. 'They're coming to the island?' I said.

'Imminently,' he said. 'They have backing from Lloyd's of London, to report on the progress of the shipping. They'll be based at the lighthouse at Altacorry, sending signals out over the Sound. We are at the very forefront of technological advances, Nuala. We must not be backward. We must grasp the nettle with both hands!'

So here I am, up near the Big Garden where the plum and the apple and the greengages grow, with a clear view over Church Bay and of any boat that appears. The morning is still, the island stretching out green to the lower end in the east, rock and heather to the west. Below, by the Waterguards' houses, the Tailor has the cart backed into the water, alongside Dougal's boat and old Susie the horse is standing steady as she's bid between the two shafts. The Tailor is balanced on the wheel and he and Dougal are unloading turf from the deck of the *Curlew*, and they have it heaped up on top of the cart and the horse barely moves except to worry her harness and blow steam out her nose at the cloud of midges that have gathered round her head. Dougal swivels from side to side with every sod of turf he unloads, the lock of blond hair on his forehead lifting as he moves. The Tailor has his jacket off, two sleeves rolled up to his elbows, his cap pulled down low, the white hair sticking out above his ears.

It's hot work for an old man on a June day.

And then I see a wake on the water, the red bow of Jamesie's boat rounding the gap in the Bo reef, making for the pier. Dougal and the Tailor pause, feeling the swell and then they turn and raise their hands in greeting as the *Sally-Anne* comes into dock behind them. Two dark-dressed, hatted figures climb out of the second boat and nod towards Dougal and the Tailor and stand on the slipway and look around them as if they're expecting something. One of them, the shorter and the heavier of the two, takes off a bowler hat and runs his hand through thick red curly hair. I can see his walrus moustache from here, a pair of round glasses perched on his nose. He stands with his fists on his lower back, stretching, his feet planted firm on the pier. He has a military look about him, naval, maybe, a stiff white collar, a bowtie at his throat. He is not dressed for the island. The other man is a good head taller, at a guess a decade and a half younger than the red-headed one, clean-shaven, fine-boned and in a peaked cap, an entirely different species of a person altogether. His jacket is short and neatly tailored, his tie tucked into his waistcoat. He looks across the bay towards Mallacht, takes in Ballynagard and Church Quarter, the stone belfry of St

Thomas's, the graveyard with its crooked white stones. I follow his eyes over the Manor House, its chimneys gleaming white in the sunlight, the dark and the light of the alder and the sycamore in the Planting behind, the yellow broom above. If he looks up now he will see the roofs of the school and the Pound House on the upper road and the wall of the Big Garden and me, watching him, my blouse pale against the black stone, my head bare, my hair drying on my shoulders, curling in the sun. But there's a rattle of wheels from the south, from the bend below Gort Beg, and he turns and there's Tam Casey on the lighthouse cart rolling along the limestone road. The two strangers take a step towards the *Sally-Anne* and Jamesie reaches a black box up from the deck. The older man takes it, handles it delicately, like it could be packed with clocking hens that might squawk and flap at the disturbance. Then Jamesie hands up another box and they stack them on the quay. Tam Casey pulls up alongside, they load the boxes carefully one by one into the cart and rope them on, Dougal and the Tailor watching them from the boat. The older man climbs up beside Tam Casey, the younger man into the back of the cart, his hand on the boxes to steady them. Then the cart moves away, slow, round past the boathouse and climbs the hill of the Shore Avenue into Glebe. They are heading, I know, to the Light.

Ginny has been full of it, pushing the newspaper over the table to me like a child wanting a story. Ginny is as canny as anyone I know, but she has never learned to read English and she relies on me for the news. She gets the papers when the Rector's wife is done with them. I don't know how she managed to insert herself so far up the queue. The whole island is waiting for the papers but Ginny managed it, however she did it. I read her the headlines and she dictates the stories she wants to hear and then she sits there on the closed-up settle bed, pulling on her Scotch cutty, the tobacco glowing red with every draw, making a sound like the sea sucking back over the stones at Owcydoo. It's occurred to me more than once that I could make the stories up – relate all kinds of fabricated nonsense to Ginny and the Tailor that would have their hair standing on end, tell the story whatever way it suits me to tell it. I could have the Queen declare that she had tired of her home on the Isle of Wight and was searching for suitable accommodation on the fair isle of Rathlin. Ginny would have it spread around the island in no time, but then there'd be hell to pay for making her a laughing stock. Ginny is fond of talk, but she doesn't like to be the butt of it. Every time I turn a page of the paper she licks her own fingers, and every time I finish reading, the same thing comes out of her mouth: 'That's the news and there's nothing new about it. Already three days old by the time we get it.' You'd think she had shares in Lloyd's the way she follows the shipping.

'"Barbados, Monday,"' she repeats after me, '"The steamer *Bernard Hall*, from Liverpool." Did you hear that, Tailor?'

'How long is that now?' says the Tailor, sitting at his table in the light of the window, not stopping to look up from his work.

'That's twenty-two days,' she says, 'since we saw it pass Altacorry Head.'

'Twenty-two days, to be in Barbados. Imagine that.'

'Sure, it's no time at all,' as proud as if she was the captain of the steamer, responsible for taking it all that way herself, and her that has never been further than Ballycastle, seven miles across the Sound.

The Tailor has some reading English, enough to make out orders for cloth, bills of sale, pattern books, but not enough to comfortably read the papers, so I sit in the kitchen on the gouged-out seat of the creepie stool, and I read to them both. My mind drifts out through the sash window and over the Sound, and at times I hardly know what I'm saying till I hear them telling it back to me. And it occurs to me then that in my bullish contrariness I've gotten myself a husband and his sister for companions that are not all that far removed in age from the grandparents whose care I recently had.

The papers say that the boxes Marconi's men have brought will shoot their words out over the Moyle like pellets out of a gun, that their speech will land on the other side of the Sound, as far as Fair Head itself. Ginny says it's not right to separate a person from their words, to put that much sea between the two. A body could say anything then and feel no responsibility for it. Who's to say, she says, that at that remove, those words belonged to a person at all? How would you know what's the truth when there's a gap the size of the Moyle between them? A word is a thing to keep close, always, she says.

Marconi writes in the papers that the new technology will change all our lives for the better. Ginny snorts and says will it draw the water from the well or milk the cow or keep the pig out of the turnips? As if that's all there is to living, as if survival is the best that any of us can hope for. I would like to look into the faces of the strangers; I would like to see the face of a man who has the power to cast his words out across the sea. But I don't want them to see me, standing here, curious, so I step under the arch into the Big Garden, behind the fern and the buckie rose that grow along the wall, and I wait there until the rattle of the cart dies away.

When I'm sure they're gone I come back out on the road. Down on the pier, the Tailor takes old Susie by the collar and I hear him say, 'Mush' in the still air and the horse begins to back out of the water and not a sod of turf moves. Such a biddable animal, old Susie, and never tells a tale. I pull out a spray of yarrow, take in the scent of it. They say if your love is faithful and true that yarrow will cause your nose to bleed. Nothing happens. I don't expect it to. The Tailor will have to go easy on the road with the cart piled high with turf. I'll cut over by Crocknascreidlin, be home a good half-hour before him.

I'm climbing the hill when I hear a boot scuff on the road behind me and when I turn there's the girl again, the one from the Tailor's house, struggling up the hill with a canvas bag on her back. I stop by the roadside to let her catch me up and she passes me by without a word of greeting, without a look in my direction. At the top of the hill she disappears around the bend and the whitethorn hedge trembles as she passes. She looks like she's headed for Portavoolin but when I reach the rise there's no sign of her. I'm beginning to get used to having her around.

Ginny continues to sleep at night on the opened settle bed by the fire in the kitchen, the four wooden sides up round her like a cot: 'That lower room's shocking cold at night,' she says. And so we have settled into life together, the three of us under one roof. The Tailor goes about the island with the cart, taking measurements for suits. From time to time old Benson sends word that he wants a jacket made up and the Tailor takes the boat to the mainland to visit him and any other clients he can pick up. Ginny spins and weaves the cloth as fast as she can pedal. What the Tailor doesn't use is sold at the fairs in Ballycastle and on Islay.

To begin with Ginny said she'd teach me to spin, and for a time she kept to her word. She showed me how to wind the yarn on to a quill so it would come away without sticking, how to slip the quill into the shuttle, ready for her to use. But she doesn't seem in any hurry to give up her loom. And now it's: 'Cart up a bucket of water from the spring, Nuala,' and, 'Redd out the ashes, will you, only empty the slops on top of them, to keep the dust down?' and, 'Nuala, will you run down to the shop and get me a fly of tobacco,' and, 'Have you the oatcakes pressed, yet?' I don't mind hard work, I never have, but I was thinking that a trade would be a useful thing to have and now there's no sign of me getting one.

Nor no sign of a baby either. I know that's what Ginny's thinking. In the five months since our wedding night, the Tailor has barely laid a hand on me. He's an old man, it's true, but I never expected indifference. Ginny will blame me for the lack of a child. She'll be waiting a long while, I fear, if she's waiting for the Tailor to make a move.

You'd think Ginny hadn't two farthings to her name the way she walks about the place. The old hat pulled down over her ears, a meal bag tied round her middle for an apron. It takes her till noon to straighten, she's that bent with all the time she's spent over her work. I don't think she was ever young. I can't imagine it. Shuffling about the house the whole time, rising dust, making like she can't lift her feet off the ground, but if she heard tell of a wedding or a wake, she'd be the first out the door.

Ginny's not much of an advertisement for the Tailor's work; that duty has fallen to me. It's not the worst of my chores. The Tailor is a fine needleman and he cuts the cloth well to fit. His measuring of me was the one time he took any interest in my shape and even then he noted down the figures absent-mindedly, like he was noting the measurements of a mannequin. I'm better kitted out than I've ever been in my life in serviceable plaids and tweeds.

Ginny too has a keen interest in my shape. Every morning since the wedding she has eyed my waist to see if there is any change in the outline of me, as if a child will sprout to full size overnight, and every morning she's disappointed in her appraisal. 'There's been McQuaids on this island since the time of Sorley Boy himself,' she says.

And now she has her eye on a bigger prize. There's talk of old Benson being forced to sell to the tenants. He's hardly ever here now. The Manor House is empty. Ginny's forever asking for news in the papers of landlords selling up. She can't wait for the Tailor to get his hands on the deeds of the cottage at Portavoolin. I think she's determined to stay alive till the name of the next generation is on a piece of land, however long it takes.

I'll bide my time with Ginny. She's old. Dougal says she was born the year before his mother and she was sixty-two when she died last December. She can't stay above the ground for ever, no matter how twisted she is. But for now, I'm as trapped on this island, in this house, as I ever was before.

## Nuala

## June 1898

Ginny has been up and down to the harbour like a magpie building a nest, collecting newspapers and shiny scraps of gossip from the Rector's wife, bringing them back to show us. The Englishman, Kemp, the red-headed one, went back to the mainland the same day I watched the men arrive. The dark one, the Italian, is still up at the Light, sleeping in one of the keeper's cottages. I've seen him walking the island, staring at the ground, stopping now and then to pick up a pebble or a piece of gravel, slipping it into his pocket, moving on. He has a jacket that looks like a gamekeeper's, with pockets all the way down the front. Dougal says he's been counting the hills between the Light and the Rue, between Altacorry and the Bull, measuring them as well. He has Tam Casey walking after him with a measuring tape, and he is writing all the figures down in a little black-backed book.

'Do you know?' says Dougal, in the Tailor's house kitchen, 'that the distance from the watch house to the wall up at the Light is one hundred and eleven feet?'

'I did not,' says the Tailor.

'And the distance,' says Dougal, 'from the watch house to the lighthouse is one hundred and five feet.'

'I didn't know that either,' says the Tailor. 'Why is it significant, Dougal?'

'I don't know,' Dougal says. 'The Italian is a great man for the calculations.'

Over on the mainland, the Englishman has a spar up on the cliff at Fair Head, and a mast on the Coalyard at the weighmaster's cottage. He has the cottage rigged up to receive the messages whatever time they start sending them. They say he has put blinds on the windows and built an outside toilet for himself and whitewashed all the walls. I don't know what difference the colour of the walls will make. Maybe the words will be able to find the weighmaster's cottage better if they can see it. The lighthouse cart has met every boat, has been on the road steady with loads of equipment, spruce and bamboo sprits and pine masts that they say have come all the way from Norway. There was great concern over something called 'cells' that seemed very important to operations. 'They need fifty of them in Ballycastle and fifty of them on the island,' Dougal says.

'What are they for?' asks the Tailor.

'For sending the signals,' Dougal says.

For days Mr Kemp has met every train from Belfast and still there is no sign of the mysterious cells. 'He's in the post office in Ballycastle every turn round,' says Dougal. 'Telegramming the stations in Belfast and Ballymoney. "No cells. Where are the cells?"' Then finally, the whole lot arrived on the last train at nine in the evening. Dougal was enlisted to help unload them at the station and then row them over to the island, Mr Kemp presiding over the cargo, like it was newborns they were handling and not a load of equipment.

'What did they look like?' says the Tailor.

'Like – boxes,' says Dougal. 'Like more boxes.'

'What's to become of us, anyway?' says Ginny. 'We'll be overrun with men and boxes, shooting words from one end of the island to the other, to the mainland and back again. The air'll be black with words. It'll get to be that we'll be batting them away like midges on a summer's night.'

I can't help but smile at the thought of Ginny being chased and bitten by a swarm of words. I doubt if even the fear of that would cure her of her gossiping. I picture the black letters in the air, the 'l's and the 'm's and the 'b's, turning like starlings over the Sound in the evenings, swirling like eddies, all of one mind, rising to roost in the trees. Branches lined with letters like leaves, clusters of them like fruit.

'What are you smiling at?' Ginny says to me.

'Not a thing,' I say.

One morning, a week or so after the arrival of Marconi's men, Ginny's sitting up on the closed settle bed supping a bowl of buttermilk, her heels knocking against the wood. She has all the good varnish scraped off the settle bed with the heels of her old rough boots. 'When you've the cow milked,' she says to me, 'fill a can of cream and gather half a dozen eggs and bring them up to the Light.' It's not like Ginny to play the part of the generous neighbour, but it's not long before I understand her. She is thinking in terms of trade. 'The foreigners could mean good news for us,' she says, 'whether it be the devil himself they're communicating with.' I milk the cow and hunt the hens and gather the eggs and prepare to leave. 'Don't go up by the roddins,' she shouts from the door after me. 'You're no goat, although you think you are. There'll not be an egg left whole.' I've never broken an egg yet, but it's not worth getting into that with Ginny so I turn on my heel away from the shore path, and head up along the millrace. 'And cover your hair,' she shouts again. 'I think sometimes you forget you're a married woman, Nuala Byrne.'

I climb the rise behind the house and walk up to the low road. When I know I'm out of sight, I drop the shawl off my head and wrap it round my middle, feel the sun warm on my face. It's nearly twice as long to the Light this way but the fields through Ballycarry are dotted with buttercups and bog cotton, and the crickets are sawing like fury in the grass and it's a good day to be out in the air. The white road unwinds like a ribbon of silk as I pass through the domed pillars at Dixon's gate. There's hardly a ripple on the surface of the small lough. From half a mile back I can see the Lloyd's mast sixty feet up in the air, the wire that courses from there to the top of the Light, the halyards that anchor it to the ground. The Light rises up out of Altacorry, first the steel dome with the lightning rod above, the glass of the lantern turning and winking in the sun. Closer, I can see the balcony beneath, the red-painted belt of the upper tower, the white of the lower tower below, the small squares of windows looking out. Next, the nine stout chimneys of the keepers' houses, the roof of the watch house to the east towards the cliff. A length of rabbit netting with a line through it runs from the mast to the watch house window looking for all the world like the nets the foorins in the upper end used to set to catch the puffins in the spring. The whole contraption looks like a becalmed ship dropped out of the air somehow, missing only its sails, the hull sunk with the force of the fall into the soft peaty ground, everything gleaming, shiny and bright in the June sun.

The keepers' houses are the best on the island, after the Manor House and the Rectory. They are built from good cut basalt stone, with wide sash windows and slated roofs and clay chimney pots and bedrooms all on an upper floor. From the Light, you can see every ship returning from the North Atlantic on its way to dock in Belfast, or the Mersey, or the Clyde. On a clear day like today you could be forgiven for believing that you could stand on Altacorry and stretch out your fingers and touch Kintyre in Scotland, fourteen miles away on the other side of the channel.

I pass through the gate of the compound wall and walk up to the first keeper's house where Ginny has told me the foreigner is staying, but there is no sound when I knock on the open door, so I call and then step in. All is neat and still and quiet in the keeper's house kitchen. In the light from the wide windows I can see that the floor is paved with fine quarry tiles. The hearth is swept clean. I set the eggs and cream down on the stout kitchen table and step through into the passageway where a set of wooden stairs and spindles leads to the upper floor. Through another door is the parlour with deep wooden windowsills hung with blue patterned curtains, a green rug on the floor, a cast-iron fireplace with brass candlesticks on the mantelpiece. As I'm standing there, taking it all in and thinking that Mrs Kernohan, the keeper's wife, keeps a tidy house, there is a sudden crackle and a hiss outside the window and a fan of sparks flies past, like what you'd see at the door of the forge up at Carravanankey, except these are yellow and blue and fly high into the air. I stop with my hand on my heart beating. It seems a strange and dangerous place.

I leave the cottage and walk towards the watch house. The mast lines are anchored to the ground with white concrete blocks, each of them cast deep with Lloyd's name. There's a smell in the air, a whiff of something gassy, rotten, stronger when I pass an old sail that's been rigged like a low tent just off the path. More wires pass from here to the watch house itself, a low wooden hut on the cliff edge where the keepers take shelter from the weather. I knock on the door and a voice shouts out, 'Enter.' I go in to a man sitting sideways at a table, his head bent over an apparatus of some kind. There's a different tang to the air inside, the smell of wood and something metallic, and the smell too of paraffin and molten wax. The man, who I recognise as the dark-haired Italian, is tapping a little black-handled telegraph key. Brripp-brripp-brripp-brrrrrr goes the instrument and then a bluish-yellow spark leaps out and then there is a stream of them, jumping between a brass-balled instrument on the table. The man does not look up. I don't know how much English he understands, but since Gaelic is unlikely to be an option, I say to him: 'Ginny McQuaid sent you eggs,' which seems somewhat foolish in the circumstances, 'and cream,' I add, as if that will justify the interruption, make the matter more important.

'Thank you,' he says in perfect English, the touch of a foreign accent. 'Please, leave them there.' He points without raising his head, to a counter on the wall to my left where sits a brass handbell on a wooden stand, the type you see on shop counters. His hair is dark and curls over the collar of his shirt.

'I left them in the house,' I say, and then I turn to go.

'Wait!' he calls. The tapping stops. 'Can you hold this?' He says the last word like 'thees', but apart from that he sounds just like the Englishman, Lewis, the photographer who came to the island once, who wanted to photograph us all outside our cabins with the glashan hanging open-mouthed, drying on the walls. Without looking up, or waiting for a reply, the Italian pulls a copper wire from the instrument and reaches it to me, and ducks his head under the table to pick up a metal box the size of a small suitcase. I take the wire, not knowing what else to do, hoping that nothing will fly in or out of it while I'm there. The black wooden boxes I watched them unload at the pier sit opened on the table and in, and on, and around them are arranged wires and drums, brass balls and copper coils and spindles. It is like the insides have been taken out of two or three longcase clocks: pendulums, cogs, the entire workings rearranged and rigged up for some new and unnatural purpose. Then the Italian is back up and has the case on the table. He takes the wire from me and attaches it to what looks like a little glass tube with a glass handle on it, angled like a gun. Then he puts his hands together. 'And now, we wait,' he says, and then he looks at me.

He has a pair of metal-framed spectacles on the bridge of his nose, another, thicker-framed pair on the top of his head. He has green, drowsy eyes and thick dark eyebrows and black wavy hair that is parted to the right but that falls down over his eyes and at the back, grows halfway down his neck. His mouth is wide and full of white teeth, and now that he's smiling a little at me I can see that the lower row is crooked. There is a shadow above his lip. He opens his mouth to speak and as he does there comes a faint tapping sound from the box on the table and a spool begins to whirr and move. A strip of pale blue paper spools out from under a wheel, emerges with ink marks, short and longer dashes. He jumps up, feeds the tape through his fingers and laughs. 'The rain is on its way,' he says. He glances at a clock on the wall, writes something into an opened, blue-lined ledger on the table.

I don't think much of his weather report. I look out

through the window of the watch house at the cloudless sky beyond Altacorry. There are charts and maps pinned to the boarded walls on each side of the window, letters and symbols, nothing I understand. Then I turn and push the door to go out. 'Wait!' he says again. 'Please, forgive me,' and he stands, removes his glasses, stretches out his hand. 'Gabriele Donati,' he says. 'Pleased to make your acquaintance.' He is about my height, a little taller, a little younger, maybe. I take the hand, which is small and fine for a man's, and he smiles at me.

'Nuala Byrne,' I say, because no one calls me by the Tailor's name, and then I add, 'McQuaid.'

'*Nulla?*' He stares at me and starts to laugh. '*Nulla?*' he says again, and then stops at the look on my face. 'I am sorry,' he says. 'I'm so sorry, but in Italian, it means "nothing". I have never heard this before. Is it really your name?'

'It is,' I say quietly, 'it is my name. It is short,' I tell him, 'for Fionnuala. My grandfather chose it and I can assure you that it does not mean "nothing". Fionnuala was the daughter of King Lir. She and her brothers were charmed into swans. They spent three hundred years on the Sea of Moyle, the sea outside that window.' This is a long and curious speech for me to make and I'm not sure why I am telling him this, except that I'm annoyed at his laughter and it's important he knows that my name is not a joke. And then I remember what the papers said, about the black box throwing words out over the sea. I look with suspicion at the yards of wire looped around the lower supports of the table, at the copper line that stretches out through the window to the rabbit netting on the mast outside. And my cheeks redden at the thought of my foolishness being loud-hailed through the streets in Ballycastle the way the circus people advertise their performances, the mainlanders laughing at my vanity. What a frightening thought that is – that a woman can think herself alone in a room with a man and find that a whole town full of people are listening.

He looks like he's hiding a smile. 'Shall we begin again?' he says. He makes a strange kind of metallic click with his heels and bows low and then straightens. 'I am very pleased to meet you, Princess Fionnuala,' he says, and he reaches out his hand again and this time, when he takes mine, he turns it over and brushes his lips across the knuckles. '*Gabriele*, although here,' and he shrugs, 'to everyone, I am Gabriel.'

I nod at him, not knowing what to say, not wishing

any more words to escape, and I am turning to go when, 'Do you cook?' he asks.

This is an odd question. What woman doesn't cook? 'Of course,' I say, eyeing the instrument again.

'The keeper's wife has abandoned us. Sickness in the family. She has taken the boat to the mainland. Can you come to prepare a midday meal? We will be two, occasionally three of us.'

I nod towards the arrangement on the desk. 'Can they hear us?' I say, quietly.

He looks puzzled. 'The keeper's wife?'

He is making fun of me. 'The people, on the mainland?'

Again, he hides a smile. 'Oh! No, no, that is not how it works.' My face must tell him that I'm still not sure. 'Look,' he says, and reaches over and pulls out the wire from the back of one of the boxes. 'We are no longer . . . connected.'

'I'll have to ask,' I say, 'about the dinner.'

'Please do, and save me from Mr Kernohan's cooking. If I have to eat one more potato . . .'

I look at him, startled. 'What else would you eat?' I ask him.

He sighs. 'What else, indeed?' And a dreamy look

comes into his eyes and then he says, 'You will ask, yes?'

I say, 'I will.' And he puts his glasses back on to his nose and makes to sit down again at the table.

I walk out into blinding sunshine, wispy clouds to the south, the heat strong on my bare arms. The hut and the wire and the mast are quiet. With no eggs to carry, I head across the fields towards the shore. I have a feeling as I am walking that I'm being watched. I look back and see a figure up at the lantern but when the light turns again, it is gone. Mr Kernohan, I think, or Tam Casey, maybe, and I don't like the idea of that. Tam Casey's not long on the island. He's an Assistant Keeper, from near Dublin, I think. Dougal says he worked on the Baily Light at Howth, that there was some kind of accident there. He has a mark on his forehead, above his right eye that he's vain enough to have grown his hair to hide. He has been talking about the great work they're going to do, he and Marconi's men, and how they're all going to make their fortune and be famous. A cooling breeze starts in the rushes round the vanishing well, blows my hair across my face. When I raise my hand to push it back, I catch the smell of paraffin, of molten wax.

The ground around Castlequarter is barren and

rocky, some of Drake's dirtiest business occurred here. You can hardly put your foot down without stepping on bone. This is a story that Granda used to tell us, a story hard to hear, even three hundred years on. Sorley Boy's people were holed up in the castle, under siege, and with no well inside the walls. They knew they could not hold out. They parleyed with the English, were guaranteed safe passage to Scotland, came out, unarmed, in groups of ten, and once in the hollow out of sight of the castle, were silently slaughtered one by one. They know they were tricked. I can hear them now, loud and bitter, still shouting out for vengeance. I close my ears against them, muffle their shouts with the louder crash of the waves on the rocks below.

There has been no sign of the girl since the day I saw her up near Crocknascreidlin, and unlike the noisy castle people, I have never heard her speak. I don't know what this means.

I'm sliding down the roddins below the castle when the first fat drops of rain begin to fall, sudden and hard as stones, pelting off the rocks, bursting around my feet, the smell of freshly turned soil scenting the air. I turn to see a rainbow in the east, the sun still shining through the rain, everything below it blue, above it everything grey, a perfect arc of colour, splitting the story of the sky in two. There is no shelter to be found. By the time I pass the blackened stones of the kelp kiln at Portcam, I am drenched to the bone. I pull off my shoes and pick my way around the rocks that are slippery now with bladderwrack, over the fading sea pink and the ragwort and the purple thistle, and wade back through the shallow pools to Portavoolin. Then just as suddenly, the rain stops and the sun reappears and as I turn towards the cottage I see that the hedges are beginning to steam in the heat. I walk through a cloud of midges in through the Tailor's house door.

In the cottage, the air is changed; I can feel it as I come in. The girl is there, sitting on a stool by the window, her back to me, staring out at the shore. The Tailor is beside her, cross-legged on a cushion, a sleeve board across his knees, his head bent over his sewing. I look at the Tailor and I look at Ginny, taking her ease on the settle bed. Neither of them looks at the girl. They pass no remarks as to her being there at all.

'You got caught in the thunder-plump,' says Ginny. 'What are they doing up there at the Light?'

I go to the fire, stand with my back to the heat, the reek beginning to rise off my sodden skirts. 'They are prophesising the weather,' I say, and I look over at the girl.

Ginny snorts. 'They can prophesise all they like. Clod another sod of turf on there, will you, Nuala? That teem of rain has brought a damp air in through the door and it's in an odd way of burning, that fire.'

The girl's long thin fingers are curled in her lap. She looks, I have to admit, a little bit like me. I take it into my head that she's something to do with my family in Newfoundland and I think of all the stories I've heard of the signs and warnings that come before a tragedy. They say Angus Magowan saw his brother, thousands of miles away in Boston before he got word that he'd died, and I say a silent prayer that all is well with them. She is a listener, not a talker, by the looks of things. I go out for the sods of turf and when I come back in there's no sign of her. The floor near the window is marked with the damp imprint of a boot. I throw the turf on, and go in to the upper room but there's no one there and no one in the lower room where the loom stands quiet.

'What are you gadding about for with your mouth open?' says Ginny.

I go back and stand by the fire. 'Did you know Mrs

Kernohan's away? They've asked if I'll do them a dinner,' I say.

The Tailor is basting a jacket for Jamesie, tacking long white stitches into the lapels, ironing the seams flat. An iron sits on a rest to his right, another on the hotplate by the fire. He is threading a needle. He runs the yarn through his mouth, and holds the needle with the eye flat and drops the yarn down through it like you would a rope through a boat hook. When it's through he wraps both ends around his forefinger three or four times to form a loop, pushes it off with his thumb and pulls it tight. 'What would they pay?' he says, looking up at me.

'A shilling a head,' says Ginny from the settle bed.

The Tailor looks at her. 'They wouldn't?'

'Indeed they would, who else is going to cart food up to them there, and Mrs Kernohan away to tend her sick mother?'

'So you did know?' I say to her.

'Ah, you're a canny one, Ginny,' says the Tailor. 'Will we try it?'

'Go up to the Light tomorrow and tell them,' says Ginny to me, 'a shilling a head. And be sure not to be talking to them about anything that goes on here.'

'They can only send the messages when the wire's connected to the box,' I say.

'Is that so?' says Ginny, eyeing me. 'Who were you talking to up there?'

'One of the electricians.'

'You'll do well to keep your talk short all the same,' she says, 'wires or no wires.'

'I'll be safe enough, I reckon,' I say to Ginny, 'in the kitchen at the keeper's house.' And I lift the bucket and go out past them to fetch water from the well.

The Italian has the door of the watch house open in the warm weather and from the keeper's house kitchen I can hear him trying to teach Tam Casey the code they use for the messages. He says this is a temporary measure, till Lloyd's send someone to take charge of the station. He doesn't know when that will be. He has a chart with the twenty-six letters of the English alphabet all in rows and the numbers from nought to nine and underneath each of them are the short and longer dashes of the code. The short dashes they call dots, though to my eyes they're not really dots at all. There's code for punctuation as well. Tam Casey has learned them all off the page but he can't get it right on the telegraph key. His dots are too long and his dashes are too short and he doesn't leave the right spaces in between. From the open door I can hear him swear at his mistakes, the electrician's voice, calm, measured beside him. They have a bell rigged up from the watch house to the kitchen so that when they're inside, taking their meals, they do not miss a message from Mr Kemp on the mainland. I understand a little now about the system, that the words need to be sent in a certain way, translated into Morse, and that even then, it doesn't always work as smoothly as they'd like. I redden at the memory of that first day in the watch house when I asked the Italian if we could be heard in Ballycastle.

Most days the best I can do for them is fresh lythe or glashan roasted in the coals, a pot of floury Champion spuds. But this day, Dougal gets me a rabbit and I put it in the roasting pot with a bunch of rosemary that's been dried on the rafters in the Tailor's house and the smell of it fills the kitchen. Granda's knowledge of herbs comes in handy – what's bitter and what's sweet, what would take the roof off your mouth, make your tongue curl or your stomach churn, what can be added, what's to be avoided. I'm at the fire, stirring the pot on the crook. I'm thinking of the days me and Granda used to go gathering together up through Ballyconaghan and I forget myself and where I am and I'm singing a low song my mother used to sing and I hear a step on the threshold and, 'What are you singing?' the Italian says from the door.

'*Na Gamhna Geala*,' I tell him, glancing over my shoulder at him.

'What does it mean?' he says.

I have to think about this for a moment. 'It means "The Bright Calf".'

'You're singing a song about a cow?' and even I have to smile at that, but I still have my back to him and he doesn't see.

'It's the song of a woman remembering how she used to herd the cows out on the hillside, when she was young, before she was married.'

'It sounds sad.'

'It is.'

'Why is she sad?'

'She made a wrong choice,' I say.

I hear him pull the chair back from the table, the creak of it as he sits.

'Can you sing it in English?'

I go on stirring the pot, though it doesn't need it. 'It's not an English song.'

'How did you learn it?' So many questions.

'My mother used to sing it, a long time ago.'

'Is Gaelic your first language?'

'It is.'

'Where did you learn English?'

'In school. We weren't allowed to speak Gaelic there.'

'Do you think in Gaelic?'

I turn to him then. What a strange man he is. He is sitting at the table, smiling at me. He has taken off his jacket and his tie and loosened the collar of his shirt above his waistcoat. His white sleeves are pushed up to his elbows, the skin on his arms darkened by sun. I consider the question. What is the language I carry about in my head, I ask myself? Does a thought need language, before it is spoken? Before it is propelled by breath?

'How would I know?' I ask him.

'What language do you dream in?'

'In Gaelic, I think.'

'Then that must mean you think in Gaelic too.'

I can see the pinch at his nose where his spectacles have left a mark. The other pair is still on his head.

'So you are like me,' he says. 'We have both left our languages behind, to make ourselves understood. We are already speaking in code.' He doesn't pronounce the 'h' in 'have' and he has a way of adding an extra sound to the end of a word, to the last word in a sentence so that 'code' sounds like 'coda'. But his speech is very clear, clearer than many's the one on the island who's been speaking English since their schooldays.

I don't say anything in answer to him. What answer is there to that? I've never considered myself a translator. I turn back to the pot and give the rabbit a poke it doesn't need.

'You sing beautifully,' he says.

'You speak very good English,' and then a thought occurs to me. 'When you're sending the messages,' I say, 'do you send them in English or in Italian?'

'We can send them in any language,' he says, delighted with the question. 'But ultimately they must be translated into Morse.'

I've seen the chart with the code. I've heard Tam Casey's swearing attempts to use it. 'That's the name of the code you're using?'

'Yes.' His chair scrapes back again. 'I will show you,' he says, and he disappears out the door. When he comes back, he has a length of the blue tape in his hand that I watched feed off the wheel on that first day.

'Look,' he says, and he shows me the long and short dashes that make no sense. 'It is not a language made up of letters, but of symbols. This, for example, look here: dot, dot, dot, dash, this represents the letter "V".'

'Why is it repeated? There's a whole string of "V"s there. That can't be a word in any language, is it?'

'It is what we use to test the signal, to make sure that contact has been made.' He stretches the tape out to show another string of dots and dashes further along. 'This is the combination for the word "yellow" – see where the "l" is repeated? It is the code we use to describe the quality of the signal. "Yellow" means the message is only readable in part.'

'So you're using code to send code?'

He smiles at me. 'Precisely,' he says.

'How can you understand it when they're all bunched together like that?'

He shrugs. 'It is a little like reading music. You learn to decipher it. It just takes a bit of practice.'

I want to ask him more about this but I hear Tam Casey's boot on the scraper at the door. 'Thank you,' I say to him, and turn back to the pot.

I hadn't thought about it before, about the way that Gaelic is lodged in my head. I think about how Miss Benson used to try and shame the language out of us at school. She'd come into the lessons and if she heard any of us speaking in the old tongue, she'd string a stick she'd marked for the purpose around the offender's neck. 'You and your old foreign gibberish,' she used to say, even though it was the opposite of foreign, even though old Benson had learned to speak Gaelic himself. We didn't want to appear backward. We avoided speaking it in front of her or the teacher, but we spoke Gaelic at home and the whole cut of the road to school and the whole cut back again. There's some people in the Upper End have no English at all, but very few can read or write in Gaelic. It's nearly all been schooled out of us. Granda Frank taught me and Dorothy, though. We used to sit either side of him at the table in the summer evenings, chalking out the letters on our slates. He said it was a thing worth keeping. You never knew, he said, when you might need to communicate something that you didn't want a stranger to understand.

As I serve up their meal, the Italian taps a rhythm on the wood of the table. 'Di dah,' he says across to Tam Casey.

'Da-dah,' says Tam Casey.

'Da-di-dit,' says the Italian.

'Di-di-dit,' says Tam Casey.

The Italian sighs and shakes his head. 'Almost,' he says, 'but it is the difference between "m" and "a"; "s" instead of "d", and those are not mistakes that you can afford to make.'

I could have told him that Tam Casey knows nothing about rhythm. I've seen him at the dances in the big barn, leaning against the wall, following the jigs of the girls with his eye, like he's biding his time, like he'll make his move when he's ready, the whole while tapping his foot out of step with the music. He is tall and narrow and straight and wiry. I've watched him unload box after box off the lighthouse cart and never break a sweat. I've never heard him say anything that was crude or insulting, but there's a smile playing always about his lips that could have been a smirk if it was let. He must be around my age, thirty or thereabouts, but any time he pulled a girl up for a dance, it was always one of the young ones, and when it came to 'The Waves of Tory' he would spin so hard on his heel, and swing his partner at such a rate that she would never be able to keep up with him and would end by screeching at him to stop as her heels left the floor. I stayed out of his way at any gathering. His is not the kind of attention that a woman would want.

'The potatoes here are very starchy,' the electrician says. 'They would make good *gnocchi*.'

'Good what?' says Tam Casey.

It's an Italian recipe, he says. He looks over and says he could teach me if I like? I've never heard tell of a man teaching a woman how to cook anything. He says to bring some wheat flour next time with the potatoes and the eggs and he'll show me.

'Do you mind me asking?' says the Italian, gesturing with his fork at Tam Casey's forehead, where I can see now that his hair is pushed back, the skin raised like a plucked hen's, tracks on the side of his forehead like the pulled quills might leave. 'What happened?'

Tam Casey tugs his hair back down. 'The fog cannon at the Baily misfired,' he says. 'The ramrod caught the side of my face.'

'I am sorry to hear that.'

Tam Casey shrugs. 'The chap who packed it didn't do it right. He wasn't as lucky as me.'

'Killed?' asks the Italian. Tam Casey nods. 'Poor

chap,' the Italian says. They eat in silence for a moment or two while I'm scraping out the pot.

'Do you speak Gaelic?' he asks Tam Casey, suddenly.

'I have a few words,' he says, 'but we were reared speaking English.'

'Ah,' says the Italian, and I know what he's thinking. He's thinking about translations. He's thinking about the dots and the dashes and the chart of the code that hangs on the watch house wall.

'If you don't mind me saying,' says Tam Casey, 'you speak very good English yourself.'

The Italian smiles. 'Thank you,' he says. 'I have Mr Marconi to thank for that.'

'Mr Marconi?' says Tam Casey. 'He's Italian, surely, like yourself?'

'Half Italian, half Irish,' the foreigner says, 'or Scots-Irish, I should say.'

I could have told Tam Casey this. I've read all about the Wireless Telegraphy Company in the papers, how it's been funded by Marconi's mother's people, the whiskey Jamesons of Dublin.

'Scots-Irish?' says Tam Casey, and gives a coarse laugh. 'He'll fit in well on the island.' It annoys me the way he talks about the island like he knows it, like he knows us. He's a blow-in and always will be, no matter how long he stays.

'We had a sort of deal,' Gabriel says, 'his mother and I. Guglielmo would speak to me in Italian and I would answer in English. We would correct each other's pronunciation.'

'Why did his Italian need correcting?' asks Tam Casey. 'Didn't he grow up in Italy?'

'He spent a lot of time with his English cousins in Livorno. Italian was practically his second language, a fact that was not popular with his father.' The bell rings and the electrician jumps up.

'Finish your meal,' he says to Tam Casey. 'I will answer it myself.'

I busy myself rinsing out the pot and dry it off with the cloth that's there. I don't like to be alone with Tam Casey. I can hear him now sucking the meat off the bones as I work.

'That's a nice bit of rabbit,' he says from the table.

'Dougal caught it,' I tell him.

'He would,' he says. 'Sure Dougal would get anything for you,' and he smiles at me in a way that makes my skin creep. 'You're a fine cook, Nuala Byrne. The Tailor's a lucky man.'

I don't bother with an answer; there's nothing to say to that so I go on wiping the pot. There's no sign of the electrician coming back. I lift his plate, cover it with a lid, set it over on the hotplate by the fire. I don't look up at Tam Casey but I can feel his eyes on me the whole time I'm moving around the kitchen and his eyes make me feel like it's his hands that are on me instead. I wonder that the electrician doesn't seem bothered by him. 'I'll go on,' I say. 'I can finish up the rest when I come back tomorrow.'

'You're in an awful hurry to get back to the Tailor today. What's the old man's secret?' And he leers at me. 'I've heard he's good with his needle, is that it?' Tam Casey has very small teeth for a man of his years. They are pointed, like a kitten's. I never let on I hear him. I take up my basket and go out the door.

Tam Casey is as soapy as a peeled parsnip. I think I know the type of him. He's the kind of man that always wants what he hasn't got. The second a woman would give in to him would be the second he'd lose all interest in her. He knows the island is not a place to get a reputation. He's being careful here, but for all that I dislike him, his words work on me the whole way down the path to Portavoolin. The Tailor is not a man of large appetite, not in any regard. I wonder at him not making some kind of attempt at me. He takes no interest in me at all, no more than if I was a cat. I'm not even sure he knows what to do with a woman. What did he want to marry me for? I'm beginning to think that if it hadn't been for Ginny's interference, he would never have married at all.

In the Tailor's house Ginny says, 'What are they at up there today?'

'Speaking in code,' I say.

Next day I go up with wheat flour and eggs and find the Italian in the kitchen. He says to boil the potatoes as usual and to keep the water and to let him know when they're done. Then he comes in and says we need to peel them while they're hot (as if I'd peel them any other way) and mash them and let them cool. He heaps the champ on the wooden board, knuckles a hollow into the mound of potato and cracks an egg into it. He sprinkles a handful of flour and kneads and folds it all together. He divides the mixture into eight and rolls each into a log, the size and thickness of his thumb. Then he flours them again and pushes the tines of a fork into each one. He runs the back of his hand across his forehead, to brush the hair out of his eyes. There is flour on his nose and on his brow. I do not tell him this.

'Now we drop them back in the pot of boiling water. When they float,' he says, 'they are cooked. But what do we use for a dressing? Do you have any oil?'

'Only the liver oil from the glashan,' I tell him, 'that we use to light the cruisie lamps.'

'Fish oil?' He makes a shape with his mouth. 'No, that will never do.'

'What do you have at home?' I ask him.

'Tomatoes,' he says with what sounds like real sadness, 'basil leaves, olive oil.'

'Old Benson used to grow tomatoes in a lean-to up at the Manor House,' I tell him. 'His cook used them to make chutney. I tried one once but it was an odd flavour, no sweetness in it at all. Anyway, the house is empty now. There's no tomatoes to be had.'

'I have eaten English glasshouse tomatoes,' he says. 'They are to the Italian tomato what gooseberries are to grapes. One vital ingredient is missing – sunshine.'

'Well, we haven't got them,' I say, 'tasteless or not, so what will you have? Cabbage?'

I think he knows I'm joking. I hope he does. I walk down to the Pound field above the Manor House, to where the wind has carried the three-cornered leek out of the flower garden to grow by the side of the road and I bring a bunch back with me, chop it up fine, scatter it through the dish with a knob of butter. 'Like wild garlic,' he says and smiles and cleans his plate.

Tam Casey is less impressed. 'A waste of a good spud,' he says.

At the cottage Ginny says, 'What are they at up there, today?'

'Boiling balls of potato bread,' I tell her.

The Englishman, Mr Kemp, arrives on the early boat; I see the cart pass on the road. When I go up with the dinner there's no sign of any of them but when I have it nearly ready, all three of them appear. They've been walking the island. It's the first time I've seen Mr Kemp up close. He's a man of about forty years, I'd say, his red hair curling and receding at his temples, his moustache waxed and trimmed. He has glasses like the Italian's, round and fine and perched on his nose, a striped tie at his throat.

He takes my hand: 'Pleased to meet you, Mrs McQuaid,' he says. Hardly anyone calls me by the

Tailor's name; to the islanders I will always be Nuala Byrne. He is formal and courteous and kind, but he has the biggest boom of a laugh I've ever heard. The three of them are in good spirits and full of chat. Mr Marconi, it seems, has summoned Mr Kemp to Kingstown, near Dublin, to the yacht races.

'Is Mr Marconi a betting man?' says Tam Casey as the three sit down at the table.

Mr Kemp laughs his foghorn of a laugh. 'He hasn't the slightest interest in gambling, only in telegraphy. We will rig up a station on a tug boat and follow the races, signal the commentary to Dublin as we go.'

'You can send signals from a moving vessel?'

'Of course! We have done it before, have we not, Gabriel?'

The Italian nods. 'At Alum Bay. We rigged up two of the coastal steamers that ran from the island into Bournemouth and Swanage.'

'Kingstown will be nothing new,' says Mr Kemp, 'but Mr Marconi is a clever man. He understands the importance of keeping the newspapers on his side. He knows how to put on a show. The *Express* will have printed accounts of the races as soon as they are over, the *Evening Mail* in London the same, and while the yachts are still out far beyond the range of any telescope. Speed is of the essence – speed and flexibility. They are our biggest advantages over the conventional telegraph.'

'You both know him well? Mr Marconi?' says Tam Casey. I can tell that he is enjoying this, sitting down to eat with the men who work with the famous inventor, as if some of their knowledge and skill will rub off.

'We've been working together for two years now,' says Mr Kemp. 'But Gabriel's known him since they were boys.'

Gabriel looks up from his food. 'His father is from Porretta, like me. They come back every summer. His mother takes the waters there.'

I don't know what it means exactly, to take the waters. Maybe it's like going in the sweat house. Maybe it clears the skin, though I don't imagine that Mrs Marconi or her like ever get much dirt on them. When Dorothy used to come over to the island in the summer, and after we'd helped with the kelp-making, we'd get into the sweat house to get ourselves clean, to ready ourselves for the Lammas Fair. Dorothy still swears by the sweating, though there's no black in her skin these days. She says we'll suffer neither ache nor pain so long as we sweat once a year.

'One summer,' says Gabriel, 'when they were visiting in Porretta, there was a storm. Guglielmo and I built a zinc lightning conductor on the road, rigged it up to a bell in the house where the family was staying. Every time the lightning flashed, the bell rang in the house. It made his father quite mad. The old man could not see the value in his son's experimentation, in the endless wires and kites and bells.'

'Ha! He feels differently now, of course,' says Mr Kemp, 'now that he can see the potential commercial value.'

Dorothy and I were caught in a storm once, up near Cantruan where we were sent to herd the sheep back from the cliff top. The sky was almost black by the time we got there, the sea in Altachuile Bay darker still, the beam from the lighthouse to the east growing stronger by the second. As we moved back down towards the old monastery, the sky suddenly crackled and lit up, a single jagged vein of white light above us, the rain pelting down. I set off to run towards a clump of alder trees but Dorothy shouted at me to stop, grabbed me by the shoulders, pulled me down onto the heather. Another crash, and when I looked up, there was a fork of lightning right above the nearest tree, like the alder was sucking the light down through it, like it was thirsty for all that power. And then a burst of sparks and flame, like dry kindling when it catches in the hearth, and in seconds the branches and leaves were alight, a puff of smoke from a crack in the bole, the tree burning from the inside out.

'Isn't that dangerous?' I say out loud, still thinking about the tree. 'Fooling about with lightning?' Tam Casey throws me a black look, like this conversation is no business of mine. Mr Kemp smiles over, kindly.

'It is if you don't know what you are doing,' says Mr Kemp, 'but Signor Marconi is a genius, plain and simple. He is also the hardest-working, most persistent person I have ever met.'

'I look forward to meeting him,' says Tam Casey. 'When do you think he will come?'

'After Kingstown, I should think,' says Mr Kemp. 'Which reminds me. We will need someone to man the Coalyard station, while I'm away. Would you be willing to do it, Mr Casey?'

'Of course,' says Tam Casey, and draws himself up.

'Gabriel tells me you are working hard at learning the code?'

'I'm making good progress.'

'We will organise a room for you, in the town. I leave for Kingstown the day after tomorrow.' Tam Casey's face looks fit to burst with the importance of it all. I go back to my work so I don't have to look at him. 'Good,' says Mr Kemp. 'Of course,' I hear him say to the Italian, 'you will need another operator here, for when you are travelling between the two stations.'

'There's Dougal?' I hear Tam Casey say.

'Dougal is a great help with the manual work,' says the Italian, 'but I am not certain how well he would do with the code. What about Mrs McQuaid?'

For a moment I don't realise that he's talking about me and then I do, and I drop the bowl into the water of the basin.

'Mrs McQuaid?' says Tam Casey. I turn to look at them.

'Why not?' the Italian says. 'There's very little time and we need someone close by. Mrs McQuaid has picked up a lot of it already, I think, just by listening over the past while. What do you say?' I avoid looking at Tam Casey's face.

Mr Kemp is twirling the end of his moustache in his fingers. 'Around a third of the telegraphists in the Post Office are women,' he says. 'We always found them to be as quick, if not quicker, than the men.'

'I . . . I don't know,' I say. 'I'd have to ask.'

'And if your husband has no objections?' says Mr Kemp.

It's not the Tailor I'll have to negotiate with, but Ginny of course. 'I'll see.'

The Italian turns to me. 'I do not think it would be a difficulty for you. A shilling a day if you agree to it?'

'That's what I get,' says Tam Casey.

'Indeed,' says the Italian. And to me: 'You will let us know?'

I walk home over Castlequarter and look out over the Sound, at Fair Head rising up, princely, out of the sea, at the line of coast beyond Carrickmore where I know the weighmaster's cottage to be, and I think about what it would be like to learn how to send messages in the air over the seven miles of water between here and the mainland. I go into Ginny and the Tailor, not knowing what the response to this will be.

'What would you have to do?' says Ginny.

'Learn the code,' I tell her, 'and send messages using the Morse key, and write down the messages that come in.'

'A key?'

'The telegraph key. A small one. It's not really a key at all. It's a sort of hammer. The same as the one in the post office in Ballycastle.'

'So that's what they're at. Sending our business to the post office in Ballycastle for all and sundry to hear?'

'They're not sending the messages to the post office. That's the regular telegraph. They're sending them without wires, to the Coalyard station, to Mr Kemp.'

'I thought you said he was going to Kingstown?'

'He is. Tam Casey is taking his place.'

'Well, that's no better.'

The Tailor sets aside his work. 'How can Tam Casey at the Coalyard in Ballycastle hear a hammer tapping from the lighthouse in Altacorry, be it big or small?'

'He doesn't hear it.'

'Then how does it work?'

'I don't know. I heard the electrician say that the messages are carried by waves in the air, that you can't see them.'

'Waves?' says Ginny. 'In the air?'

'Would it be,' says the Tailor, 'like when you're in

Oweyberne and you throw your voice in and the cave holds it for a second or two and then throws it back out at you again?'

'Maybe,' I say.

'Except instead of throwing it back, the black boxes throw them on across the Sound?'

'Pffff!' says Ginny. 'How could waves in the air carry words from one side of the Sound to the other?'

'I don't understand it either,' I say.

The Tailor laughs. 'At least the hawks won't be able to eat the waves the way they used to eat the carrier pigeons,' he says.

Ginny ignores this. 'I don't know that it's right, you a married woman, up there in the watch house with him and his hammers and his keys.'

'Whatever you say,' I tell her.

'Did he mention a price?'

I tell her what he said. 'Same as Tam Casey gets.'

The pair of them look at each other. 'Mrs Kernohan will be back before too long,' Ginny says, 'whatever way it goes with her mother. They won't be needing the dinners for much longer. We'll give it a try, maybe, see how it goes. Sure, Mr Kernohan's about. He'll keep an eye on you. And it's only till Mr Kemp is finished with the races? But mind and don't be repeating our business to them up there.'

Ginny is as tight as a duck's arse. Any opportunity to make money, and she's there, making it. But I have to bite my tongue and remind myself that she and the Tailor, like my own people, have known real hunger and that hunger has a long memory. She remembers her family being driven out of Kebble, Benson's sheep put there in their place. She remembers the potato blight, the boats in the bay, hundreds of islanders leaving at a time, my father's people among them. She remembers the building of the famine wall round Kilpatrick, the islanders living on birds' eggs from the stacks, auks they caught in nets off the cliffs, limpets they pulled off the rocks at low tide. Every time she tells it her eyes sink deeper into her head. I have heard her tell the story of how her father kept lookout for the United Irishman, Thomas Russell, the time they held the secret meetings in Brackens to plot against the landlords. It makes her more determined, I think, to hold on to this piece of land, to grab anything she can. She feels she's suffered for it, her and her people. She looks at me like I'm her passage to the future.

## Nuala

### July 1898

The first morning of my new position I am up early, my hair washed and brushed and my shawl pulled over my head before Ginny notices or can pass any remarks. I should balk at the way she uses me, like a hired hand to do her bidding, but since her bidding on this occasion is to my own benefit I will go along with it for now. I am curious about the goings on in the watch house. Since Ginny has neglected to teach me her trade, perhaps I can learn another. I've nothing to fall back on when she and the Tailor are gone, and I would like to find out more about the foreigners, about their dangerous experiments.

When I walk into the watch house, the electrician is already there, sitting in his neat tweed jacket with his back to the door. He's busy with an iron file sawing at a disc the size of a shilling, a small dark mound of metal filings building on the table top. 'Good morning, apprentice,' he says without looking up. He stops then, and with what looks like a fine paint brush, sweeps the filings onto a sheet of paper, curls the paper into a spout and pours them into one of the small glass tubes I saw him use that first day. It reminds me of something I've seen once before and then I have it: the tube on the barometer in the Manor House.

'What is it?' I ask him, taking off my shawl, tying it round my waist.

'It's called a coherer,' he says. 'It is made with two thermometers, fused together with a hand-bellows.' He fits the tube up with small metal plugs at either end, attaches wires to these. 'This,' he says, standing, 'forms part of the receiver, and this,' as he points to the brass-balled instrument on the table beside it, 'is the transmitter. Are you ready for your first lesson? We'll deal with that first. You've seen a Morse key before?'

I nod. The time they had it installed in the post office

in Ballycastle, Mrs Rory let me and Dorothy in round the back of the counter to look at it. Just a little round wooden knob like a doorknob, mounted on a brass lever on a block of wood. We were both a bit disappointed. We agreed afterwards that we had expected something more eventful though we didn't say so to Mrs Rory, who stood over the apparatus at the time like she'd given birth to it herself. She didn't show us how to operate it. 'No hands are to touch it but mine,' said Mrs Rory. 'I have been trained.'

Beside the Morse key on the table in the watch house is a wooden stand like the abacus we used to have in the schoolroom but this one frames the four brass balls, the outer two mounted from either side of the frame, the middle two from above so that none of them rests on the frame itself and no two touch each other. You could pass a sheaf of papers between them, maybe, but nothing as broad even as a fingertip. 'The Righi oscillator,' he says, 'or spark-gap transmitter, if you like.' I am hoping it's not important for me to remember these words. I do my best to pack them into my brain. A wire leads from the mount on the left-hand side down to the ground. 'The earth,' he says, and then he points to the wire that is attached at the other end, the one that disappears out the watch house window. 'This line is connected to the high vertical conductor – the mast head.' I can see the rabbit netting stretching up. He points to a sort of barrel resting on its side that sits towards the back of the table, wound round with what looks like copper wire. 'This,' he says, 'is the induction coil by means of which the electric sparks are produced and beside it, is the cell.' The cell that had caused so much consternation to Mr Kemp on the mainland is a metal box wrapped in orange paper. I can just make out the word 'Obach' and an instruction that begins, 'Note Care Must Be Taken When . . .' but the rest of the writing is blocked by the apparatus in front.

'Come,' he says. 'Watch what happens. Put your finger here,' and he points to the little black-handled key I saw him operate on the first day. I look at him, remembering the sparks that flew out the watch house window.

'It is perfectly safe,' he says, and smiles. 'Trust me. I will tell you what to do.'

I put my finger on the knob of the little lever.

'Now,' he says, 'press down,' and I press it and there's a crack like a gunshot and a string of blue sparks leaps between the four brass balls on the device beside me and on the other side of the watch house, a bell begins to tinkle. I let go of the lever like it's bitten me and the bell is immediately silenced.

'You said it was safe,' I say to him, my heart pounding in my chest.

'Your face!' he says, laughing. 'I am sorry, Nuala. I can never resist.'

'What rang the bell?' I ask him, trying to keep my voice even, determined to be businesslike, even if he is not.

'You did, when you pressed the Morse key. You released the current from the cell. The electricity created electromagnetic waves that were strong enough to ring the bell.'

I walk between the table under the watch house window and the small counter to the side where the bell sits. I walk all the way around it. I look right underneath. There are no wires or cables or pipes. There is nothing to connect it to the lever on the table.

'Where are the waves?' I ask him.

'All around you,' he says. 'You cannot see or touch or feel them but they are most definitely there.'

'How do you know?'

'Didn't you just hear the bell ring? We know they are there because of what they do.'

I shake my head and stare at the empty space between the table and the bell. He is asking me to believe in the invisible and yet he says it with such an air of matter-of-fact, it is as if I am the one who is at odds with the world and he is the one speaking reason.

'How can you be sure?' I ask him.

'Can you see my words when I speak them?' he says.

'I can't, but I can hear them.'

'How is that?'

'I have ears.'

'How does your hearing work?'

I open my mouth and close it again. This is not a thing I have considered.

'Can you hold a spoken word?' he says. 'Can you catch it in your hand?'

'A word is made of breath,' I say. 'A word is a thing you feel in your throat, a sound you hear in your ear.'

'To begin with, yes, but can you feel my breath from where you are standing?'

I am standing by the counter beside the bell. I shake my head.

'The sound must reach you by some other means, therefore? The vibration is carried by molecules in the air,' he says, 'by invisible sound waves that cause your eardrum to vibrate.'

I put my hand to my ear. An eardrum is not a thing I've given any thought to. I try and picture what it might look like. A bodhrán, maybe, with the skin stretched taut, and his voice is causing it to vibrate? 'And these are the same waves that rang the bell? That carry the words to the mainland?'

'No, if that were the case then there would be no need for us. I have begun badly, Nuala. Let me try to explain. When sound travels, it meets resistance in the air that gradually fades out the sound waves. So if I stand at the top of the lighthouse and shout, the sound will only travel a short distance. You would hear me at the watch house, perhaps as far as the castle, but Mr Kemp will not hear me at the Coalyard station in Ballycastle. The distance is too great. The sound waves will not reach him.'

'There used to be a man,' I say, 'who lived at Ushet in the lower end, who had a voice big enough to be heard in Murlough, three miles beyond on the mainland.'

He laughs. 'Is that true?' he says.

'They say he used to call to his brother to come over and help with the harvest.'

'He was unusual.'

'Very.'

'You will agree, then, that for most people, their voices will not carry so far. Sound waves fade. Electromagnetic waves, on the other hand, do not. They travel through matter: air, earth, water. Nothing stops them, nothing at all. They are carried in the ether that surrounds the earth. They cannot be diminished. If we had a mast high enough and power enough to send them, we could transmit signals to the other side of the world using electromagnetic waves.'

'To Newfoundland?'

He laughs. 'Yes, if you like, to New York, to Sydney, to Paris, to Bombay.'

'Two thousand miles,' I say. 'You really think you can send them that far?'

'There is no question of it. How long for a letter to reach Newfoundland?'

'Seven days, maybe ten.'

'And the same back again? With the new technology, we will be able to reach it in seconds.'

'You'll be able to send a message there, and a message back again?'

'It is Mr Marconi's greatest project: *il grande salto del Atlantico*. It will take some time to develop the system but there is no reason to doubt that he will achieve it. In the meantime,' and he smiles at me, 'we are employed by Lloyd's to conquer the Sea of Moyle. Let us take a look at the receiving apparatus.'

He talks me through the equipment that sits to the right-hand side of the table: the metal drum he calls a relay that detects a signal, however weak; the telegraph instrument that strengthens it; the little glass tube filled with nickel filings that he has attached to the relay and to the earth, and to the high wire netting outside and, crucially, he says, the little tapper that taps the tube, that breaks the signal as required, that makes the use of the Morse code possible. The more he talks the more I see of what I do not know, can never understand.

He has a way of explaining things like it's important to him that you comprehend so I do my best for him. I don't know how he can go through life carrying so much knowledge about in his head. It must make him heavy, though he doesn't seem it. I concentrate hard on the words, and bit by bit, it does begin to make a kind of sense, the way he says it. His waves penetrate solid objects, liquids, gases, he says. They travel through people, hillsides, houses. They are no respecters of walls or of borders, or of boundaries. They go straight through. I put my hand again to my ear, consider what he's told me, what I've seen, what I've heard him say. I begin to believe that he could persuade me that black is white. I think he could talk me into believing anything.

He's not the best-looking man I've seen. His nose is a bit too long and thin and his ears are big and his parting is all wrong but he has humour in his mouth that smiles even when he's not smiling and his eyes are wide and green. His 'r's are all trills like the wagtail makes. When he talks about the waves, his eyes fill up with light. It's like listening to a song, hearing him speak. He talks about the ether the way the priest talks about faith, the way my mother used to sing about love.

He is trying to explain to me how the code works, how the taps from the telegraph hammer travel through the air. 'The sounds are transformed into beats,' he says, 'like a . . .' He can't find the word and he steps towards me and reaches for my hand. He turns it over, puts two fingers on the inside of my wrist, gently squeezes on the blue vein there. 'That,' he says. 'What is the word for that, the blood that pumps through your veins?'

'Pulse?' I say.

'Pulse!' he says, and I slide my wrist out of his hands before he can feel the change in it.

He explains that the pattern of dots and dashes and spaces gives a very special character to the code.

'You must send the complete sound of each letter, then pause before you send the next, a longer pause between words. Each sequence has a particular rhythm of its own. Listen.' He takes the knob of the telegraph key between the tips of his fingers and thumb. '"R": di-dah-dit; "L": di-dah-di-dit. Just one pulse between them but two different sounds, can you hear? Two different beats, two different rhythms. Let me show you.' He pulls the chair back from the table. 'Sit,' he says. 'Feet flat on the ground, back straight, and put your hand here.' I place my hand over the key. 'Now,' he says, more gently, 'rest your elbow on the table, relax your wrist, your forearm. That's it. Take the key between your thumb and your second finger and hold it loosely, by the fingertips. The forefinger you use to send the code. Now:' He puts his hand over mine and taps the key. '"R".' I nod at him. 'And "L". Yes?' His hand moves again. 'Can you feel the difference?' I can. It's only a tiny thing, a breath, a heartbeat, but I can feel it. 'Now you try,' he says to me. I tap the key the way he's shown me. 'Good,' he says. 'But relax your hand.' I tap the key again. He reaches for one of the metal discs and slides it on to the back of my wrist. 'Again,' he says. I tap the key and the disc slides off. He puts it back on my hand. 'You must practise to keep your hand level, relaxed, otherwise you will tire. You will get what is called the glass arm.'

I look up at him, trying to disguise a smile. 'The glass arm?'

'It is not a mistake in language,' he says sternly, 'it is what all the operators call it. Cramp in the forearm and wrist.' I turn back to the telegraph key. 'Are you laughing at me?'

'Of course not.'

'It is very serious.'

'I understand.'

'Good. You have a feeling for it, Nuala, as I knew you would. And it is as much about feeling as it is about hearing and seeing. The spaces are as important as the sounds. Get the order right and the spacing wrong and there's a world of difference to the meaning. Now, I will be a hard taskmaster. Try it for me again.' I do what he says but it is hard for me to concentrate while he is leaning over me, his breath on the side of my face. I practise, replacing the disc each time it slips off, until finally it stays on the back of my hand.

I go to the cottage and Ginny says, 'What are they doing up there, today?'

'Ringing bells,' I say.

I go about my business in the Tailor's house thinking about what Gabriel has said about the importance of the spaces. I am thinking about the voices I sometimes hear in my head, and about the girl I see who does not speak to me. Gabriel doesn't need to tell me that silence has a value, maybe the highest value of all, since nothing makes sense without it; since without pause, it is all meaningless clamour and noise.

The one time I can remember stepping off the island with my mother, we took the train from Ballycastle, through Garry Boy and Dalriada all the way to Alexander's in Ballymena. It must have been shortly before they left for Newfoundland. She must have been buying things to take with her, things she couldn't get in Ballycastle. Or maybe she didn't want her sister, Dorothy's mother, to know that they'd already made the decision to leave. I can remember my boot on the scuffed wooden step climbing into the carriage; the whistle as the train climbed the slopes of Glentow, the steam billowing out behind us. I remember the way the light slanted in through the frosted glass in the high carriage windows and cast a pattern of petals and leaves on to the white-painted panelling below. I remember the hard wooden benches under us and the smell of coal and soot, and the taste of flour round my mouth from the oven pot scone that Mother'd brought with us for the journey, and the sweetness of the buttermilk to wash it down. I remember the wonder of the jointed carriages that snaked for miles through the countryside. Maybe that was the point of the journey, maybe that's what my mother was doing: making memories for me to keep for after they'd all gone. But best of all I remember Alexander's shop.

It was the size of the chapel inside, with stained-glass windows that coloured the air, that sent shafts of red and green and yellow on to the walls and the floor, except instead of pews all in rows, and an altar with the priest's back to us, there were big square wooden counters and glass display cases that came up to the top of my head. Each one was piled high with bolts of fabric in every colour. It was like being in a maze. The underwear was kept in brass-handled wooden drawers behind the main counter. Mother was talking to the shop assistant, running her hand over fabric, testing the weight and heft of it. And then there was a clatter above my head and when I looked up, I saw that the ceiling was crossed with wooden tracks suspended from wires and that shooting along one of them was a little wooden ball. I tugged Mother's elbow and asked her what it was and she said it was the order, making its way to the cashier. 'Watch,' she said, so I watched. Mother made a decision about the fabric and handed over the money. The shop assistant in a neat ruffled blouse and fitted skirt took it from her and wrote on a docket, and then lifted one of the little wooden balls I'd seen and twisted it open into two halves. She slid the money and the docket into a metal cup inside, pushed the halves back together and dropped the ball into a wooden and metal carrier at her side. Then she pulled a cord and the ball shot up and out and disappeared along the line to the cashier in the middle of the store. A few minutes later, the ball came hurtling back and dropped down through a long narrow net on the counter. The assistant picked it up and gave Mother her change. I'd never seen anything like it. I didn't want to leave the shop; I could have watched them all day.

I look up from the table in the Tailor's house where I'm patting the oatcakes into shape and the Tailor has his eyes on me. 'Where do you go?' he says.

'What?' I say to him, startled, and then Ginny shuffles in from the lower room and says you could die of drouth in this house and is there no word of a drop of tay and that's the end of that.

When I go back up to the watch house I tell the electrician about the cash system they had in Alexander's, and ask him if his waves carry messages like this. And he says, 'You can think about it that way if you like, if it helps you to understand. The crucial thing to remember is: these signals travel without wires.' And even though I've witnessed the bell ring in the watch house without anything touching it, and even though he's told me all about the soundless, invisible waves, this is the part I can't get right in my head.

There is no docket that passes between the island and Ballycastle, no paper, no letter, no note. The words need not be written or even spoken in order for them to be understood there. They are thoughts transformed into beats, long and short, like a gull's wing makes in the air. With Signor Marconi's magic boxes, Gabriel's words become something else, they are signals, dots and dashes that appear on a spool of tape on the other side of the Sound at the weighmaster's cottage and are read and converted and then spoken. His words in the mouth of Tam Casey. An act of devilish ventriloquism. There's a thought to stop you in your tracks.

In the Tailor's house, or in the keeper's kitchen, the words I say do not travel beyond the walls. They fall to the floor, are swept out by the draught, are separated by the winds off Portavoolin, off Altacorry Head. They are as short-lived as the breeze itself. When I write a letter to Dorothy, I make marks on a page that only a person who can read Gaelic will understand. I seal it and carry it to the post office at the harbour and pay the penny lilac at the counter. Cissy Turner will stand there in front of the wooden pigeonholes, under the shelves bearing balls of string. She will take a good look at the address before she drops it in the mail bag that Jamesie will lift and carry to the boat and row out over the sea. At the harbour in Ballycastle, the bag will be loaded on a cart and bounced all the way up Quay Road, past the new villas and the trees to the post office in the Diamond where it will be emptied and the post sorted and my letter delivered only then. How many hands will have touched it before Dorothy can open and read it and smile? How long till she hears that the air on the island is still, that Sam Curley has broken his arm boating a cow for the market, that the new baby at the Rectory has the croup? It could be two days, if the weather stays fine, three weeks or more if the wind is up, by which time the still weather will be long past and Sam Curley's arm will be on the mend and the Rector's boy bouncing once again on his father's knee. A letter is a thing you can carry, you can touch and see, you can smell. It requires too great a leap of my brain to believe what the electrician asks me to.

Dorothy has seen a telephone in a store in Belfast. She says that one day we'll all have telephones in our houses and she and I will be able to talk whenever the notion takes us. There'll be no shortage of gossip then, she says. I think that day's a long way away, but strange as it seems, I can understand that a little better. Those messages travel along wires. However far apart the two speakers are and whatever magic occurs between them, there is something physical to connect them. The new wireless telegraphy makes use of thin air. The new wireless telegraphy asks that we believe in what we cannot see.

I ask Gabriel why this work is important and he says, 'One day it will be possible for every lighthouse on the coast to be put in communication with passing ships, for those ships to communicate with each other. Think of the lives that may be saved. This is Mr Marconi's main objective. And in the meantime,' he smiles at me, 'there is money to be made in knowing things, and the person who knows those things the soonest has the best chance at making most money.' I tell him about old Cissy in the post office shop and how she knows every move that's made on the island, but I can't think how she'd make money out of it.

'Why do people go there?' he says.

'To drop and collect the post. To hear the gossip.'

'And do they leave with their hands empty?'

'They leave with tea and sugar and tobacco.' I'd never thought of Cissy making money out of news before.

He tells me that Lloyd's need to know the whereabouts

of the ships and the safety of their cargoes and the date on which they're likely to dock. 'Information is power,' he says. 'Information is money. The person with the knowledge, the intelligence, holds the key to the bank. Wireless communication has the potential to improve all our lives. At the very best, it has the potential to save lives. Signor Marconi's work is driven by this.'

He has a ledger by the inker and a little pot of flour-and-water paste, and he shows me how every strip of paper that feeds off the spool is to be cut and pasted into the book, with the letters that the dots and dashes represent written in above. Sometimes he writes notes in pencil underneath, or on the following page, messages that seem cryptic in a language he begins to teach me. In the first column must be recorded the height of the mast (this rarely changes so I'm to put two marks to indicate it is as it was recorded before). In the second, the exact time of the receipt of the message (12.10 p.m.), in the third the content of the message (2 'V's). The final column is a note about the strength of the signal (2 dots in first 'V' missed; 2nd dot of 'H' missed; last dash split), and always at the bottom of the page a general report on the weather (Weather clear but raining; South-west gales & heavy seas; no sun). Now and again, there is a colour recorded and he writes them out for me: the colours of the rainbow with an extra two. Red means a perfect signal; crimson is good but with some parts missing; orange is imperfect but all of the message is readable; yellow is partially readable; green is a strong signal but unreadable; blue is strong but unreadable and missing; indigo is weak; purple is partially readable but missing; violet means nothing at all. He looks at me, 'Will you remember that?' he says.

'Violet is *nulla*,' I say to him. 'I'll remember that.'

He smiles. 'How do you say "nothing" in Gaelic?'

'The same way you say nothing in any language, without moving your lips.'

He laughs at this. 'I'm no match for you,' he says.

'There is no word for "No" in Gaelic,' I tell him, 'and no word either for "Yes".'

'That's impossible.'

'It's true.'

'How do you answer a question?'

'By saying that you will or you won't.'

'You're making fun of me.'

'I'm not.'

'So you can't say "No" to me?'

'Not in Gaelic. Luckily, I speak English as well.'

I wish I could spend all my time in the watch house talking with him, doing work that is neat and ordered and appreciated, that makes its way quietly down a page in numbers and columns, that does not require the rattle of buckets or shovels or basins or crocks.

July unspools itself slowly, the air warm, the earth damp and dry in turn. Ginny complains of the pains in her bones, the Tailor tramps the island looking for work. I pass my days between the cottage and the watch house, beating a path over the roddins that my feet could walk unbidden by me.

The Tailor, who can throw away nothing, on the grounds that it could come in handy some day, has a crate in the byre filled with parts of boats and carts and all sorts of things. In it I find the rusted thumb latch from a door. It's the closest I can get to a telegraph key. In the evenings I sit by the fire in the Tailor's house with the chart that Gabriel has given me and I beat out the rhythm of the letters with my fingertips and like this I learn the code.

* * *

'Can I ask you something?' I say to Gabriel this day.

'Of course.'

'Why do you need two pairs of glasses?'

He takes the thick-framed pair off his head and hands them to me. I put them on. The world is suddenly blurred, like it is when your eyes fill with tears. He says there are times when he needs to see more closely, for the intricate work of filing and measuring and for these he uses the thin-framed pair, the ones that are on his nose. But it would take too long to look at everything that closely so for the other times he uses the pair that he's handed to me. I take the glasses off and pass them back to him. 'They're making me feel seasick,' I say. 'Everything is cloudy.'

He's looking at me through the thin framed ones. 'To me, everything looks perfect,' he says.

In the cottage Ginny says, 'What are they doing up there, today?'

'Scrutinising things,' I say.

The electrician is testing me to see if I have learned the code. He sends a few 'V's to Tam Casey to gauge the strength of the signal and then a longer message.

'What did I send?' he says.

'You're very interested in the weather.'

He laughs and hands me the earphones. 'We will see if you are as good at listening.' He takes the wire from the induction coil and attaches it to the receiver.

The message comes through on the earphones, a series of brrrrps and burrs like a cricket might make and the tape begins to spool out from the wheel. Gabriel stands in front of it, so I cannot see the ink marks. I listen hard, trying to translate the pattern of sounds and pauses but it doesn't make much sense to me. 'I think he says it's cold,' I tell him. 'Something about the wind?'

Gabriel pulls the tape through his fingers.

'He can't close the window in the signal room,' he says, 'because of the wire to the mast. He's afraid he'll catch a cold.'

I say nothing about this but my face must register something of what I'm thinking – that Tam Casey's health is none of my concern.

'You do not like him,' Gabriel says to me.

I shrug. 'Whether I like him or not makes no difference to anyone.'

'It makes a difference to me,' he says, his eyes on mine.

'I don't like him,' I tell him.

'I thought so,' he says. 'What is it you dislike?'

'I don't trust him,' I say. 'I feel his eyes on me and . . . There's something about him I don't like.'

'I have no complaints about his work.'

'He's careful around you. He gives you no reason to complain.'

'It seems harsh to object to a man expressly because he gives you no reason to do so. If I do not offend you, is that reason for you to take offence?'

'You're twisting my words.'

'You are hard on him, I think.'

I shrug.

'Shall we find out if he has heard from Mr Kemp?' he says. 'You can write it down first if that helps.'

So I write out the message and then I send it and Gabriel nods his head. The message comes back to say that Mr Kemp has telegraphed. He has erected a mast in the Harbour Master's garden in Kingstown, in preparation for the races, commissioned a tug called the *Flying Huntress*, set up an instrument room in its cabin. The National Telephone Company has laid a special telephone wire from the land station to the offices of the *Daily Express* and *Evening Mail*.

There's something about spars and iron caps and sheers that I can't make out but the electrician can't make it out either. 'You are very quick at this,' he says. 'It takes some operators weeks to learn.' He is a good teacher, though I don't tell him this, and I don't say anything more about Tam Casey. I don't want Gabriel to think me unkind. We make out at last that Mr Marconi's been out in the tug as far as the Kish lighthouse, that he's sent a message to Mr Kemp at the land station, another to Dublin and one to Horace Plunkett in the House of Commons itself. The electrician laughs when he reads this. 'He is showing off,' he says.

'Does Tam Casey have the same equipment as this over in the weighmaster's cottage?' I ask him.

'Exactly the same. He can send and receive both but not, of course, at the same time. It is a matter of switching the wires as we do here.' He talks to me about senders and receivers. 'It is a very civilised form of communication,' he says. 'You cannot talk while you are listening and you cannot listen while you talk. You have to know when it is time to do one or the other. It is quite revolutionary.' He smiles.

'And these two machines – yours and the one in

Ballycastle – they're – I don't know how to say it but – they're tuned to each other?'

'Not exactly. In theory, anyone with a receiver could pick up my message. In the same way that anyone who reads could open a letter and read it.'

'You're saying it's not private?'

He smiles. 'There are not very many people with this equipment in the world, and certainly no one else in Ballycastle. But you are right. We need to find a way to prevent interference, to tune in and out of wavelengths the way you might tune a piano. It is one of the things we are working on. It is the next obstacle to overcome.'

I think about the signals travelling by wavelength, about the ability to hear them only with the right equipment, and suddenly I understand something about the voices I hear in my head, about the girl who has appeared to me. I have a kind of tuning that other people don't have. That's all it is. I understand him better than he thinks. There are times when I can block out the voices, other times when they are loud in my ears. Maybe this electrician can teach me a thing or two. I won't be pestered with the voices of the dead. I look out the watch house window, over the restless sea where the black-tipped kittiwakes are fishing, dropping like stones into the blowing spray.

'So there's no need to watch any more?' I say to him.

He follows my gaze out the window, considering the question. 'No,' he says. 'Indeed, no need at all. The watch house has become a place to listen.'

The days pass in a haze of signals and talk. I go to the watch house in the mornings; in the afternoons I return to the Tailor's house. The girl appears from time to time. I've almost gotten used to her now. She seems to have taken it into her head to try and help me, like the kindly *gruagach* that Granda used to tell us about that lived in the Manor House. On my way back with a bucket from the well, it is her hand I see on the handle; her face across from me as I shake out the bolster on the iron bed. She doesn't look anything like the *gruagach*, though: she is tall and straight and slender and serious. Although she does not seem inclined to speak, she has begun to smile at me in an encouraging way, the way you might smile at a child whose understanding of the world is limited, a child who cannot see what you can see, cannot know all that you know.

Sometimes when Gabriel tells me things, I think I've

heard them before. Although it's not so much that I've heard what he's said, but more that I've seen him say it. He stands at the watch house window looking out, his back to me, his hand on the frame, and the picture is suddenly clear and familiar, like a photograph, or a memory, even though I know that that's not possible, that we've never stood in exactly this way before, he and I, saying what we're saying.

I am still having trouble with the idea of the invisible waves.

'If I were to throw a bottle off the cliff here, into the sea, would it remain there?' he says to me.

'Of course not. The current would carry it over to Islay, or to Fair Head, or south to the Rue, depending on the tides.'

'You believe that water will carry a bottle, undirected by human hand, why not believe the air can carry something as light as a word?'

'You can touch the water, put your hand in and it's wet, it tastes of brine, it smells of kelp. Sit in the mail boat even on a still day and you can feel the pull of Slough-na-Mara under the boards at your feet. You can see the white water where the two tides meet. Throw a lump of bracken out and you'll see how the current takes it. No one who's ever crossed the Moyle between here and the mainland would doubt the power of the sea.'

'Close your eyes,' he says.

'What?'

'Close your eyes.' So I close them.

'Can you see me?'

'My eyes are shut.'

'That's not what I asked.'

'I can't see you.'

There is a pause and then his voice, closer: 'How do you know I am here?' My eyelids flicker. 'Keep your eyes closed,' he says, and again, 'How do you know I am here?'

'You've just spoken to me.'

'Ssh. Listen. How do you know I am here?'

This is a stupid question. If he'd moved to leave I would have heard him, the rustle of his tweeds, the metal tip of the heels of his boots on the wooden boards. I can smell the metallic tang on his fingers from his filing of the nickel disc, the faint scent of wax, of India rubber off his clothing, but I shut my mouth tight and listen. I hear the clock tick on the wall, and the sea, gentle, on the rocks below Altacorry, the cry of a fulmar overhead. I can feel the full light from the window on my face so I know he's standing close to me. There's not a whisper of sound from him. He could have vanished into the air. He could have transported himself down through his machine the same way he does with his messages. He could be in Ballycastle right now, looking back over the sea at me. But still, I know he's there.

'It's a question of faith,' he says, 'of belief.' I keep my eyes closed tight. His voice is close to my ear. 'Can you feel this?' A breath on my cheek.

'I do,' I say, 'I can feel that.' And for a moment everything is sharp and familiar, his voice coming to me in the watch house, me standing there with my eyes shut, as if we've stood like this a dozen times or more. There are messages in the air, there's no question of that, a sort of closeness like the kind that comes before a storm, a listening, a waiting, a holding of breath. I hear him move away and I open my eyes. He is back at the window, looking out over the sea. 'These waves that are in the air, in the ether,' he says, 'are a kind of invisible energy. They are every bit as powerful as the waves you see outside. They cannot be diminished by the fact of our not being able to see them.' It's a lot to take in. I look at the silent bell in the watch house. He is making the airwaves seen and heard. He is giving form and voice to their ghost.

There is a piano in the parlour of the keeper's house. In the still July evenings, when the big meadow is filled with the sounds of the heather-bleats, we hear music drifting over from the direction of the Light. The salt air has not been kind to the instrument, but Gabriel has tuned it, after a fashion, and plays it as best he can. He has brought different music to ours. Some nights, he is joined by one of the young Harrisons on a fiddle, and I stand at the door of the Tailor's house and listen to the rise and fall of their music, as Gabriel tries to teach him the tune. Strange, delicate notes they are, hesitant, like they're not sure of where they're headed, repeated over and over, growing stronger through their repetition, round and round like the spinning wheel but then different, changed, although it's hard to say how, and whether the change is in the hearer, in the growing familiar with the music, in the anticipation of what comes next and not in the melody itself.

'What is that tune you play in the evenings?' I ask him this day, and he looks up, surprised.

'You can hear it? At Portavoolin?'

'Of course,' I smile at him. 'Music needn't go by the road,' I tell him. 'It comes over the roddins, same as me.'

He laughs at me. 'It's a sonata,' he says. 'Beethoven. It helps me to relax.'

Word goes round that there's to be a dance in the big barn. Dorothy comes over on the boat, makes arrangements to stay with Mrs Davey, the Rector's wife, who's a good client and friend of hers. Ginny and the Tailor have opted to stay away from the dancing. They'll come up afterwards to the Light. I call for Dorothy at the Rectory and we walk along the road from Ouig, arm in arm, like old times. It's a still evening, the sun dropping round as an orange behind Doonbeg in the upper end, gilding the sea. The chitchat of eider ducks fishing for mussels in Church Bay, a splash of white as a seal slips off a rock, the water parting and closing behind its dark whiskered head.

'Have you any news for me?' she says.

I know what she's hinting at, but there is no news of that sort, and I don't want to tell her anything of relations between me and the Tailor.

'Not a thing,' I say to her. 'Tell me the news of the town.'

So she tells me about the renovations at the chapel and about Mrs Corcoran who has become a regular in the shop, and about Tam Casey, who sets out from the Antrim Arms opposite her shop every morning to head to the weighmaster's cottage with his chest puffed out as far as it will go. 'You'd think he was the Duke of Wellington going out to defeat Napoleon at Waterloo.'

'Long may he stay there,' I say to her.

'You're still helping out, up at the watch house?' she asks me.

'I am,' I say, and I tell her what I've learned about the invisible waves and the way the messages are carried.

'You always were a great scholar, Nuala,' Dorothy says to me. 'Your brain is wasted here.'

We go into the barn where the Harrisons have set up with an accordion and a mandolin, a bodhrán and a fiddle. Mr Kernohan is calling the dances, smart in his keeper's uniform and cap.

'Everyone up. It's "The Waves of Tory",' he calls.

Dorothy and me join the end of the line as the dancers face each other across the room. Then Mr Kernohan appears with Gabriel at his side. 'Show him the ropes, will you, Nuala? It's his first time at a ceilidh.'

Gabriel shrugs, smiles at me. 'I have no idea what to do,' he says.

'It's the easiest dance to learn,' Mr Kernohan tells him, 'marching and swinging, that's all there is to it. Nuala will keep you right.'

He places Gabriel at the end of the line opposite, beside Mrs Davey, and walks back to the front of the room.

To my right, Dorothy takes my hand. I see Mrs Davey take Gabriel's. He looks across at me with mock panic in his eyes and then begins to laugh. As soon as the music starts up, the dancers begin to whoop, bob up and down.

'Forward and back,' calls Mr Kernohan, and the two lines dance towards each other, Mrs Davey skipping forward, dragging Gabriel with her, pulling him back again. His eyes widen at me. 'And again,' calls Mr Kernohan, before Gabriel has gotten his feet under him and forward and back we go. 'Jig set!' shouts the caller. 'One, two, one, two, three, four.' We jig on the spot, Gabriel looking around, baffled, lifting his knees, kicking out his leg now and again. Then, 'Pass through,' shouts Mr Kernohan, and the two lines move forward to meet each other, the dancers on our side with their arms raised to let the dancers opposite pass through. 'You're doing grand,' I say to him as he passes under my arm. Then it all begins again, with us facing the opposite way. He is always at least two steps behind everyone else, but he looks like he's beginning to enjoy himself, understanding the pattern, when Mr Kernohan calls, 'Couple one,' and I step forward to take his hand.

'What happens now?' he says.

The dancers begin to clap and stamp their feet in time to the music.

'Put your other hand on my elbow,' I say to him, 'I'll show you how to spin.' I begin to turn, pivoting on my right foot, propelling us both around with my left, until he gets the rhythm of it and starts to spin us too, and my heart starts thumping as he turns faster and faster and the room and the dancers become a blur of colour and noise. Though he swings me hard and my feet are flying, I feel safe with him, like he is gauging my strength against his own and knows the limit of my speed. Then the music changes, we slow, I let go of his hand and, head still spinning, march us up through the other couples, the dancers we pass falling into line behind us. We separate at the top of the line, rejoin at the bottom, form an arch with our hands and arms for 'under and over', stretch and duck through the other couples. 'You'll like this,' I say to him and smile. 'It's the waves.'

The dance ends with every couple grasping hands and elbows, swinging around the floor, the younger of the dancers spinning wildly, the older of them, standing aside, hands held to chests, smiling at the exertion. Then we all clap the band and the dancers.

Gabriel turns to me and bows, that strange click of his heels. 'Thank you for the dance lesson,' he says.

'You're welcome,' I say.

Dorothy leaves Mrs Davey, walks up and takes my arm. 'So that's the Italian?' she says.

'It is,' I say to her. 'Come on, we'll get a drink.'

'I can see the appeal of all those hours spent up at the watch house now,' Dorothy says, and gives me a wink that I never let on I see.

When the dancing's over, Mr Kernohan invites us back to the Light and we traipse up through the island, me and Dorothy and Mrs Davey and the rest of them, and Ginny and the Tailor arrive in on our heels. Dougal is there and Jamesie too, and Cissy from the shop and a couple of the Harrisons who are not yet tired playing. I sit down on the long couch under the window between Dorothy and Ginny. Gabriel sits down at the piano.

The Tailor takes a chair beside Jamesie. They're doing the rounds with the drink and Mr Kernohan shouts over, 'Give us a song, Nuala Byrne,' and, 'Yes,' says Gabriel at the piano, 'the one you were singing that other day.'

I shake my head. 'I'm not in the form for singing.'

'What song was that?' says Ginny.

'A Gaelic song,' Gabriel says, and laughs. 'Something about a cow. What was the name of it?'

I can feel the colour rise in my cheeks. 'Just an oul' come-all-ye. I don't remember.'

'Not a lullaby?' says Cissy, slyly, and the whole company laughs.

'There'll be time enough for that,' says Ginny, but she's looking at me sideways like she'd like to take the eye out of my head.

'Come on, Dougal,' says Jamesie. 'Give us a song yourself.'

Jamesie and Dougal are brothers, but there's a hardness about Jamesie that comes from the McQuaid side that neither Dougal nor the Tailor got. Ginny has it. There's an edge to their dealings with people, a sort of competitiveness. It comes out of fear of being mocked themselves, I think. It makes them cruel.

Dougal is one of the quietest men on the island. He hardly ever speaks until he's spoken to. I don't think he's ever looked me in the eye. He could carry a boat on his shoulders, he could fell any man on the island with one swipe of his arm, but ask him the time of day and the colour starts up in his cheeks and he looks any road but the one you're on and mumbles and slopes away as fast as he can. He looks all the time like he doesn't know what to do with his strength, like the weight of it's an embarrassment to him. I'm not expecting for a second that he'll stand up and sing; it's unfair of Jamesie to suggest it. But the next thing I know, he's up on his feet, elbow leaning on the mantelpiece and what do you know if he doesn't strike up a song. He has a small voice for a big man and we have to strain to hear the words, low and frail in Gaelic. Gabriel is listening too, and though he can't understand a word of it, I can see in his face that he hears the feeling behind it, a story of joy turned to sorrow, a story of love and loss. When the song ends and Dougal sits down and lifts his glass and takes a swallow, that's the only sound in the room before we're all on our feet, clapping.

Jamesie and the Tailor are up to something on the far side of the hearth. The pair of them are in the corner of the room, the Tailor with a look of concentration on his face, Jamesie with his back turned to me now but talking earnestly to the Tailor, going over some manoeuvre or other. The Tailor looks over at me and Jamesie turns and looks me up and down and winks. Jamesie Duffin has a houseful of big strapping red-headed sons. His wife looks like a rag that's been steeped in water and wrung out and hung on a hedge to dry. It occurs to me that he may be giving the Tailor some sort of intimate instruction. He lifts the bottle and crosses the floor and fills Ginny's glass again, as if she hasn't had enough already. Things liven up after that. The Harrisons give us a few half sets on account of the size of the room, the younger ones going about, kicking the stour up around us. By the end of the night Ginny's collapsed in the corner of the couch and has me affronted with her snoring. Mr Kernohan says to leave her to sleep it off – we've no way of shifting her anyway. I avoid looking at Gabriel. I don't know what he makes of us, of me and of the Tailor who hasn't spoken a word to me all night, and of Ginny, drunk by the fire.

Dorothy and Mrs Davey walk with us as far as the fork in the road. Me and the Tailor walk down to Portavoolin by ourselves, the light from a full moon shining white on the chalk road. I am thinking about Gabriel and about what he said in the watch house. His waves travel at the speed of light, he said, seven times around the earth in a second. I'd never before considered the question of the speed of light. I thought that light was either there or not. I never imagined its needing to travel. I must remember, I think to myself, to ask him about the moon. I like to listen to him when he talks. I remember his hand on my hand in the watch house and the tremor that passed from his fingers to my wrist like the flick of a tail underwater.

'It's a grand night,' the Tailor says.

'It is,' I answer him.

And then he does a strange thing. In the moonlight, I feel him reach for my hand and squeeze it. We walk on awkwardly together, on either side of the grass ridge that runs down the middle of the loanen, the Tailor still gripping my hand. But the ridge is wider than the gap between us, and after a minute or so of stumbling, our feet slipping on the grass and the loose gravel at its edge, he lets my hand drop.

We go into the cottage and we're heeled up in the bed as usual, the Tailor with his back to me blowing out through his nose, our first night alone in the house after nearly five months of marriage, when the noise of his breathing stops and he turns towards me.

'Will we give it a go, Nuala?' he says.

'Give what a go?' I say to him, but I fear that I already know what he means. By way of an answer he starts to footer with the buttons of his combinations and struggles up on top of me and tugs at my shift and the next thing I know, he's between my legs and going at it like he's working the plunger of the churn. I grab hold of the ticking under me and turn my face to the window where the big round face of the moon is shining in. So this is it, I think to myself, this is what all the fuss is about. Dorothy's book was right about the discomfort although there was no mention of the noise or the sweat. Finally, the Tailor gives a grunt and a groan and he rolls off me, gasping for air and lies on his back looking up. And when he's recovered his breath he says, 'Well, that's that, then,' and it's only seconds till he takes up the snoring again. I lie there in the dampness of the sheet, looking out the window. I am thinking that there must be more to married love than this dull throbbing pain I feel. It was Jamesie put him up to it, I'm certain, goading him on up there at the keeper's house.

In the morning I gather up the sheet and have it washed and dried and back on the bed before Ginny staggers down the loanen near evening time. It's none of her business what passes between me and the Tailor. It comes to nothing anyway. A morning or two after I feel the usual cramp. I throw the first of the monthly rags on the fire with greater gusto than I ever did before. I know Ginny sees it. She misses nothing. She counts the days between the rags with more keenness than I do myself.

I read the paper to Ginny and the Tailor and it is full of the news of the Kingstown experiments, news that was signalled over the water from Ballycastle days earlier to the electrician and me. The rehearsals for the races, Mr Marconi's wireless demonstrations, Horace Plunkett out on the tug, the whole affair a huge success. When the fog descended on the third day, the *Daily Express* in Dublin had news of the winners long before the spectators watching along the coast. Mr Kemp has dismantled the stations and has seen Mr Marconi off on the ferry to Holyhead, is now on his way back north. It won't be long till Tam Casey is back among us. I wonder could Mr Kemp be persuaded to keep him?

* * *

'Can I ask you something?' I say to Gabriel when I'm back in the watch house again.

'Of course,' he says.

'What causes the smell?'

'I hardly notice it any more. Come,' he says, and he walks to the door, leads me outside. He stops at the sail that's stretched over the grass, picks up a corner, ushers me underneath. Inside are dozens of thick glass boxes, each of them covered in a layer of tar. There must be fifty of them in total, greenish in colour, a web of wires running across the tops. 'Cells,' he says, 'holding lead plates, filled with sulphuric acid. What you smell is hydrogen sulphide – the gas it gives off when the two react.'

'What do they do?'

'They generate volts – the electrical charge you released when you tapped the lever on the coherer.' He looks up. 'The aerial picks up enough electromagnetic waves to power a receiver over short distances. For longer distances, we need a little more muscle.'

'It reeks in here.'

'Thank you,' and he smiles. 'You have very serious eyes,' he says.

I remember then that there was something else I

wanted to ask him, 'What's faster than the speed of light?'

'Nothing that we know of – yet,' he says. 'But one day, someone will find it and when they do, we will be able to move through time as easily as we move through memory, as easily as we move from room to room.'

'That's impossible,' I tell him.

He says 'impossible' is a term relative to time. It is impossible for a man to fly, he says, but it's only impossible *now*. In the future, that will change. Impossible is subject to trial and error and then it is no longer impossible and then we move on to something else, some other impossible-for-now.

'Do you think the dead have found it?' This is a risky question, but it's been on my mind for some time and now the words are out of my mouth and there's nothing I can do to bring them back.

He looks at me strangely. 'Found what?'

'The thing that's faster than the speed of light. Do you think they can move through time? Or that their voices can?'

'What an extraordinary question,' he says. 'Why would you ask that?'

What would he say if I told him about the girl I see,

the voices I sometimes hear? Would he think me mad? Would he look at me the way the youngsters did in the schoolyard all those years ago? I shake my head. 'Just nonsense,' I say to him, and I duck back out from under the canvas, away from the dreadful reek.

When I was small, my head the height of my mother's waist, I went with her to the Manor House to collect the linens, her with a creel on her back. She told me to wait in the back hall. There was a door a little open into a room at the front of the house, the smell of leather and polish and wax, so of course, I pushed it and went in. The big windows looked out over the green to the south, over the wall to the harbour beyond, on the opposite side of the Bay. The other three walls of the room were lined with books – even the fire set in the grate had shelves above it. It was like being inside one of the caves, except instead of rock and moss, the walls were studded with pages. I walked around, running my hand along the spines, feeling for the engraved letters under my fingers. I couldn't read then but I knew what reading was. I knew that those letters held the key to whole worlds, that this was another means of keeping a story, different from the way my grandfather stored them in his head. In the corner of the room, away from the window, stood a globe on a three-legged wooden stand, a brass hoop that arched over the top and held the sphere in place. I didn't know what it was then. I thought it an odd sort of patterned ball, sky and oatmeal-coloured. I tried to lift it out, found that I couldn't. But when I saw that it moved under my hand, I spun it round, gently to begin with, then harder and harder till all the colours blended into the colour of the skin on the back of my hand. Next thing I knew, there was a sharp tug at my elbow, my mother pulling me across the rug, scolding me under her breath.

'And, perhaps most importantly,' Gabriel is saying back in the watch house, 'the waves follow the curvature of the earth.' I think of the globe in the Manor House, imagine it surrounded in a haze of electric charge, think of the haze carrying signals. 'Which means,' he says, 'that it is only a matter of time until we can send our signals across the Atlantic, all the way to America itself. It is a simple question of mathematics,' he says. 'The higher the mast connected by wire with the transmitter, the greater the distance of transmission.'

'How high a mast would you need to send a signal from here to Newfoundland?' I ask him.

'Newfoundland again?'

'That's where my family are.'

'How is it that they are there and you are here?'

'They left when I was small. There was nothing for them here. I was supposed to follow later, but that didn't work out.'

'You married the Tailor?' I nod at this. 'You must miss them?' he says.

'I hardly remember them.'

'You must miss them, all the same?'

'I suppose I do.'

He takes a deep breath. 'Let me see,' he says. 'Double the height of the wire and you quadruple the distance of transmission. A wire suspended from a mast at eighty feet in height will transmit over a distance of twenty miles, a hundred and sixty feet, eighty miles and so on. Newfoundland is around two thousand miles distant.' He lifts the stub of a pencil off the table top, starts to scribble calculations. 'In theory, we would need a mast at around a thousand feet in height, roughly a fifth of a mile.'

'A fifth of a mile? From here to Bruce's Castle, say, except straight up into the air. And with that you could reach St John's?'

'In theory,' he says, 'if there were another Eiffel

Tower on the other side of the Atlantic there would be nothing to prevent us sending messages from Paris to New York, through the ether, and without ocean cables. Although in practice, it is not quite as simple as that, otherwise Mr Marconi would have succeeded by now. And then there is the power required.' He smiles at me, wrinkles his nose. 'Imagine the smell of all those batteries.'

Letters from Newfoundland come rarely to the island and with news that's weeks out of date. My mother writes about the men's work in the fisheries, about the seals and the whales they spot off the islands. Mulholland Point and East Quoddy Head and Lubec wink a triangle of light at them, she says, like the lights at Altacorry and the Maidens and Kintyre, and she complains that none of this is like it is at home. She writes of the days they go mackerel fishing off the rocks at the harbour with our cousins. And behind it all is what she's not writing, not saying, an apology for leaving me behind, for not sending for me sooner. I have been the salve to her conscience, the part of her that stayed to mind and to companion her mother and father into their old age. Gabriel needn't talk to me about deciphering code, about transatlantic messages. All my life I've been translating signals between here and the other side of the ocean. 'You cannot leave and still be here,' is what Granny used to say to every letter that came, full of their homesickness. I imagine what it would be like to message them the way Gabriel sends messages to Tam Casey and Mr Kemp, to know how they are and what they are doing in the moment of their doing it instead of days later when the thing is almost forgotten. It's a kind of wishing and a kind of magic to think like this, though Gabriel says it will happen. God knows where any of us will be when it does. Years and years under the earth, no doubt, where even Mr Marconi's waves cannot reach us.

I don't remember my family leaving but I remember a new quietness at the table, room at my elbow, more light in the cabin, which we got used to bit by bit. Me standing on the creepie stool while the spuds were emptied into the middle of the table, the saltiness of the glashan in three bowls of thin broth; Granda saying, 'They'll be on the steamer now'; Granny peering out the cabin window like she could pull them back with her eyes. It's an odd bittersweet thing to grow up with old people. The taller you get, the more bent and frail they become, like there's only so much space or straightness to go around, like their bending is to make room for you. I was taller than both of them by the time I left school and still they called me Nuala Beag – Little Nuala – till they were both gone from the world. Those were strange letters to write to Newfoundland, to tell my mother she'd lost her own parents, one after the other. It was odd to think of me sending news that the whole island had and that would take two weeks to reach her. I counted the days between us, the days between my grief and hers. I can't pretend I didn't write them with a certain amount of relish. I can't pretend I wasn't impatient for her suffering to begin.

## Nuala

### July/August 1898

My prayers have not been answered. Tam Casey is back. He's in the keeper's kitchen when I walk up, no sign of Gabriel.

'Just me for dinner today,' he says, more full of himself than he was before.

'Where is Mr Donati?' I say.

He looks at me like it's not my place to ask such a question. 'He's lying down with a bad head, if you must know,' he says.

I bite my lip and prepare the meal as quickly as I can, but Tam Casey's in the mood for talking. 'How did you all get on while I was away?'

'Grand.'

'How did you find learning the code?'

'Grand.'

'You'll not be needed in the watch house now I'm back.'

I say nothing.

'You're a woman of few words when it suits you, Nuala Byrne.'

I hate it that he uses my own people's name to me. He has no right to it; he's not from here. But I say nothing to him. He is trying to goad me into speaking, I think, and speaking to him is not a thing I want to do. I want to be as far from him as I can be. It puts a shiver up my spine to be in the same room alone with him.

The bell rings in the kitchen and he rises with great importance and walks out to the watch house. I would like to ease Gabriel's sore head if I can. I throw the shin bone I've brought with me and the vegetables into the big pot and top it with water and a handful of barley and leave it on the fire to stew. Then I go back over to Portcastle to where I know there's still a bit of sweet kelp left drying on the walls, and I pluck a piece and bring it back and put it on the table. I give the broth a stir. It's bubbling away, looking after itself. And then I have an idea, a whimsy, to write Gabriel a note in Morse with instructions for him to chew the dulse to take the pain out of his head, so I tear a strip from the top of an old newspaper and take a pencil from the drawer in the bookcase. I write it quickly; I don't want Tam Casey to see it. I look out the door up to the watch house and there's no sign of him coming back. I take my courage in my hands and walk out into the passage and, heart thumping, creep up the stairs. There's a door at the top, which is open a little, and when I peer in I see Gabriel lying on his back in his clothes on the bed. He has one arm across his eyes, the other across his chest. His dark hair curls on the pillow. There's a lump of white quartz on the nightstand beside him. I slide the scrap of paper in under it, and as I do his arm moves and his eyes flick open, and he looks at me and then his eyelids close again. I slip back down the stairs. As I'm gathering up my basket, about to leave, Tam Casey walks in, picks the kelp up off the table. 'What's this for?' he says.

'It cures headaches,' I tell him.

He gives me a sneer I ignore. 'You're quite the healer,' he says.

I walk the other way round the table from him. 'The broth's ready any time you want it,' I say and I leave by the open door.

Ginny gets hold of the newspaper from the Rector's wife and I'm reading to her and the Tailor as usual, when I turn a page and am stopped by an illustration of a thin, dark-haired man. He is seated at a table, his back to the viewer, the tail of his jacket visible through the open back of the chair. His head is bent over an instrument – a copper cylinder, a box, a frame – and he is tapping out a message on a Morse key. The scene is so familiar to me that for a second I think that the *Daily Mail* has had a spy on the island and that it is Gabriel who is pictured there. Then I see the name 'Marconi' and realise it is the great man himself. Two ladies stand behind him, side-on, both in leg-o'-mutton sleeves so wide as to look like they might take flight, the first with her hand on the back of the operator's chair, leaning over his shoulder, a simpering look on her face. A wire leads from the instrument out through the top of a window where the line becomes dotted to show that it stretches for some distance and ends at the mast of a yacht on the water (the print reads), four miles away.

The caption between the two scenes: 'Sending a Message to the Prince'.

'What are you gawping at?' says Ginny.

I read the print below the drawing. 'It's Mr Marconi,' I say. 'He's with the Prince of Wales.'

Next day when I go up to the Light Gabriel is there in the kitchen. He smiles his hello, thanks me for the kelp.

'I thought I had dreamed you,' he says to me, 'but when I woke I found the note.'

I tell him to chew a piece of dulse every day and he'll never suffer from headache.

'You know a lot of things,' he says.

'I do,' I say to him back.

Tam Casey comes in, sits down at the table. 'Still no word from Mr Marconi?' he asks Gabriel.

'No,' says Gabriel. 'Mr Kemp has heard nothing from him. I thought he would follow on, soon after Kingstown.'

'He's on the royal yacht.' The words are out of me before I can stop them. Tam Casey throws me a look of contempt.

'What did you say, Nuala?' asks Gabriel.

'He's with the Prince of Wales, on the *Osborne*. The

Queen sent for him. Ginny has the paper. I read it to her last night.'

'I'll go down for it,' says Tam Casey. He takes off out the door and jumps on the cart, leaving his dinner sitting. So I tell Gabriel the whole thing that I read to Ginny, about the Prince falling down the stairs at the Rothschilds' in Paris and about his bad leg and how he was recuperating (I take care with the word) on the royal yacht and how the Queen had wanted regular medical reports. So she'd sent word to Mr Marconi to come to the Isle of Wight and he'd erected a one-hundred-foot pole in the grounds of Osborne House and set up a station in the saloon on board the royal yacht. And they were all busy sending messages forward and back, the Queen and the Duke of York and Princess Louise and the Prince of Wales himself, even when the boat was moving.

'*Santa Maria!*' says Gabriel, and smiles. 'He is a master publicist.'

I think of the sketches I've seen in the newspapers, of the old Queen in her white veil, with her hair piled high, the crown disappearing into her curls. It's a thrill to think that Mr Marconi is with her.

Tam Casey comes back from the harbour, breathless,

the paper in his hand, and he reads the whole thing out to Gabriel like Gabriel couldn't read it himself.

'"The message,"' he reads, '"was deciphered to Prince Edward by Mr Marconi himself. It read: 'The Queen hopes the Prince has had a good night and hopes to be on board a little before five.' The Prince has presented Mr Marconi with a tiepin in reward for his efforts."'

'Ha!' says Gabriel. 'The clever rascal. He has converted even the Queen. This augurs well for future investment. There will be no stopping him now.'

There's talk at the table of Mr Kemp, who arrived back in the town from Kingstown some days ago. He has progressed to the chapel spire in Clare Street in Ballycastle, hoping for a better signal. I have a picture in my head of the Englishman, hanging off the spire the way I've seen Paddy the Cliff hang off the stacks at Portnaboe when he's gathering gulls' eggs. And it's too much for me, the thought of Mr Kemp, his red hair sticking out from under his bowler hat, glinting in the sun like the copper wire that's never far from his hand.

'What's funny?' says Gabriel, and Tam Casey raises his head from the paper to look at me.

'Nothing,' I say, startled, not realising he was watching. 'Nothing at all.'

'Tell us,' Gabriel says, but I won't, not with Tam Casey listening.

'You should smile more often,' Gabriel says, and I turn away from them both.

'Is there a barber on the island?' Gabriel asks me this day.

'Con Dolan comes once a month,' I tell him, 'and sets up at the harbour, but you've missed him. He'll not be back now for three weeks or more.'

He runs his hand round the back of his head. 'Mr Marconi will think I have gone native.'

'Is he coming?'

'There's no word from him yet, but these experiments were never intended to be long-lived. I expect we'll be called away soon.'

'I used to cut my grandfather's hair. I could do it for you, if you want.'

'Do you have shears?'

'I could use the Tailor's. I'll bring them up tomorrow.'

He sits in the straight-backed chair at the window, his back to the kitchen fire. I tie an old apron of Mrs

Kernohan's round his throat. He reaches me a comb, folds his hands on his lap. I dip the comb in the basin to dampen it and then run it straight up from the nape of his neck, tiny whorls of hair underneath. 'How much do you want off?'

'An inch or so?'

I stay behind him for as long as I can, combing and snipping, the hair falling down on to the apron on his shoulders, or sliding off on to the floor. I have to pull his ears out a little so I can trim the hair behind and above and it's awkward then, with the Tailor's shears, the blades of which are wide and are meant for cutting bolts of cloth. The point of one blade catches his skin.

'Sorry,' I say to him.

He puts his hands up. 'I'm quite fond of my ears,' he says. I can tell that he's smiling.

I dip the comb in the basin again and then I have to move around so I can cut the hair at the front. I have to reach up a little more to do this, and comb his hair forward to get a straight line and I can feel his breath on my wrists as I do it. I am doing my best not to look at his eyes, at his mouth, which seems to me to be always smiling a little, but then I do look and see that his eyes are closed. So I dip the comb again and pull it through the hair and I'm finished cutting when I hear a foot stop dead on the threshold and I take a step back, expecting Tam Casey, but when I look it's only Dougal, standing there with his two arms the one length, opening and closing his mouth like a murran stranded on the shingle after a storm.

Gabriel opens his eyes. 'Nuala is giving me a haircut,' he says.

'I'm sorry,' Dougal mutters, and turns as if to go out, his face reddening as he does, as if he's walked in on an intimacy, as if he's seen something he shouldn't.

'Not at all,' says Gabriel. 'We're finished, are we not?' And when I nod he rises from the chair. 'What is it, Dougal?' He pulls the apron away and walks to the glass-fronted bookcase to see his reflection.

Dougal turns back into the room. 'Tam sent me to say, there's a ship passing.'

'Thank you, Dougal. I'll be there directly.' He runs his hand over his head. 'You have done a good job,' he says. 'Is there nothing you cannot do, Nuala?'

'Not that I know of,' I say, and I put the shears down on the table and pick up the bisim to brush the hair off the tiled floor. Gabriel goes out past Dougal and I realise, after a moment, that Dougal is still standing sideways in the doorway, looking down at the ground. I can see him trying to screw up the courage to say something.

'Do you think it's right to . . . ?' he begins, and then stops.

I give him a scornful look. 'To sweep the floor? Someone's got to do it.'

Dougal looks pained. 'I didn't mean that, I meant . . .' but he can't find the words to say what he means and my look is enough to silence him.

'Away out of here, Dougal, you're only in the road of me.' And he skulks out the door, after Gabriel.

Who does Dougal think he is, giving me advice? There's no law that I know of that says a woman can't cut a man's hair. When he's gone, I pick up a lock of it, slip it into my apron pocket. There's no harm in that, is there? It's only a lock of hair. Still, I'm glad it was only Dougal that walked in.

Mr Kemp is on the move again, to a rental house on North Street. Gabriel says the problem was the lack of a signal room, that the belfry at the chapel was too small for all the equipment. He has found a good spot in the White Lodge, a private house with plenty of space. He has borrowed the jib of a crane from the harbour to act as a lower mast, suspended an aerial from a bedroom window down the cliff side. He is signalling almost non-stop. The log book in the watch house is nearly full.

Then word comes that General Benson is paying a visit to the island. He is curious about the experiments and has asked for a demonstration.

'You will help me?' Gabriel says.

'What about Tam Casey?'

'Tam is not as skilled with the Morse key as you. He can pick the general up from the harbour. It will give us time to prepare.'

The general arrives in the trap. I've seen him before in Ballycastle but never in full military dress. He steps down in a red coat with brass buttons, a gold collar, gold braid at the cuffs. The left side of his chest is studded with medals. He is a little bent and leans on a gold-topped cane in his left hand, smooths his thick white moustache with his right, runs his hand over his bald shiny head, a little tuft of white hair over each ear. He nods to Tam Casey, who picks a white-feathered helmet off the seat of the trap and hands it to him. The general tucks the helmet under his left arm, salutes Gabriel as he stands outside the watch house, gives out a hearty laugh.

'Thought it an appropriate occasion for the full regimentals,' he says to Gabriel. 'Given that it's a day for conquering the waves, as it were.'

We are introduced and he steps into the watch house in his knee-high boots, his white britches spotless from the journey. Tam Casey follows him in. There's not much room with the four of us in there and no need that I can see for Tam Casey at all.

'I have been following Mr Marconi's progress with great interest,' the general says, 'ever since the trials on Salisbury Plain.'

'We made great strides there,' says Gabriel, 'and new discoveries every day since. You have already had a demonstration from Mr Kemp, at the White Lodge?'

'I have. Most impressive. And savoured a number of Mrs Walker's scones while I was there.'

'Nuala, if you would tap out a few "V"s?' says Gabriel.

'A fine assistant,' says the general, and his eyes travel the whole way down my skirts. I am weary of being leered at in this way, but no good will come of slighting the general, so I take the chair in front of the Morse key and wait for Gabriel's instruction.

'Mr Kemp will have explained the system in detail, General, but there are many finer points.' With both hands, he pushes his glasses further back on his head. 'Could I ask you to keep your eye on the coherer, the little glass tube, just here?'

The general takes up position, and at a nod from Gabriel I begin to tap the key. The blue sparks jump and stream at what I now know to call the induction coil.

'Hah!' says the general. 'The fireworks begin.'

'Can you see this little tapper?' Gabriel asks the general.

'I do,' he replies. 'It is striking the glass.'

'Indeed, and every time it does so, the filings drop to the bottom of the tube.'

'I see that, yes.'

'This tiny device,' says Gabriel, 'is Signor Marconi's invention. When the charge passes through the metal filings, they jump and cling together. They act as a conductor for the electrical pulse. Without the little tapper, they would remain stuck together; they cannot separate themselves once the charge has passed through. When the hammer taps the glass, however, the impact is enough to release the filings and they drop to the bottom of the tube, ready for the next pulse to pass.'

'Like a valve,' says the general. 'Such a simple thing.'

'It is, as you say, a simple thing, but also extremely effective.'

'Mr Marconi has his detractors?'

'I am aware of that,' Gabriel says.

'What do you say to those who claim that he has invented nothing, that he has simply assembled various pieces of apparatus already patented by others, that he has no genuine ideas of his own?'

A nerve in the corner of Gabriel's eye twitches. 'Signals have been sent before Mr Marconi's time, it is true,' he says. 'Other inventors have rung bells and set alight bulbs and released traps to free pigeons – where the signal was strong enough, they have produced enough magic tricks to entertain a roomful of children. But without this little tapper that breaks the circuit, this tiny invention by Signor Marconi, there would be no such thing as conveying a message using Morse code. Meaningful wireless communication over dozens of miles is impossible without it.'

'The final piece of the puzzle?' the general says.

Gabriel nods to me to end the signal. 'There are those

who would say that arranging things in a new way does not make a man an inventor and it does not make him a genius. I say it is precisely this that makes Mr Marconi so. He has been my friend for a long time. I have watched him experiment over the years. He is as a man possessed. He knows there is an answer, and that if he wears away at it long enough he will find it. I have been with him when he has filed and adjusted and perfected his equipment to the last millimetre, when he has worked through the night and into the next day and the night after that, oblivious to cold or dark or thirst. He will not rest until he has spanned the Atlantic, General. And I plan to be there to witness it.'

He talks to the general about the trials on Salisbury Plain, about the ten-foot balloons and the calico kites they sent up covered in tin foil to keep the wires aloft, how the gales blew them to pieces. He tells him about the mast at the Needles on the Isle of Wight, one hundred and twenty feet high in the air, how Signor Marconi and Mr Kemp put to sea in a tug boat, travelling further and further out every day for weeks in all kinds of weather, until they could get signals clear to the mainland four miles away. At Kingstown, he says, there were times when the *Flying Huntress* was twenty-five miles from shore and they transmitted over seven hundred wireless signals.

His hands are always on the move when he's explaining things. I am listening to him speak, at the way he sometimes misses the sound of the 'h' at the beginning of a word, at the way he replaces an 'x' with an 's'. He is lost in what he's saying. He could be anywhere, saying this.

'If you've already proved it can be done,' says the general, 'that you can send signals over a distance of up to twenty-five miles, then, with the greatest respect, why have you come here? Ballycastle is seven miles away at most.'

'We need to prove that it has a commercial use,' Gabriel says. 'Lloyd's are paying for these experiments.'

'And have you done so?'

'You saw the weather yesterday, sir?'

'A real pea-souper.'

'The ships pass close enough to the island to signal the keepers with their flags; even in thick fog they can be seen from here quite clearly. But in those conditions, the flags on the island cannot be seen by the lookout on the mainland at Torr Head. The keepers have the information but they do not have the means to pass it on. It is useless to them if it cannot leave the island. Ten ships passed us yesterday. With our equipment, we signalled news to Ballycastle of every one, and from there Mr Kemp was able to wire their progress to Lloyd's in London.'

'Your waves are unaffected by fog?'

'If anything, the signal is clearer.'

'What about rain, snow?'

'We were in Bournemouth in January of this year when the blizzards brought down the telegraph wires. Mr Gladstone was visiting and had taken ill. London was clamouring for news of him. We were able to send wireless messages to the Royal Needles where the telegraph links were still intact. London received hourly bulletins of the ex-Prime Minister's health.'

'Astonishing,' says the general. 'Wireless telegraphy. Its potential, for commerce, for the military: the mind boggles.'

'In his experiments with the Italian navy, Signor Marconi has exploded gunpowder at a distance of a mile and a half, without the use of wires, but by means of electromagnetic signals.'

'This is a terrifying possibility,' says the general. 'It's a damn good thing he's on our side. Tell me something of the theory behind it.'

Gabriel smiles. 'Mr Marconi is not an academic,' he says, 'he is a practitioner. There is no theory. Theory gets in the way of invention. There is trial and error, there is experiment, there is finding out what works, there is keeping an open mind. In this way, a theory may be devised. But we do not begin there. We leave that to the professors who will have to rewrite their books.'

The general looks at the apparatus, leans on his cane. 'The world moves too fast for me,' he says, shaking his head. 'I am too old. I cannot begin to comprehend what this might mean for future generations.'

'Would you like to send a message, sir? To Mr Kemp on the mainland?'

'I would be delighted. What should I say?'

'Anything you wish.'

'Ask him . . . ask him if Mrs Walker has done any baking today?'

Gabriel turns to me. 'Nuala?'

I can feel Tam Casey's eyes on me as I send the message through. I'm aware of his fingers moving, tapping out the letters on his wrist, testing me. There's a pause in which Gabriel switches the wire from the transmitter to the receiver, and then a further pause while we all sit, eyes on the inker. Then the little wheel begins to move and the inker starts to print and the tape begins to whirr forward, spooling out on to the table. Gabriel makes no move to pick it up but nods, instead, at me. I feed it through my fingers, translate the dots and dashes into meaning. 'She says if you call on your way through, there'll be a barnbrack waiting for you, General.'

The old man guffaws. 'I shall savour the truth of that message on the other side of the Sound,' he says. 'Well done, Assistant, very well done indeed.'

They talk some more, the general moving around the watch house, leaning on his cane, inspecting the equipment. Finally he nods to Tam Casey. 'We'll have to make a move if we want to make the gap in the tides,' he says. And to Gabriel, 'How much do I owe you?'

'Nothing at all,' says Gabriel. 'I would not dream of it, sir.'

There's a twinkle in the general's eye. 'I insist,' he says. 'I heard Lord Kelvin paid Mr Marconi when he sent the message from Alum Bay. That must have put his nose out of joint. If your invention progresses as you say it will, it will render his telegraph system obsolete.'

'Lord Kelvin was most gracious, sir. He paid telegram prices. A shilling.'

The general reaches into the pocket of his tunic, slips the coin into Gabriel's hand. 'A shilling it is,' he says.

It's nearly the end of July and the weather is fine. Dorothy writes to say that she will come over Saturday evening for the sweating. She'll stay at the Rectory again, she says. She has no desire to be kept awake by Ginny's snoring.

'What are you sweating for now?' says Ginny. 'The Lammas Fair's not for nearly another month.'

'We don't have to wait for the fair to get in the sweat house,' I tell her.

'What have you been doing to get dirty?' she says to me, and I give her a sharp look.

She says she's killed with aches, the *fuair*, her two hands are twisted like crab claws. 'If there's a pain about at all it'll light on me,' she says. She says it's years since she's been in the sweat house, and if we're stoking it up she'll get into it herself. The men are all away to the christening of a net. 'We'll get peace to ourselves,' says Ginny.

I take a lit turf from the fire and put it in an old Blue Bird tin. Me and Dorothy fill two creels of turf and carry it up to the little lough at Glackaharan. We can see the beehive shape of the sweat house as we come off the road, the march wall leading away on either side, a screen of alder to the roadside giving a bit of shelter, some cover. The low stone entrance is overgrown with nettles and harebells, there's been no one near it since the summer before. We clear the briars and crawl in under the low lintel on our hands and knees, sweep out the old ashes and roots with a fern, pile some twigs and dry grass on top of the still glimmering turf I've brought and take turns to blow on it till it catches. Then we stack more turf around it and go outside and lift the sod off the roof to give it a draught. We sit down on the wall and wait for the heat to build and the smoke to clear.

Dorothy has met Mr Kemp. He is lodging in the Antrim Arms; she has seen him come and go. 'He walked into the shop one day looking for cotton-covered hat wire,' she says, 'and I sold him a coil of it.'

'What did he want that for?' I ask her.

She straightens herself up on the wall and sticks a lump of moss under her nose for a moustache.

'"It's perfect for our experiments,"' she says in her very best English accent. '"The cotton acts as an insulator. It saves me the trouble of coating the wire with wax."'

She has me doubled over with her shenanigans. I nearly fall off the wall. She wants to know all about the experiments up at the Light so I tell her everything I know: about the waves in the air and how the code works and what Gabriel says about how the new wireless telegraphy will change communication for ever.

'Gabriel?' she says, and raises her eyebrows at me. 'What are you up to, Nuala?'

'What are you talking about?'

'I've been here a few hours only and it's Gabriel this and Gabriel that, and not a word about the Tailor.'

'What is there to say about the Tailor only that he's grand?'

'He is. He's more than grand. Him and Ginny have got themselves a slave, by the looks of things.'

'I'm not afraid of hard work.'

'I know that, Nuala, but more importantly, it's the Tailor that you married.'

'I don't need reminding of that.'

'Do you not? You know, Nuala, when you came to me that day in the shop I tried to tell you not to be hasty, that there might be other chances for you.'

'I'm very happy, thank you, Dorothy, with my situation.'

'Then you should be careful around the foreigner. You don't want to give him any notions.'

'What sort of notions?'

'You know fine well what I'm talking about, Nuala Byrne. Don't forget I've seen the pair of you – at the dance. Just mind yourself, that's all I'm saying.'

I slide down off the wall. 'The fire's caught,' I say to her. 'Ginny will be wondering where we've gotten to.'

We go back down to Portavoolin hardly saying a word. The Tailor has the exact measure of every body on the island but he knows not a thing about what causes a heart to beat faster or a pulse to quicken. It's true that Gabriel's on my mind a lot. I wonder if he spends much time thinking about me.

At the cottage we harness up old Susie the horse, put Ginny in the slipe cart and take her back up the rise. By the time we get up, the turf's burning well and the inside of the sweat house is as hot as an oven. We rake out the ashes and put the sod back on the roof and then it's down to our undergarments, all three of us, and into the heat. Dorothy crawls in first and helps Ginny in. It's a sight for sore eyes crawling in behind her, I can tell you. But we get in and get settled on the earthen ledge and wait for the sweating to begin. I love it in there, the rough stone wall at your back, the heat of the slabs under your feet, the glow of the few remaining embers on the clay floor, and then the slipperiness of your skin as the heat seeps in, the way the breath catches in your throat. They say the monks built these centuries ago to cleanse their bodies and their souls, a kind of unspoken prayer, a meditation, and I can understand that as I sit there, breathing in the heat. It must be like being in the womb, I think. It must be like going right back, as close to the beginning of being as it's possible to get. You can forget everything you ever learned except how to breathe out and breathe in. We sit in there till we can't stick the heat a second longer and then me and Dorothy have to oxter Ginny out and into the shallow lake, her feet hardly touching the ground. The skin on her arms and neck and belly is all slack and loose and the two paps are hanging down on her the like of what you'd see on an old sow. The backs of her hands are as risen and veined as two cabbage leaves, but the skin on her back and shoulders and shins is white and taut and smooth and there's a little mark on her shoulder that I haven't seen before, the shape of a tadpole, the colour of a tea stain. I see Dorothy look at it too. I wonder if any man has ever touched Ginny, if any hand has moved over her skin since the time she was a child. Who is there to love her? I think to myself. I don't want to end up like that. I want to know about love. There's more to it, I'm sure, than what passed between me and the Tailor in the cottage the night of the ceilidh in the big barn. There has to be more to it than that.

We must have been making a bit of a racket, what with all the screeching when we hit the cold water. Dorothy fell over and sat right down in it and then Ginny did the same. They must have heard us up at the Light. I'm kicking sprays of water over Dorothy and she grabs me by the leg and pulls me down. When I lift my head out of the water, I see a movement over the heather towards Altacorry, and there's Gabriel, looking straight at me, up to my neck in lough water and hardly a stitch of clothes on me. I don't know how long he's been there. I don't know what he's seen but there's a look that passes between us that needs no charts to decipher it. Dorothy sees me stare and turns her head and sees him too, but Ginny has her back to him and is too busy shivering to notice anything. I silence Dorothy with one shake of the head and Gabriel turns and goes. And I make a decision there and then that I won't heed Dorothy's warning. I won't end up like Ginny. I'll do what I must to colour my grey life, to find out what love feels like, no matter what anyone says.

I see him about the island with his geologist's hammer, collecting samples of rock. His pockets are always full of stones, white gravel or flint that he's picked up as he walks, blue porcellanite he has collected from Brockley. He says there used to be an axe factory there, maybe five thousand years ago, that they sent the stone axe heads to all parts of Britain and Ireland. He says that at one time, the island was divided in two; that Ballynoe was under the sea. It looks like that sometimes still, when you're walking from the east through Ballycarry, like Glebe and Ouig and Demesne have all dipped under the Moyle. And for the old people it might as well be like that still, so little do the upper islanders want to have to do with the lower. He says that the chalk on the island is made up of millions of shells and sea creatures, that the ridges on the field at Imraham show how high the sea once rose. He says that the pillars at Doon Point were formed by volcanoes at the same time as the Giant's Causeway, millions of years ago. He says you can tell the whole history of a place from what you find in the rock, in the earth. He has a habit of rolling a pebble between his fingers. I've seen him do it when he's thinking about something, or trying to find a word in English. I think that's funny, that he has to search for words, when he's the one gathering them up, sending them off across the sea.

Not long after the day at the sweat house, I mention the icicles to him, the ones to be found in the cave at the Wet Cove, down by the shore at Ally, beyond the Saddle Stack. He asks me what I mean by icicles and I tell him and he says, 'Stalactites! Are you sure? I must see those.' I tell him to meet me at the Blue Hole at dawn, before the day's work begins. I can see him hesitate.

'Would that be all right?' he says.

I shrug. 'I know the caves better than anyone.'

'I would love to see them,' he says.

It's the first day of August, almost light by five. I know the road over to the Wet Cove well. The water at the Blue Hole is still and clear, moving gently over the shingle, the only sound the snorts of the seals that are lying up on the grey rocks. No one would pass any remarks if they saw me out with my basket gathering boor tree leaves – the entrance to the cave is almost hidden with them. And what if I chanced on Gabriel while I was out, and him known for his rambling and his scuttling about looking for rocks? Who would remark on that?

We have to get down on our hands and knees to crawl into the cave. Once we're in we can stand up easily enough. He produces a candle and a small tin box of matches and strikes one on the cave wall. I've never been in a cave in candlelight. The rocks reach down like living things, like long brown fingers from the roof and taper into points, water dripping off the tips on to the cave floor. He hands me the candle to hold, puts both his hands on the rock. You can see where people have broken the icicles off over the years and taken them away. I tell him Dougal said he saw a man selling them at the Causeway and Gabriel gets very annoyed about that. He says they shouldn't be touched. He says, in his strange accent, that they are a 'national 'eritage', without the 'h'.

'They say if you keep walking through the cave,' I tell him, 'you'll come out on the other side of the island.'

'Is that true?' he says.

'There isn't a candle made that would last that long. No one's ever been brave enough to try.'

There are names and initials and the shapes of hearts gouged into the dark walls and into the roof of the cave.

It is quiet here, not even the sound of the sea. He says something in his own language and I ask him what that is. 'Love,' he says, and pauses, 'that shows no mercy to the gentle heart,' and then, 'How would you say that in Gaelic?' so I tell him. He repeats the words, rolling them around in his mouth though they can make no sense to him and then he says, 'Between us, we are always translating.' He says we should go. He reaches to take the candle from me and a bead of wax falls on my hand. I jump at the shock of it.

'You are burned,' he says, and I laugh and shake my head.

'It's only a drop of wax.'

He leads me to the cave wall where he wedges the candle into a nick in the rocks and examines my hand. The wax has formed into a small molten coin. He tests it with his thumb.

'The best thing is to wait until it cools,' he says, 'and then it will peel off quite easily and, hopefully, not leave a mark.'

I look at my hand, red and roughened with work. 'It's not the first time I've got a splash of wax,' I say.

He nods, says he's sorry, and sighs. The light from the candle flickers.

Then instead of making for the mouth of the cave as we both know we should, he reaches over and takes the full weight of my hair in his hand. 'Soft and cool,' he says, and smiles. 'I thought it would be wiry, a tangle of cables.' I lift my hand and close it over his and he takes it and opens it and brushes his thumb over the tips of my fingers, traces the lines in my palm up to the wrist, pushes back my shawl, follows the blue vein to the inside of my elbow, bends his head, kisses me there. Then he raises his head to mine and kisses my lower lip and then the upper. He kisses my chin and my cheek and my ear. He draws his fingers along my eyebrows. He cups my cheek in his hand. And what does it matter then about the limpet shells and the flint and the fish bones under our feet, or the blackened spot on the ground where the fishermen from the mainland have lit a fire and camped one night, or the steady drip drip of water from the roof of the cave? Nothing matters at all except his fingers peeling back the layers of my clothes, his lips on my skin, his hair brushing my flesh and his voice in my ear, saying my name, over and over, saying, 'Nuala, Nuala, *nulla*.'

# Nuala

## August 1898

Ginny's at the loom, a frown on her face like always when she's weaving, the two feet pedalling like bejasus and the shuttle going forward and back, clackety clack, clackety clack. The door's propped open with the cracked loom stone, and every now and again she stops the shuttle to hear what the Tailor is shouting in to her from where he's working under the kitchen window. I'm at the table, brushing up the flour from the sodas with a goosefeather, funnelling it back into the stoneware jar, all the time thinking of Gabriel.

'What did you say?' shouts Ginny.

'Roddy Calahan has six cows dead in the lower field,' says the Tailor.

'I don't believe you!'

'I'm telling you.'

'Hit by lightning?'

'Must have been.'

'Ah, that's shocking. I heard an awful blatter and I said to myself, "That's very close, getting." It must have been then.'

'It would have been all the same if it had been Roddy himself in the field.'

'It would. Ach, the poor beasts. That's a terrible loss.' She goes back to her pedalling and then stops again. 'Do you know what I'm going to tell you?' she says.

'I don't,' says the Tailor.

'That's something to do with the interference of those foreigners up at the Light.'

'It wouldn't surprise me.'

'Have you ever heard the like of that happening before?'

'There was that time Jem Hafferty's dog was killed when the lightning hit the tree, do you remember?'

'Ach, I know, but six beasts? All at the same time? I'm telling you. The height of that mast – it's drawing the elements down. The weather's been all over the place since they arrived. They'll not finish till they have us all killed with their meddling.'

'Like as not,' says the Tailor.

There's another clatter and shuttle and then, 'Ach, Nuala, I can get no relief from these feet.' This is the signal for me to fetch the Tailor's shears, to get down on my hands and knees on the floor and start hacking at her old twisted toenails. I hate this job. The skin on her shins is white and shiny, mottled on her calves, bulging with dark veins at her ankles. The splinters of nails fly round the room, ping off the walls; they'd put your eye out if you got in the way of them, and the smell of her feet is shocking. But I know that if I do it, she'll be in better form and I can get away to Gabriel. I half fill a bucket from the rain barrel outside, add hot water from the kettle and then I take down the shears and go in to her.

I know all the dry caves in the lower end and we make sure never to meet in the same one twice in a row. The mainland fishermen from Ballintoy and Dunseverick use the caves at this time of year but they fish long hours and don't come in until the light starts to fail. I tell

Gabriel where to meet me and he comes. I keep an ear and an eye out for the splash of an oar, the scrape of a boat over shingle. One day, when we've arranged to meet at the castle, I hear that Jem McDonnell is over there, fishing off the frasses at the gun rock, so I slip up to the watch house to warn Gabriel, but Mr Kernohan is there with him. I go into the kitchen on the excuse of collecting a pot, and I write him a message in Morse that says, 'Kinkeel tomorrow, same time,' and slip it into the pocket of his jacket that's hanging on the back of the door. He knows to look for it. He knows to check his pockets always before he comes to meet me. He knows we have to be careful. He knows, in any case, that I'm not there for a pot.

He meets me at the cave at Kinkeel. It's a scramble up the scree to the mouth of it, but we are safe there; the cave is not much used. There's a pool of still water at the entrance but once through the earth is dry and packed, mossy in places where the rainwater has run off. Where the cave turns away from the mouth into the hillside it is as dry and sheltered as the cottage at Portavoolin. The remains of a fire blacken the ground, a few scattered, forgotten creels and ropes, an old bed-tick the fishermen would occasionally use when they're holed up for a night. The roof and walls are packed with black stone like coal. He says the caves on this side of the island are carved out of basalt, the white caves on the upper end from limestone. He talks to me about lava, cooled from volcanoes erupted millions of years before, and he runs his fingers over the stones, cups them in his hands. I tell him the stone-cutters call it 'rotten rock', that there's too much iron in it for building – it doesn't withstand the sea air well.

Kinkeel Cave is a loud place for the dead. The islanders hid here from the Danes when they came but the Danes found them and fired straw at the entrance to smoke them out. Those that stayed were smothered and those that fled were cut through with knives. The place is scattered with bones. The islanders avoid it. It's odd that the living should believe that the dead restrict themselves to dark places. The dead are free to move wherever they like though they seem to be partial to the place of their undoing. They like to have their stories heard. Usefully for Gabriel and me, their stories keep people away from those places. I left a rough old shawl there, hidden in a nook in the side of the cave and it does for covering the bed-tick. And there's a ledge that a finger of sun reaches and it is still, so still, that you can hear the ringing call of the choughs on the cliffs above and the sea moving slow down below you. I ask Gabriel what he did with the note I put in his jacket pocket. He says he mashed it up with some potato, poured salt over it and ate it; it tasted as good as the gnocchi I'd made him, he says.

He talks to me about his home, a place where lemon trees grow out of cobbled courtyards and tomatoes redden on vines, like apples, in the sun. He talks to me about his people, his father and grandfather who worked the land on the steep slopes above his village, clearing chestnut trees, growing maize and oats; about his mother who worked in the baths in the town. So his people are not so unlike mine, a hard-working breed of the soil. His father was insistent that Gabriel would be educated and join the navy when he left school. But when his friend, Marconi, wrote to ask if he would join him in his experiments he didn't have to think twice, he says. He was more than happy to come.

'Tell me about your people,' he says.

'There isn't much to tell. They were farmers and fishermen; my mother was a washerwoman for the Bensons, before they went away. Granda Frank was a cobbler. He had the cure and he gave it to me.'

He frowns. 'The cure?'

'He was a healer of sorts.'

'Ah, the kelp,' he says, 'for headaches. He taught you that?'

'He taught me everything he knew. Lavender for dizziness, bilberry leaves for the kidneys, turnip for a weak bladder, raw onion for the bowels.'

'It's like poetry,' he says, and smiles. 'Please. Do go on.'

I take a swipe at him and he catches my hand, kisses the knuckles, one by one. There's a big blue vein on the inside of his left arm that I follow with my fingers in the dark as he talks. The hairs on his shins and on the front of his thighs are short and wiry and black. The calves of his legs are nearly bald, rubbed by the cuff of the boots he wears. His feet are bony and arched. There are no hairs on his toes or on the insides of his thighs and only a little on his chest. There is no unnecessary flesh. When I run my fingers along the bones below his neck I think of the yoke you'd put on a plough horse. He says '*Clavicola*,' and I say, 'Ssh'.

I like to put my lips behind his ear, on the bony, unfleshy part of him and rest them there. I like to move to his eyebrow and the bridge of his nose and do the same. It's not a kiss; a kiss is what I plant on Dorothy's forehead, a touch and a release. It's more of a resting, a moment of peace, somewhere between a blessing, and a caress. He has the patience and the wisdom to lie still beside me for a little while I do this, before he begins to move again. I like the boniness of him, the real, hard presence of him. I slide my fingers down his spine, feel every bump and groove, right down to where the boniness ends between his narrow hips. He groans and turns and slips his hand between my legs. I grip his lips between my teeth, taste the warmth of the blood under the thin skin there, grip his sides with my knees. His tongue is rough on my skin, telling me stories I never knew were possible, speaking in a language that is entirely new to me. The tremble that grows and passes between us is like the first test notes of the fiddle, the song warming in the singer's throat, the drumming on the skin of the bodhrán, till we find a rhythm that suits us both, till we both start to thrum at the same frequency, absolutely in tune. And then there is a certain pressure in a certain spot that can no longer be borne, and the colours come, all at once, like the splintering of a stained-glass window, falling towards us, fracturing the light. By now, I've walked every inch of him with my fingers. I know him as well as I know this island, every bump and groove of him. He is all home to me. There are as many ways to make love, it turns out, as there are ways to speak: in whispers, with urgency, half-awake, with forgetfulness. In the short time we have had together I think we may have tried them all. Touch is a language all of its own. He has left his intention on my skin.

I like to take his glasses off. Up close, you can see the two colours in his eyes – green around the pupil like a kind of sunburst, bleeding out into grey. I would never tire, I think, of looking at his eyes, in his eyes, to see what moods there are there. I think if I had more time, I could learn to read his whole history, the way he reads the rocks of the island.

'What do you see?' he says to me.

'Everything,' I tell him. 'Everyone who's ever stood in front of you, everyone you've loved.'

'Then you see yourself, Nuala Byrne,' he says, and pulls me to him. My heart skips at the sound of my own name in his throat. I cover his mouth with mine.

I ask him to tell me about London and he tells me about the gaslit cobbled streets, about the underground railway that rumbles deep in the earth, about the electric arc lights outside the Gaiety Theatre. He says the air is dirty there, thick with coal smoke and the smell of horse dung. 'In the city,' he says, 'no one looks up. You could live a whole life at roof level, and never be discovered. There's an entire world going on above people's heads. When we were working on the roof of the General Post Office,' he says, 'we could have been plotting to detonate the city; we would never have been discovered.'

'What were you doing on the roof?' I ask him.

'Sending signals, of course,' he smiles.

He says he has fallen in love with this place on the edge of the Atlantic, on the edge of the world. 'The sky is higher here,' he says. 'There is more space and light. The day seems more. It is loath to leave. It clings to the ground past eleven at night, lingers in the early hours, begins to grow again by three. Anything could happen in such an airy place. Lives could be reinvented. Stories could come true.' He causes me to look at the place I've lived in all my life as if I'm seeing it for the first time. He puts new eyes on me.

'Tell me a story,' he says. So I tell him the tale of the fisherman at the upper end who caught a mermaid in his net and took her home and removed her tail and hid it in the scraghs of thatch high up in the byre next to his house. They were happy together, I tell him, and had two children, a girl and a boy. Then one day when the fisherman was out, a storm got up and the wind lifted the thatch and the mermaid-wife spotted the tail and took it down to the shore and put it on and slipped back into the sea.

'How did he remove her tail?' he asks and I tell him I don't know, that's just how the story goes. 'It seems strange that she would leave her children.'

'She had no choice. The pull of her own people was too strong.'

'Are her children not her own people too?'

I hadn't thought of it like this. 'Not yet,' I tell him. 'They can't be. Your own people are the people who come before you, not the ones who come after.'

'But it must be true both ways?' he says. 'You and the Tailor . . . you . . . ?'

I shake my head. 'Don't ask me that. There's nothing between us.'

'What will happen,' he says, 'if you have a child?'

'Then I'll have a child,' I say.

'I cannot stay here. I must go where Signor Marconi goes.'

'I know that.'

'I cannot take you with me.'

'I know that too.' He says that Signor Marconi is as a man possessed, but I've seen the light in Gabriel's eyes when he talks about their experiments. He will not rest until they have achieved everything they have set out to achieve.

'So it is clear?'

'Message received. Red each way,' I say.

He smiles. 'What will you do?'

I don't want to think about this. I don't want to think about life on the island without him. I don't want to think of the days of rising and lying back down again in the Tailor's house with no Gabriel in the hours in between. 'I'll do what I did before,' I say. 'And now it's your turn.'

'For what?'

'To tell me a story.'

'I know only true stories, not fairy tales.'

'Are you saying that my story isn't true?'

He smiles again, then takes a deep breath. 'Very well,' he says. 'I will tell you a story that will make you smile. I was on duty one night at Bournemouth, in charge of the wireless room, alone, when a man burst in through the door carrying a revolver.'

'This will make me smile?'

'Be patient. He was shouting at me, saying he had not slept a night since we had begun our experiments. Our wireless messages, he said, were giving him pains in his legs.'

'Ginny says her chilblains have gone mad since you arrived.'

'Chilblains?'

'Pains, in her toes.'

He laughs aloud at this. 'People will always be suspicious of new things.'

'The man with the gun – what happened?'

'I told him that I'd heard of this problem, but that it was within my power to cure him.'

'You have a cure for pains in the legs?'

'For his pains, yes, I did.'

'So we have that in common.'

'I suppose we do. Stop interrupting me. I told him that first, he must remove any items of metal about his person: coins from his pocket, the gun from his hand. He gave them up readily. And then I cured him.'

'How did you do that?'

'I asked him to place his hand on the capacitor. I gave him the greatest electric shock he'd ever had.'

He does make me smile after all. 'And did it work?'

'He went away very contented. We never heard from him again.'

'And so you are a healer, as well as a magician.'

'I am many things that you still do not know.'

'And never will,' I say to him, and he kisses me on the mouth.

'Do you really think there will come a day when you will be able to signal all the way to America?'

'I do not doubt it for an instant,' he says. 'And when we have conquered distance, then we will conquer time.'

'There you go again, "conquering time".'

He props himself up on his elbow. 'What did you mean that day in the watch house when you asked me if I thought the dead could move through time?'

I shake my head. 'Nothing,' I say. 'I was trying to be clever. I was trying to impress you.'

'You were serious,' he says. 'Why did you ask?'

'It was just talk,' but he takes my chin in his hand.

'You don't trust me, Nuala.'

'I do trust you.'

'Then why won't you tell me the truth?'

I have never told anyone about the voices I hear. Not even Dorothy knows. What will he say to me if I tell him? What will he think of me then? 'There are times,' I say, taking a breath, 'when I hear things that no one around me hears.'

'What kind of things?'

'Voices, in my head.'

'What do they say to you?'

'They're not speaking to me, exactly. It's just that I happen to overhear them. They're looking to be heard, I think. Sometimes they're hard to make out.'

'And you think that these voices are the voices of the dead?'

I nod. 'It's the only explanation I can think of. When you talked to me in the watch house about tuning into wavelengths, it made a kind of sense to me. I know it must sound mad . . .'

He shakes his head. 'It doesn't sound mad at all.'

'It doesn't scare you?'

'Does it scare you?'

'I've gotten used to them.'

'There are so many things we cannot explain,' he says, 'that seem impossible for us to understand. We are only beginning to learn how this extraordinary universe works.' He takes my hand. 'You are not mad,' he says. 'You're just impossible-for-now.'

He says I have a curious face, broad and pale, changeable, and a mouth that betrays what I'm thinking. He traces his finger down the length of my nose and says it is too wide for beauty but that I am saved by my cheekbones that lift when I smile, by my blue eyes and dark lashes, my thick, black, curly hair. He says I'm like a woman in a Rossetti painting: there is something compelling, something that draws the eye. I don't know who Rossetti is but it doesn't sound very flattering to me. I tell him that with this kind of talk he could charm the birds out of the trees, and he laughs and says, 'Drawing-room perfection is dull. Your face is filled with stories.'

He falls asleep in the same position I saw him in that day in the keeper's house, one arm over his head, the other across his chest, whistling through his nose. It looks uncomfortable. He has told me he learned to lie like this in the signal room at Poole so he wouldn't enter into too deep a slumber, so the bell would wake him for the messages coming through. I shake him and tell him it's time to go, that I'll be missed. He says he'll miss me more. He says we will have to be vigilant. 'Vigilant,' I say, 'that's a good word.' He says we mustn't take chances but I think the opposite is true. I think we have to take every chance we get. The old people say there'll come a day when there'll be only one man and one woman left on the island. That would be a happy day if it was me and him who were to be left and nobody near us.

I tell him to wait till I'm well over the fields, bid him go round by the road. Near Coolnagrock I see the figure of Father Diamond, the tails of his long frock coat flying, walking towards me.

'What are you doing out here, Nuala Byrne?' he says.

'Going to the holy well,' I tell him, 'to get the cure for the Tailor's warts.' It is my first direct lie to the priest.

'Come with me now and we'll walk together,' he says. 'We'll say a decade on the way.'

'I will,' I say, thinking of Gabriel, hoping he stays close by the road and is in the direction of the harbour by now. 'Where are you going yourself?'

'To separate two men that are fit to kill each other over the ownership of a march hedge.'

'Good luck with that, Father.'

We walk on in silence for a bit and then, 'I hear you have a job, up at the Light, Nuala?'

'I do, Father, the electricians pay well.'

'You're doing them a meal?'

'Until Mrs Kernohan gets back.'

'And learning about the signalling too?'

'Just while Tam Casey was away.'

'He's a very serious young man, Mr Donati.'

'He is, Father, very serious.'

'They say he's fascinated by the geology of the island, that if you get him started on about the rocks, you'd be there listening to him all day.'

'That's true, Father.'

'Do you be in the watch house on your own with him much?'

I say nothing.

'Because that wouldn't be right, Nuala, you know that, don't you, and you a married woman?'

'I'm not in the watch house at all, Father. I'm in the keeper's kitchen.'

He looks at me closely and shakes his head. 'Just so long as you know, Nuala Byrne. I'm keeping an eye on you.'

'Thank you, Father,' I say.

'You know what happens to women who get themselves a bad name. You wouldn't want to end up like Goretti Nelson, God bless her.'

'Good God,' I say to him. 'I would not.'

'No need to take the Lord's name in vain. Now, we'll

make a start.' And he makes the sign of the cross and starts up with the Apostles' Creed.

Goretti Nelson is a woman you would see from time to time going about at the fairs, her hair matted and thick with dirt and she herself sodden with drink. Granny would threaten us with her as children, when me and Dorothy wouldn't settle at night. 'I'll get Goretti Nelson in to you,' she'd say. 'She'll put manners on the pair of you.' We were terrified of her. We thought she was a kind of witch. They say at one time she was married to a glensman, that her husband drove her out. They say that now she'll lie down with any man to get money off him for drink. I don't want to end up like her, with neither hearth nor home. We will, as Gabriel says, have to be vigilant. We will have to watch our step.

We have to live two lives, and this is fine with me. This new life is so much better than the one I was living before he came to the island. I think of him every hour of the day, from the time the magpies wake me with their cackling in the trees in the morning, till I see the cats going about at twilight, licking the dew from the grass. With his beats and his bells he has changed the shape of my day. We are careful in the kitchen where Tam Casey skulks around, trying to get Gabriel's good opinion. We hold ourselves straight. We do not touch. We behave like polite strangers. We orbit each other the way the moon orbits the earth, the way the earth orbits the sun, pulling towards each other, keeping our distance.

I try to think about what life will be like when he is no longer here. I try to remember how things were before he came to the island, but I am too full of him to remember that and why should I make myself miserable trying? I am living moment to moment, waiting until I can be alone with him again, impatient for his touch. I'll be miserable soon enough. This flutter in my stomach, this fullness cannot last for ever, but while it does I see no point in dwelling on what's to come. This may be my one taste of happiness. The flavour may have to last me for a long time.

We are three-quarters of the way through August and still no firm word from Mr Marconi. He has left the royal yacht, is doing business in London or in Dublin. Gabriel says he will not maintain the station on the island for much longer. He says they have succeeded in proving the commercial worth of wireless telegraphy. Mr Marconi will be keen now to move on with the cross-channel experiment. They expect to be recalled any day now, he and Mr Kemp, to set up the stations at Dover and at Wimereux. We know we do not have much time together. And now there's something else on my mind, something I'd like to do before he goes.

This day in the kitchen when Tam Casey is up the Light, checking on the lantern, I say to Gabriel, 'Do you think I might be able some day to send a message of my own, over to Ballycastle?'

'I don't see why not,' he says. 'Who would you like to send it to?'

'To Dorothy,' I say to him. 'Could I send one to Dorothy?'

'If you could get a message to her, to be at the White Lodge for, say, eleven on Friday, we could arrange that.'

So I send word over with Dougal on the boat and on Friday, Gabriel and I are in the watch house together, ready to send the signal. Gabriel taps a few 'V's into the machine and Mr Kemp replies.

'Who is there with you?' Gabriel sends.

'Miss Reilly,' comes the reply. Gabriel stands to give me the chair.

'Good morning,' I send.

'Good morning,' comes the answer.

Gabriel runs the tape through his fingers. 'It makes fascinating reading,' he says.

I shoot him a sidelong look. 'I have a message for Miss Reilly,' I signal.

'Go ahead,' Mr Kemp signals back.

I take a deep breath. I have memorised the message I want to send, and I begin to tap it out. Gabriel frowns, not understanding. At first, I think, he believes I've made a mistake. Mr Samuel Morse was a practical man, he has told me on more than one occasion. He reserved the shortest sound patterns for the letters used most in English. One single dit for 'e'; one solid dah for 't'. But I'm not signalling in English, and the 'h' takes half a minute to send. (When I complain about this when we practise, he tells me it's quicker than rowing to the mainland.) I switch the wires the way I've seen him do and the machine sits in silence. I picture the Englishman in the room in the White Lodge, his careful writing of the letters. I picture Dorothy reading the message. In the watch house, we wait.

'What does it mean?' Gabriel says.

'It's a test,' I tell him.

'What kind of test?'

'To see if your machine understands Gaelic as well.'

He laughs at this. There's a certain pleasure for me in sending a message under his watchful eye, one that he cannot interpret himself. This must be the first time that such a message has been sent in Gaelic. I redden at my own forwardness. When the wheel begins to turn again and the tape spools out, Gabriel reads the words that Dorothy must have dictated to Mr Kemp and scratches his head and writes the words down. It's an odd thing to see him writing in Gaelic. He reads it aloud and I can't help but laugh. 'What am I saying?' he says to me. 'Put me out of my misery.'

'It's a blessing,' I tell him. 'Nothing more than that. *Bail ó Dhia ort, a chailín.* God's protection on you, girl.'

'God's protection on you, girl,' he repeats, softly.

And even though it goes against what we've agreed, even though it's not permitted, I say to him in English, 'And on you, my love.' I know he's leaving me; I know he cannot stay, but at least I will have this.

We arrange to meet at Brackens, maybe for the last time. It's not the driest of the caves, but it's quiet there this time of year, hardly anyone bothers with the holy well, once the saint's day is passed. I scramble over the yellow-lichened boulders on the shoreline with a bucket in my hand, on the excuse of fetching water from the well, going finally to do what I told the priest I was doing days before. Rain begins to fall, soft and steady, darkening the stones. I step over the skull of a sheep at the entrance, the bones of a rabbit lie near the wall. It is not the most romantic of meeting-places, but it serves our purposes well enough. I reach into the cool clear water and wash my face and hands. I am waiting inside, by the cave wall, listening to the fall of the rain outside, watching how it drops a gauzy curtain over the mouth of the cave, and I hear feet scramble up the scree and see the dark shape against the light and I step forward, eager, out of the dark, but too late I see that it's not Gabriel. It's Tam Casey, and it's worse then because he's already seen me.

'Nuala Byrne,' he says, and his breath is short, like he's been hurrying, 'this is a nice surprise.' There's no way of getting past him.

'I was just fetching some water,' I say, and I can barely hear myself speak, so loud is my heart thumping in my chest. I turn to lift the bucket and bend to dip it in the well. 'I'll go on now,' I say, moving towards the mouth of the cave.

'Sure, what's your hurry?' he says, standing square at

the entrance. I say again that I have to go and the sweat is beginning to gather at the back of my head at the thought that Gabriel might appear at any minute, and at the question of why Tam Casey is here on this side of the island where he has no business. I make to go past him, the bucket between us, and he catches me by the arm. 'You were waiting for someone, maybe?'

'I was not,' I say, trying to shake him off. 'I was just getting some water. The Tailor'll be wondering where I am.'

'The Tailor must be used to wondering by now, what with all your gallivanting,' he says, gripping my arm tighter. 'But I don't think it's the Tailor that's on your mind now, is it, Nuala Byrne?'

I can smell the tobacco breath of him and the stale sweat off his clothes, and the gassiness of the lighthouse generator, and he's still gripping my arm, high up above my elbow and then he reaches up and spreads his other hand over my throat.

'Let me by, Tam Casey,' I say to him, my face turned away.

'You're shy all of a sudden, now, Nuala Byrne; you were never shy before.' His hand leaves my throat and passes down the front of my shawl and over my breast, and then round my back where he bunches my skirts in his fist.

'Let me go!' I say to him. I don't know what he's doing here or what he knows about me or how he's found me, but he's still holding me tight by the elbow and then he's moving forward and walking me back, over the rough ground, nearly tripping me, towards the cave wall.

He says: 'Easy now. You weren't shy yesterday or the day before, were you, with your two legs wrapped tight around the Italian? In Oweydoo, was it, or in Kinkeel, or in Oweynagolman, I forget which?' The knees nearly go from under me when he says that and I let go the handle of the bucket and it clatters and bounces on the hard ground.

'Let me go,' I say to him. 'Let me go this minute.'

'I don't think so,' he says. 'Not yet, Nuala Byrne, not yet,' and he pushes me up against the cave wall. 'You can see for miles from the Light,' he says, with his face up close to mine, 'over Ballycarry and Ballyconaghan, as far as Mullindress. From up there folk can look like spiders, moving over stone, scuttling into holes, disappearing underground.' He shoves his knee between my legs and grabs my skirts with both his hands and hauls them up and with his body pins me to the rock. 'I thought I'd try a little experiment of my own,' he says. 'You and your coded messages about caves and days and times. Who do you think you're fooling, Nuala Byrne?' He reaches down and when he feels with his hands that I'm bare below he gasps into my ear and he says, 'I see you're ready for me,' and I say to him, 'Take your hands off me,' and I try to shove him away, to struggle out from under the weight of him but he's too much for me.

'Gabriel,' I say, though it makes me guilty to say it. 'Gabriel will be here.'

'Ah, no,' he says. 'He's occupied. It's just me here today. Isn't one man enough for you at a time? Now ssh and be quiet, Nuala Byrne, if you value your house and your hearth and your home. Ssh now, girl and be still.' I stand, pinned, against the cave wall like the breath has been knocked out of me, thinking of what I stand to lose if Tam Casey was to spread talk about me. I can't speak and I can't move and I can barely breathe. And that's the last thing he says before he does what he does to me. The power seems to go from me and there's nothing I can do. I can feel his breath, hot on my neck, his thick tongue below my ear. The roughness of his pitted skin gouges into my cheek. There is a rock in the wall of the cave digging into the small of my back. He shoves his loathsome self into me and grunts and grunts and grunts. Behind him, the round black entrance of the cave opens out onto the sea and the sky, like a mouth open wide, screaming, with no sound coming out. I feel the bones of some small creature crumble under my heel. The wooden bucket lies toppled on the floor of the cave with the water from the holy well seeping into the dry earth.

I am slumped on the floor of the cave, my back against the rock, waiting for Gabriel but he doesn't come. I can't go to the Light because Tam Casey will be there so I go to the Tailor's house. The rain continues, drumming, steady; it brings an early dark. I shuffle about like a person asleep, like a person dead on their feet.

Ginny asks what's ailing me, my face like a week of worry. 'I have pains in my stomach,' I tell her, and this is true; I feel that I can't straighten myself for fear that I might break in two.

'Go in to your bed,' says the Tailor. 'You're not right at yourself.'

'You may as well,' says Ginny. 'You're no use to anybody going about the place bent double like a closed knife.'

But I won't go. I sit down with my back to the warm nook of the fire, my feet on the creepie stool. I pull my knees up to my chest, wrap my hands round my ankles. 'I'm better off here by the fire.' The Tailor goes in to bed. He doesn't want to get involved in a conversation about women's problems. He's glad, I think, to get peace to himself away from Ginny and me.

'You're blocking the heat,' says Ginny, and climbs into the settle bed and pulls the clothes up to her chin and commences snoring almost straight away. I sit in the hearth and listen to the clock tick and the wind gasp and sigh in the thatch. I sit there the whole night long. I have been blind and stupid, playing a dangerous game. I could see nothing but Gabriel, thought of nothing else except that he would soon be gone. I did not see Tam Casey watching, biding his time. I did not dare to let myself think of what would happen if we were caught. What has Tam Casey said about me up at the Light? I am afraid of what he will say.

I must have slept, or half-slept, or dreamed, and when I open my eyes I can see by the half-glow of the embers and by the lightening square at the window that I am no longer alone by the fire. The girl I've seen before is sitting cross-legged on the Tailor's cushion, looking into the coals. I glance at the dark of the opened settle bed but there's no sign of Ginny stirring.

'What do you want?' I say to her as quietly as I can.

She starts, as if she hasn't seen me, or hasn't expected me to speak, and then she looks at me with a half-pained expression, trying to force a smile. 'Just to be here,' she says.

'Why? What are you to do with me?'

She looks towards the lower room door, uncertain, and then back to me. 'I wanted to see you,' she says.

'Are you a warning?'

She stares at me, shocked, like I've slapped her, and shakes her dark head. 'I hope not. I don't want to be. I want to be a help.' She reaches out a hand to me but I do not take it. I do not want to touch the hand of a person who is not in the living world. What would become of me? She's a puzzle I can't figure out. I shake my head at her. Just then there's a sharp knock on the wood of the door that jolts me upright and Ginny rouses herself on the settle bed. 'Who's that at this hour of the morning?' she says, and it's just the two of us in the room. 'Did you never go in to your bed?' she says to me. 'Well, open the door, woman, for the love of God.'

I open the door to Mr Kernohan, the keeper, and my

heart jumps into my throat. He stoops in under the lintel, takes his cap off his head. He bids us both good morning, apologises for the early hour. The Tailor stumbles out from the room, pulling his braces up over his shoulders, rearranging himself.

'Good morning, Tailor,' says Mr Kernohan.

'Good morning,' says the Tailor.

'You're early on the road,' says Ginny. 'Will you take a bowl of tay? Nuala, stoke up the fire there, get the water on to boil.'

Mr Kernohan says he won't take tea, thank you, he's already had his breakfast. He says they're all out looking for the Italian as he didn't come back to the Light last night. He says has any of us seen any word of him? A fist of fear closes over my heart.

Ginny looks at me. 'Sure, what would he be doing over here?'

My thoughts are running round in my head like rats trapped in a well. What does Mr Kernohan know? What has Tam Casey said? I gather myself the best I can. When did I last see Gabriel? I answer him honestly. 'I haven't seen him since dinnertime the day before yesterday,' I say, 'when I was up at the Light.'

Mr Kernohan nods, twists his cap in his hands. 'He

was spotted up near Cantruan yesterday afternoon,' he says. 'No one has seen him since then.'

'Why would he have gone to Cantruan?' I say, before I can stop myself. That wasn't one of our meeting places. It was the wrong direction entirely.

'He's a shocking man for the rocks,' says Mr Kernohan. 'More than likely, he was after more specimens for his collection.'

'The cliffs are very steep there,' Ginny says, shaking her head.

'There's no need for alarm,' says Mr Kernohan. 'He could turn up yet. The rain came on early. He could have spent the night in one of the caves, rather than risk getting lost in the dark. We'll keep on looking. Let us know if you hear from him?'

Ginny crosses herself. 'God keep him safe,' she says.

I turn on my heel to look at her. 'Why are you saying that?'

'As I say, he'll probably turn up,' says Mr Kernohan, and takes a step towards the door. I pick my shawl up from the stool where I've left it, throw it round my shoulders.

'Where are you going?' says Ginny.

'I know some of the places he goes,' I say.

'Leave it to the men to look for him,' says Ginny. 'It's no business of yours.' But I'm out the door before she or the Tailor can say another word to hold me back.

I search every dry cave on the island, even the ones in the upper end where we never arranged to meet. I crawl in on my hands and knees where I have to and I call and call and call. In each one the walls throw his name back, broken and garbled as if to mock me: 'Gabriel, Gabriel, Gabriel,' rings around the caves. At the Wet Cove where we went that first morning, it seems his name will go on echoing for ever, trapped inside the island itself. There is no answer from him anywhere, just the rocks throwing back his name. Then I'm up near the waterfall at Slieveanaille, near Cantruan where the elvers make their way up the steep cliffs in the spring to the pools of standing water on the headland above. I'm looking down, over the edge and it seems to me that I hear a voice calling, 'Nuala, Nuala, nulla.' But the clifftop is empty, there is no one near. The breeze whips my hair across my ears and mouth, but when I push it back I can still hear the voice. Altacorry Bay is still and blue, flecked with white below the Light, Ailsa Craig rises grey beyond to the east. I move to the cliff edge and look down below but the path there is treacherous and there is nothing but rock and sea and gulls nesting on the grassy ledges. Wherever I move, the voice gets no louder, no fainter. It seems to me that I know what this means and I am afraid. I am praying now for silence.

I go back to the Tailor's house and get the full brunt of Ginny's tongue.

'What is he to you,' she says to me, 'that you have to go about the island, making a show of yourself?'

'Ginny,' the Tailor says, 'half the island's out looking for the poor man.'

'The state of you!' she says to me, and shuffles back in to her loom.

I spend a second night by the fire, with Ginny snoring in the settle bed. I am praying that Gabriel will be found, that he will be well. I make a deal with God, that if he is spared, I swear I will take nothing more to do with him. I will not go back up to the Light. And the whole time I'm wondering about Tam Casey and what part he could have had to play in this. How could he be so certain that Gabriel would not come to Brackens the day we had arranged to meet? What has he said to him against me? Has he spoken of me and Gabriel to anyone?

When the light starts to leak in through the sash in the morning and creeps across the floor, when it comes to me that Gabriel has been missing now for two whole nights, and everyone who's able searching the island for him, and every boatman accounted for that could have taken him off, I tell myself that I must prepare, that I must ready myself to hear the worst, and not betray myself.

The day after, I stay close to the Tailor's house, hoping for news of Gabriel. I put the day in busying myself with all the small jobs I have neglected to do in the days I've been spending with him, up at the Light and in the caves. There is no word until evening time, when Dougal's big head appears at the half-door, his shoulders filling up the frame. He steps in over the stoop, head bowed, greets us all, sits down by the fire, looks steadily into the flame. The Tailor is by the hearth in his wooden armed chair, his lit pipe in his hand. I am at the table, my back to the window, where I am kneading griddle scones. Dougal was out in the boat, he says, off Cantruan. The mention of the place halts my hands in the dough.

'A fine evening for it,' the Tailor says.

Ginny opens her mouth, about to ask, I know, if

there is any word of the foreigner, but something about the look on Dougal's face stops her short before she speaks. She sits down on the settle bed, looks across at him. There is silence for a moment or two, before Dougal starts again.

'When you're used to always seeing the shape of a thing,' says Dougal, 'you notice when there's a change.' All our eyes are on his face. 'No matter how small, or how far out you may be, you still remark on it,' he says.

'That's true,' says the Tailor, leaning forward in his chair, holding his pipe by the bowl, away from his face. 'What did you see, Dougal, tell us?'

Dougal was working off Stackamore, hauling in a lobster creel, he says, when he spotted something glinting in the light on the flat rock below Dan's Cave. He pulled the boat closer in, could see then what it was: the metal tip on the heel of a boot. There is a pause in which hope is still possible. The flames lick round the sods of turf, the sparks burn yellow in the chimney. Dougal is staring into the fire like he could keep it lit with his eyes. I look into his face and still he hasn't said anything that will need to be unsaid but he won't look back at me. I will him to be silent. 'Don't say another word,' I tell him in my head.

'The rock is above the waterline,' he says. 'I had to stand up in the boat to see what it was. But I think I knew already. It's a boot I've seen before.'

'The foreigner's?' says Ginny.

'The foreigner's,' Dougal says.

'Dead?'

Dougal nods his head and Ginny looks straight at me.

I lower my eyes and curl my hands into fists and push my knuckles down through the dough onto the hard wood of the table. The light is behind me, my face is in shadow; this much is in my favour. This is a test, I tell myself. I tell myself to be strong. There will be time enough to think about what these words of Dougal's mean, and this is not the time, not here with Ginny looking at me, with the Tailor smoking by the fire.

'God rest him,' I hear the Tailor say. 'What did you do?' he asks Dougal.

'I rowed over to the rock where he was lying. I managed to grab him by the collar of his jacket, heaved him into the boat, sent up a flare to warn them at the Light, rowed over to the inaan below Altacorry, pulled the boat up there.'

'That's a lonely journey, Dougal,' says the Tailor, 'with a dead man in the boat.' I can tell by the direction of his voice that the Tailor is not looking at me. There is a silence in which I dig my nails into the heels of my hands. I cannot trust myself to speak, to feign saying any of the usual things that a woman with a passing acquaintance with a man might be expected to say on hearing of his death. I must be quiet; survival depends on this. There are plenty of wild and lonely places on the island where you can go to howl if you need to, where no one will hear; places where the wind will catch the roar in you before it's half out of your mouth; places where the yells of the dead will drown out any living voice. I list them in my head to keep myself from uttering a sound: Sloaknacalliagh, Kilvoruan, Skerriagh, Doon: places of slaughter and betrayal, where the soil and the rock and the air itself hold pain against them like a shield. The Tailor's house is not the place for howling. Not here. Not now. Not yet.

'Mr Kernohan walked the whole way along the headland above me,' I hear Dougal say, 'keeping pace with the boat. He and Tam Casey dragged the slipe cart down the path to the inaan. They've brought him on up to the Light.'

'God rest him,' says Ginny, and I hear the rustle as she crosses herself.

'Sad news,' says the Tailor, and does the same.

'That's a shocking drop,' says Ginny. 'It must be five hundred feet or more.'

I sense Dougal shake his head. 'He wasn't in a great state,' he says. 'He must have fallen from near the top.'

My hands are numb and streaked with flour, my nails are caked with dough. There are four red crescent-shaped dents in each palm where the nails have dug into the flesh. I raise my head at last and look at Dougal and Ginny and the Tailor like they're three characters in a playact, like you'd see at the kole-in at New Year's Eve. I have the sudden notion that they're all about to jump up and catch a hold of each other's coat-tails and start going round the floor, rhyming, to show me it's all a joke. But this is not what happens. No one moves.

'Tam Casey has sent word to Mr Kemp. He's on his way from the mainland,' Dougal says, his eyes still on the fire. 'He has telegraphed the family and Mr Marconi from there. The steamer will come tomorrow with the coffin.'

There's a buzzing in my ears like you'd hear at a wasps' nest and the edges of the room go dim. I think of the steep path from the cliff top down to Dan's Cave, slippery from the rain shower that must have arrived there as I scrambled over the boulders at Brackens. I see a seam of red sandstone, grassy ledges, the grey stone below splattered white with gull droppings, the smell rising up to my nose. I see a black boot with a metal-tipped heel slip on rain-dark stone. I hear a shout of fear, I see soil and gravel scatter, I see a hand reach out to grab at the broom, I see the yellow flowers come away in the hand. I hear the rip and tear of stalk and root, the warbly croaks of the black-headed razorbills as they're roused, flapping, from the ledges, the crack of dappled eggshells, the yellow ooze and slide of yolk, the suck and splash of the sea round the rocks, the silence that must follow.

I step over to the bucket inside the door and stumble and almost fall. I scoop up a cupful of water. I can feel Ginny's eyes on me again as I drink. It's as if she can read the words in my head when she says, 'What was he doing up there?'

'He was a wild man for gathering rocks,' says Dougal. 'You couldn't have kept him out of the caves.'

I look quickly at Dougal whose eyes are still on the fire. He makes no sign that he knows anything about

Gabriel and me but it makes me wonder if this is his way of telling me that he knows, if he is using his own brand of code to speak to me in the presence of Ginny and the Tailor.

'The path to Dan's Cave is fit for nothing but sheep,' says the Tailor. 'Paddy the Cliff himself wouldn't go down it without a rope.'

Dougal shakes his head. 'Only an islander knows the island. We were forever telling him to tread carefully. We were always telling him that.'

Dougal stands to go, stops, stares down at his boots.

'You'll take a sup of tay, Dougal?'

'Not for me, thanks, Ginny, I'll go on home. I . . .' He pulls his eyes up from the floor, finally raises them to mine, puts his hand in his jacket pocket, takes it out again, empty. 'I'll go on home,' he says again and the door closes behind him.

'It's lucky he didn't fall in the sea,' says Ginny. 'He might never have been found.' But while he wasn't found, there was still a hope and now there's no hope at all.

## Nuala

### August/September 1898

When I get scared of all the things that are happening, of the unstoppable train of the hours passing and of the knowledge of what each new one brings, I tell the story back to myself, as if it was all over, and the pain is gone, and I'm telling it how it was. It makes it bearable. It means I can go on breathing. Dan's Cave wasn't one of our meeting places. I don't know what Gabriel was doing there. There are parts of the story blurred or missing, and I can't help but think that these are to do with Tam Casey. I think he holds the key to it all.

And so Gabriel's gone. But only in time. He's only

gone in time. If I could go back ten days, twelve, he would be here and I could speak to him, could walk up behind him as he sits at the table in the watch house, his head bent over his work. I could put my hand on the back of his neck where the hair would have begun to curl again at the collar, I could lean over, speak into his ear, tell him not to take the path down to Dan's Cave, but to come south to Brackens, to me. I could save him. I could keep him here. I could keep Mr Kemp and Mr Marconi at bay. I could stop them from coming for him, from calling him away. I could go back and then go back and then keep going back again and again. I could peel time like an apple and bend the skin to suit me so that we'd never reach the place I'm in now but stay for ever in the days before this in the Wet Cove, at Altacorry, at the Light. But who would I be then, knowing everything I know? A stranger looking back at myself, at him? Would it be possible to forget the story of what happens next? Or if not to forget, then to set it aside, to live it as you wished it would happen and not the way it did? Could I keep that secret from him? Would it be worth it? What did Gabriel say? His signals travel at the speed of light, seven times round the earth in a second. It's only a matter of time, he said – there it is again, time –

before Mr Marconi's signals will span the oceans, '*il grande salto del Atlantico*', and when that is done, we will discover something faster than this and faster than this again. And then we will be able to do what seems impossible-for-now. We will be able to bend time. I think again of the globe in the Manor House. If the earth really does move as they say, if what we're doing is going round and round, then why can't I go back round to him? Why can't I feel the touch of his hands, the brush of his hair on my throat? Why does that seem like a dream to me now? Like a story I made in my head? I would like to try an experiment of my own, to put my hand on the Manor House globe, spin time back twenty-five years and more, ask my mother for a change of heart, to bring me with them when they leave, let me grow up strong in Newfoundland, let me be there to meet Gabriel when he comes. I'll have to think hard about how to do that, about how to become a pulse in the air that doesn't fade like skin or hair but goes on beating. 'Indestructible,' Gabriel said. 'Invisible, untouchable, unstoppable, undiminishable.' If only there was a way to do that, to circle like a gull, to ride the updraughts of air and never land again.

They say Mr Kemp washed Gabriel's body himself,

that Tam Casey helped to dress him, to lift him into the coffin. Ginny and the Tailor went up to the wake. I stayed on my own in the cottage but I took care to put the Tailor's armed chair against the door until I heard them coming back. Gabriel's people didn't come from Italy; the journey was too great. They asked for him to be buried on the island. They said he had written to them often of this place; they said he loved it here. He's buried at St Thomas's, near the brae wall. The coffin was closed at the wake. That's always a bad sign. I don't want to think of him lying there on the rock below Dan's Cave for two days and two nights. I don't want to think of what the gulls did to his face. I want to think of him the way he was, with his head bent over the Morse key, sending words up into the ether. I want to think of him in the caves with his hand cupping the fall of my hair. The worst of the pain is yet to come. I'm in a gap in time, the lapse that happens between feeling the heat of the pot handle in your hand and knowing that you've been burned.

Time strides forward. Ginny watches me. I haven't done my howling yet; there'll be time enough for that. Dougal comes almost every night to the Tailor's house. No sooner have I cleared the table than he's at the door with news from the Light. Ginny and the Tailor seem glad to see him. Mr Kemp has dismantled the station at the White Lodge, Dougal tells us, and had everything carted up to the Antrim Arms in Ballycastle. So there will be no more messages relayed over the Sound. What has it all been for? Mr Kemp caught a cold on that last crossing from the island, the day the weather turned. Four hours, the boat took to get to the mainland, after which he took to his bed. Mr Marconi arrived in Ballycastle on Monday last, the eve of the Lammas Fair. They've been trying to cross to the island these two days or more, but not a boat has come or gone this last week, not since the day of the funeral. Tam Casey has been put in charge of packing up the station at the Light. I try not to think of him, strutting about, cock of the walk, full of his own importance now that Gabriel is gone. I don't go near the watch house. I stay close to the Tailor's cottage. And every night when Dougal is leaving he pauses on the threshold, like there's more to say, only he hasn't the words to say it. I think if he could he would say to me that he's sorry that Gabriel is gone. Only he can't say that in front of Ginny or the Tailor – why would he? My loss goes unacknowledged. It's the only way to save myself. So he taps his cap against his knee and goes on his way.

* * *

The Lammas floods are here: it has rained and blown for days. You can feel the season turn. A new coolness in the air, the sky these clouded evenings darkening by nine, the air these nights loud with the wings of bats, hunting for moths in the bushes behind the house. The Islay loggers have moored their boats at Ushet, as they do at Lammas every year, as if nothing different has happened. The Islay girls are going about in their plaid and their dark velvet bodices, their thick, quilted petticoats swinging from side to side, the fine silver buckles that pin their shoulder shawls glinting in the light. They're mad to get over to the Fair but like everyone else they'll have to wait for the weather. They dance the whole night in the kelp house in their stout knee boots. In another time, in another life, I would have danced the night with them.

The first of September, the first clear day we've had. And today, finally, Mr Marconi is come, too late for Gabriel, too late for everything. I stand on Crocknascreidlin and watch the boat come in. It's a good place to stand, on the hill of the screaming women, above the dark hollow of Lagavistevoir. They're as loud as they were when Drake's men came and slaughtered all the men of the island. I am silent. I let them scream for me too. They're keening for my heart. To the south the island lies low and green, rock and broom and heather to the west. From here I can see the wall of the graveyard at St Thomas's where they lowered Gabriel into the ground. He is part of the clay and rock of the island now. He is part of the story of this place.

Here's Mr Kemp in his bowler hat, the red hair sticking out either side. From the hill I can see a figure I take to be Mr Marconi, in an odd sort of tweed hat, peaked to the front and the back. He looks like a bit of a dandy, not what I was expecting at all. Then I hear the rumble of the cart on the road, and I see Tam Casey, for the first time since that day in the cave, coming to collect them, just as he did when he came for Gabriel, eighty-three days, a heartbeat, a lifetime ago. It strikes me then that they have come for the equipment at the station and I turn on my heel and I run to the Light.

Nothing is locked. The watch house is empty, everything is as it must have been that first day he came, the drawered black wooden boxes all closed up with their wires and wheels, their screws and metal drums, the smell in the air I will always associate with Gabriel, of metal filings, of paraffin, of wax. I have to have something he touched. I have to have something important to him. My eyes fall on the log book that has been left on top of one of the boxes and I slip it into my apron pocket. I go back out and crouch on the seaward side of the compound wall and wait for the rumble of the cart.

Mr Marconi is fair, not overly tall, and looks younger than I thought. I don't know why I'm surprised at this – he is the same age as Gabriel, after all. He has a clean-shaven chin and a long fine nose and clear blue eyes. He has taken off his hat now and I can see that his hair is parted to the right, a kink in it above his large ears. I remember now what Gabriel said, that his mother was Irish, or Scots-Irish, that there's Irish in him himself. He is wearing a tie and a high starched collar, a heavy suit, despite the season, a pair of stout laced boots. He looks very serious, as well he might, and a little bit distracted, his mind on other things. He is frowning as Mr Kemp talks to him and leads him up towards the Light. Tam Casey has gone into the watch house. I can hear him in there, packing up the boxes, ready to load them into the cart. I am tempted for a moment to go after the two men, to call out Mr Marconi's name, to look into the face of the man in whom Gabriel placed such belief, whose future, he was certain, was tied so securely to his own. But what would I say to him? That I am sorry for the loss of his friend? Sorry for him, when Gabriel was so much more than that to me? I can't do that. They'd think me impertinent, or worse, they'd think me mad.

I stand up, ready to make my way back over to the Tailor's house, and as I do I hear a step and turn and there at the door of the watch house is Tam Casey, a black box in his hands, sneering over at me and a shiver runs down my spine. I force myself not to hurry. I walk away with my heart thumping in my chest and cross the fields towards Portavoolin, the whole way feeling his eyes on my back. If Mr Kemp or Mr Marconi happen to look out from the top of the Light they'll see me as a speck in the distance, just an island woman out tramping the fields, toeing the baughrans over in the sun to dry them after the rain, a person of no importance to them.

Dougal says they're gone. They've taken all the equipment. There's no word of them coming back.

'Bad cess to them,' says Ginny. 'They were nothing but trouble when they were here.'

'We'll miss the extra bit of money,' says the Tailor.

I shoot the Tailor an angry look. What have I been to him only a hired hand? I'd have been better off, maybe, going to the hiring fair in Ballycastle. At least that's a clear sort of business deal where both parties know their worth. But there is good news for me: Tam Casey has gone with them. He has got what he wanted, to work with Mr Marconi. For me there is only relief that he's gone.

They're cutting the barley up on Kilpatrick, the yellow paddy frogs are jumping through the stubble with their bulging eyes and their sticky tongues; their chorus of rattles and creaks and croaks are filling the morning air. The moon sits low and yellow on Knocklayde. The weather is still, waiting. I've a sickness in my throat that is worse in the mornings when the chamber pots near turn me, and a yearning on me for dandelion tea that I'm drinking by the bucketful, except that it's coming back up my throat again as quick as it goes down.

'The fall of the leaf,' says Ginny, 'is a bad time of the year for sickness, if sickness is what it is,' and she gives me her sideways look.

It's not like her to stir herself to make a broth but she has the big pot bubbling on the fire crane and the steam pumping up the chimney. I'm to sup it up, she says, for it's full of herbs, it'll settle my stomach. But I've seen her with her back bent low above the house, pulling handfuls of cow parsley in the marshy ground. I recognise the mouse smell of it that she hasn't managed to cloak with the flavour of strong turnip and cabbage and I know well what it can do. Ginny, having the advantage of age and the luxury of doing little and observing much, and the benefit of a heart that's not cracked in two pieces, Ginny will know that there've been no monthly rags to steep or burn this while. I tell her I cannot stomach the broth, that I'll suck on the oaten cakes for now and there's nothing she can say to that. Then she says the pot's turned sour in this strange, still weather, and she throws it out to the pigs. I know now that I'm to watch Ginny. By the time the cuckoo spit comes on the thistle in the spring, there'll be a baby in the Tailor's house and it is clear to me that Ginny does not believe that baby to be the Tailor's. No woman ever conceived a child through snoring. There will be something of Gabriel above the ground. I am both more and less than I was.

## Nuala

### January 1899

The loughs are frozen over, the moorhens skidding across their surface, the waxy leaves of the water lilies caught like plants in a glass paperweight. I walk to St Thomas's in a freezing fog, my breath hanging in the air before me, as if I've already walked this road today, or some other day, ahead of myself, as if I'm in danger any moment of meeting myself coming back. Every tuft of grass is furred like a spider; the reeds stand stiff as the bristles of the bisim; a robin in the hawthorn plumped fat against the cold. The fog makes a moon of the sun, a perfect glowing globe through the mist. The trees at the Planting reach their bony arms up into the sky, the burn below them a ribbon of ice, Miss Catherine's rock garden all moss and heather, the sea at Port na Spag sluggish, curling round the stones. My belly is hard and round, the skin stretched over my bones like the goatskin on the frame of a bodhrán. You could drum a tune on me if I was hollow, if I wasn't as full as a puffin's egg. Church Brae is as glassy as a washboard. I have my hand on the stone wall for fear of slipping, a flutter in my stomach like a moth might make, a squeeze against my bladder, a tiny limb lifting like a wing under my skin.

It doesn't matter what church you are born into, all the dead of the island end up here at St Thomas's, in the graveyard below the neat stone tower with soil heaped over their heads. Gabriel is buried near to my own people, to the east of the church; no one passes any remarks to see me here. I pick my way through the crooked stones engraved with every family name on the island; past the unknown sailors washed ashore; past the wrought-iron railings of the Benson family plot; past the poor servant man, valet to Miss Dorothea's German prince, who they say died with sunstroke; young people in the ground before their time. Wealth and age and position are of no consequence here. 'There's no pockets in a shroud,' as Ginny is fond of saying. She has a plot picked out this long time for her and the Tailor, down near the shore wall. She'll have plenty of room in it whatever time she goes, if she ever obliges me by dying. Ginny's that pickled with poitin I'm beginning to think she'll outlast us all. I won't be buried with them. I've lain beside the corpse of the Tailor for long enough with little or nothing stirring. He thinks he hit the target with that one shot; let him think it, let him believe what he likes. I'll find myself somewhere else to lie when he is dead and gone for good. Gabriel's marker is a simple wooden cross, his name, the date he was found. I look about me at all the people who are not Gabriel, who are walking the island and breathing still and I don't know how this could have happened, how he is gone and they are here. I will love this child for both of us. I have more than enough love to go around. I listen out for him but he does not speak to me. It's only the voices of dead strangers I hear. There's some consolation in this, maybe. He is peaceful, perhaps. He does not think ill of me. And still I don't know why he went to Dan's Cave, how it was that Tam Casey found me at Brackens.

I miss him. I must have loved him, though I don't have much to compare it with. I knew who I was with him in the caves, skin against skin, equal; I knew what he was worth to me. There is no price on what I do for Ginny or the Tailor. I will forever be a slave to them, unpaid or hired out. It is still and quiet in the mist in the churchyard with not another soul around. No boats on the water in this weather, no walkers on the road but me.

# Nuala

## February 1899

I am making my way back from the harbour a day in February, bright and clear, when up near the standing stone, I fall into step with Dougal. I have a feeling that it's not an accident that I have met with him here.

'A fine day for it, Nuala,' he says.

'Indeed,' I say to him back.

'I'm just heading up to the Light,' he says.

'God speed to you, Dougal.'

'Have you ever been up it yourself, Nuala?'

I give him an odd look. 'Dougal, you know I have.'

He shuffles about, looking at his feet, opening and closing his fists. 'I don't mean have you ever been up *to* the Light, I mean have you ever climbed *up* the Light?'

'What would I be doing up there?'

'There's a great view,' he says. 'On a clear day like this you can see for miles. I love to look out from it. Mr Kernohan says I can go up any time I like.'

'That's great, Dougal.'

'Would you like to come? I think you'd like it,' he says. 'I think it could be important.'

This is an odd speech for Dougal to make, but there has been something on the tip of his tongue since the day that Gabriel was lost, and maybe, I think to myself, this will be the day he spits it out. 'Well,' I tell him, 'it's a fine day. Maybe I'll take a turn with you. I'll go up, so, to the Light.'

I haven't been up there in months, not since the day Mr Marconi came. The walk is slower now with the small burden I'm carrying but Dougal is an attentive companion and shortens his stride and chatters the whole way there. I've never heard him go on so much.

'There's talk,' Dougal says, 'of a new kind of signalling system being tried. A man from the Post Office called Preece wants to run a line from Church Bay to the Light, and another over on the mainland from Murlough to McGildowney's Pier. They say him and the Marconi man used to be great pals but they fell out. He's saying now that the Marconi methods are no use at all, that this new invention is the way forward. The Postmaster in Ballycastle told me about it. It's all to do with copper plates sunk into the sea.'

'What do you think, Dougal?'

'Ah, sure, what do I know? It's all gobbledegook to me.'

We stop for a drink at the vanishing well where the water is high, the tide being in. No one knows how the salt water current regulates the rise and fall of the well, but the water is cool and welcome after the walk. Passing through the stone pillars at the compound wall is like walking back in time. All is quiet at the watch house. The keepers have gone back to using flags to signal sightings of the passing ships. No wires hang from the mast. The place looks like a town after the fair has passed, the stalls and decorations all taken down: rendered more ordinary than it was before, unornamented, dull.

Dougal stoops in through the arched metal door of the tower and I follow him in. Mr Kernohan is sitting in a chair on the stone-flagged floor, turning a heavy chain around a winch. It's like the engine room of a steamer in there, all blue-painted rivets, ladders, metal struts. He's surprised to see me. Dougal explains the visit.

'Take it easy,' Mr Kernohan says to me, smiling, eyeing my growing belly. 'I don't want to have to run for the handywoman.'

'I've a while to go yet,' I tell him.

I look up to where the chain feeds out and back through the wooden casing that runs like a mast the whole way up the centre of the tower to the oil lamp in the dome above. I put my hand on the wooden banister that curves along the top of the railings and follow Dougal up the spiral stone steps that wind around the inside of the tower. As we climb and turn, the scene through the crossed bars of the windows shifts from the green of the compound grass to the blue of the sea to the east and north. I have to stop on the first landing to catch my breath. Dougal waits for me as I lean on the sill of the window and look out over the fog cannons to where the sea meets the sky. The white-washed walls of the tower must be two feet deep, the glass of the window an arm's length away. There is little noise bar the cranking of the chain, the call of the gulls outside. Above our heads, the cast-iron brackets that support the steps wind round and round and round.

On the last landing, we step out through another arched doorway on to the balcony that circles the tower. The view is like nothing I've ever seen, not from Crocknascreidlin or from Bruce's Castle, not even from the cliffs at Bull Point. Below, the keepers' slate roofs and white sashes and green-painted doors are like dolls' houses, the white pitted road like a streak of paint stretching south-west towards Mullindress. To the east Kintyre is clear above the watch house, Islay rises beyond the channel in the north. We are looking down on to the sea pink and moss that grow along the top of the compound wall. We are looking down on to the backs of the gulls that wheel below us. To the west the cliff falls away like a giant hand has clawed a lump out of the island.

You can see all the way across Ballycarry and Ballyconaghan, over the hill of the houses and the cabin in which I was born at Crockanagh. You can see the tin roof of the grain store and the horse outside turning a circle, round and round, powering the thresher. You can see over the string of small loughs, glinting in the sun like a pearl rosary, and the mound where they say the monastery stood. You can see as far as the cliff above the path that goes down to Dan's Cave. From here, a lone figure on the headland at Cantruan, would stand out against the sky. I walk around the balcony and look south over the vanishing well and Bruce's Castle, at the dark spits of land that stretch out into the sea on the eastern shore like knobbled fingers: Portcastle, Portcam, Portavoolin, Porta Utta, Brackens. You can see how a person could get notions of grandeur up here. You can see how a person might feel capable of doing anything they like and getting away with it. The whole time we are standing there, the chain continues to wind, up and down through the casing in the tower like the gut-line in a longcase clock, and the lantern above our heads never stops turning.

I am aware of Dougal next to me. 'Your mind's on Gabriel,' he says.

I don't say anything. I don't need to explain myself to Dougal.

'There's something I wanted to show you,' he says. 'I never got the chance. The day I found him, the day I rowed him round the head in the boat? After we brought him up to the Light and Mr Kernohan took charge of him, I went back down to the boat and found something lying in the keel. It must have fallen out of his pocket when I upended him. I was going to give it to Mr Kemp but then I thought it might be something to do with you . . . ?' Dougal shrugs. 'I didn't know what to do with it. It means nothing to me.'

It's nearly six months since Dougal sat by the fire in the Tailor's house and told us what he saw on the rock below Dan's Cave. And now he reaches into his jacket pocket for something he must have kept there ever since and he hands me a curl of paper I recognise, a length of pale blue ticker tape from the watch house. As I take it in my hand it falls open like a ringlet. I run my thumb along the tape to stretch it out, the familiar dots and dashes, but marked in pencil, not in ink, as they would have been if it had come from the machine. It's a hand-written message in Morse, like the ones I occasionally left Gabriel in an emergency, when I had to change our meeting place. It's a little wrinkled where it's been wet and then dried but I am able to make out the message: 'Meet me in Cantruan,' it reads, 'down the path at Dan's Cave.'

'I didn't write this,' I say aloud even though Dougal can't know what it means. I never would have sent Gabriel there. There's only one person who could have written this message and I know who that person is.

Tam Casey is to blame for Gabriel's death, and the knowledge of that lodges in my heart like a black thorn driven into the heel of a hand.

## Nuala

## March 1899

I sit in the Tailor's house in the long still evenings and take solace in the small things, in the sheen of the cruisie lamp off the varnish of the settle bed, in the pattern the sparks make when they catch the soot in the back of the chimney, in the cross of browned rushes above the door, and I follow Mr Marconi's progress around the globe. The lighthouse steamer is anchored off Church Bay and the cart rattles up and down the road bringing oil to the Light, and Mr Marconi is in France, in Wimereux, sending messages over the Channel. Am I more or less miserable than I would be if Gabriel was still with him? Would there be consolation in knowing where he was? I think of Mr Marconi as a fly or a beetle travelling over the map of the world that used to hang on our schoolroom wall, where Ireland was a patch of green and the island as insubstantial above it as a dropped sycamore seed, like something that might lift in the breeze and spin away. It was wrong of Miss Tanner to hang a map, I think, that showed the earth as a flat thing, with Alaska on the far left-hand edge of it, and Russia on the right. Poor Dougal never could understand it, how the two countries looked so far apart and were as close in reality as England is to Ireland. Even if you could have lifted the chart off its string, bent it round so that east met west at the back, it would still have been wrong, a tube rather than a globe, a hole in the centre that a child could stand in. It's a shame Dougal never saw the globe in the Manor House. It would have helped him make sense of it all.

There was a map on the wall of the watch house too. In the caves, one day, Gabriel says, 'Italy is a foot and Rathlin is a stocking,' but I don't think that's right, I don't think that's right at all. I think Rathlin is an elbow, with Church Bay in the crook of it. 'If Rathlin is an arm,' he says, 'then Italy is a glove,' and he takes my hand and kisses it from the palm to the wrist, up the dark veins, to the crook.

Tam Casey never got the lees of the island. He never took the time. Maybe he didn't know how dangerous the path down to Dan's Cave is. Maybe he didn't intend for what happened to Gabriel to happen. But, in writing that note, he made himself guilty. Is that what he was looking for when he helped Mr Kemp to dress Gabriel in his grave clothes? What would he have done if he had found it? Destroyed it, or destroyed me?

The girl is here again today. She looks at me with pleading eyes but I won't meet her gaze. Let her keep her secrets whatever they are, I've had enough of her. There's something about her that reminds me of a story, but my thinking's so coddled I can't get it straight in my head. Something I've been told that I've forgotten, by Dougal, or by Dorothy, maybe? I'll have to ask them when I see them. What is it? I can't get a hold on it. It'll come back to me, maybe. She's quiet, sitting by the fire like she's nothing else to do. She's there when I come in from gathering the kelp from the shore, gone when I go out to close the pigs up for the night. I know she's not among the living, she makes no pretence at it. I don't know what she wants from me, still. So I mark time, I step around Ginny, I sleep with the Tailor at my back. I tuck my worries up into parcels and string them up tight. I wait.

# Nuala

## March/April 1899

The house has held its breath all winter and now begins to let it out. Doors close easily against the jamb, cracks appear in the whitewashed walls, the place shrinks in the warmer air. There is a place on the doorframe where a hair was caught in the paint. The hair has long since been plucked away, but the trace of it remains. Such a small thing and it has left a ridge. You could put the flesh of your finger against it and feel it, the place where it was.

I peel away the newspaper I laid on the windowsill last June to catch the water drops off the glass and it comes away, crisp and yellowed by the sun and the underside leaves the newsprint in reverse on the white-washed sill. I make out the article where Mr Marconi has given a demonstration of the new wireless telegraphy to Lord and Lady Kelvin and to Lord Tennyson at Alum Bay. I must have read that story aloud to Ginny and to the Tailor before Gabriel came to us. I am lonesome for the person who read that, knowing nothing of what was to come. I should gather the scourer and baking soda, scrub it away, I suppose, but I like that it's left its mark. It's not dirt, it's just old news, like everything else that's gone before.

I am ripe and full like a plum with a small hard stone at my centre. It's been a bad winter for crossings and Dorothy has been busy, her father poorly at home. I write to her and ask her if she can come to see me. She arrives on a day that feels washed and new, the air clear and mild, a stretch in the hours of light, purple bugles appearing in the grass around the rise. They're starting to plough the fields, ready for planting. Dorothy says she will conduct an experiment, that I must hold out my hand, and she ties a pin with a length of the Tailor's thread and dangles it over my wrist. It swings from side to side like a pendulum. 'You're having a boy,' she says. She walks all the way to Glacklugh with me to see the handywoman, Grainne Weir, to hear what's ahead of me, what needs to be done. Grainne Weir has thick white hair and a stork mark on her cheek. Her eyes are deep set and shadowed, the lines in her face engrained with soot, or smoke or the coomb that rises off the turf. She has a newborn lamb in a box by the fire, its back still bloody, the straw beneath it soiled and dark, a smell of damp wool, something stronger. It's too weak to suckle from the ewe. She has pulled a rubber nipple over the neck of an old clear whiskey bottle, is nursing the lamb to strength. She stands me by the window, puts her cold hands either side of my belly, feels the rise of it above and below. 'It's a big bairn,' she says to me, 'and you're carrying it low. You're maybe further on than you think. That can happen sometimes.'

'I told you it was a boy!' says Dorothy.

Grainne Weir turns soda bread on the griddle, brews us strong dark tea. She must see something of the worry in my brow for when we're leaving, she takes my hands in hers and says: 'You're a great strong girl, Nuala. It'll be no bother to you.'

We are walking back over through Knockans, past Douge where they say the devil sits at night, on past the grey stone. At Shandragh, Fergusons' white hens scatter to the east and west of us, the sun is warm on our backs. Knocklayde rises round-backed, blue, out of the haze across the Sound. We can see the *Curlew* on the water, near the Dutchman's Leg, Dougal out lifting creels, on his way in to Church Bay. He gives us a wave. Dorothy lifts her hand in reply.

Dorothy is quiet, walking by my side, then: 'Nuala,' she says, 'are you worried?'

I am worried, but maybe not for the reasons Dorothy thinks. I don't know how to answer her. I'm not sure what question she's asking me. Dorothy has been quiet since the summer before, since the time I sent her the message to the White Lodge. I suppose it's a question about the pain and the risks, but I don't think that's all that's on her mind.

'Sometimes,' I tell her honestly, 'I worry about not being fit for it. And I worry . . .' But how can I finish that? How can I say that I fear Ginny and what Ginny might take it into her head to do? I'd have to tell her the reason I fear her and that's not something I can tell, not even to Dorothy. 'I wish my mother was here,' I surprise myself by saying, and Dorothy nods and we walk on, quiet, down to the harbour in time for her to catch the mail boat home.

'*Gravida*,' Gabriel would say if he was here. I have been studying his language. The Rector has a lending library the priest says we're not to go near, but what's one more transgression after all that I have done? I won't go to confession. I won't call this child a sin. I take Gabriel's log book and the slim dictionary up to the ruins of the castle and I sit on the sun-warmed stone at the gun rock and look out over the Moyle with my hand on my belly and I speak words to our baby in three different tongues and copy them into the book. He will be a musician and an explorer, a time-traveller, a geologist, a translator. He will be loved. In the Tailor's house, I push a hole in the thatch in the corner of the bedroom and I tuck the log book in above the lathes. It will be safe there for as long as there's a roof on the house. Ginny and the Tailor will never find it. Gabriel was right about the people in the city but it's true about the people on the island as well. They wouldn't think to look for anything above their heads. When they are gone I will tell our child the truth about who he is. I am determined to live that long.

I miss Dorothy. I miss her chatter and the days of drinking tea in her little upstairs parlour, and all the gossip and news of the town. I miss the ease between us. There was a time we could have said anything to each other but there's a difficulty between us now. It sits like a dog, turning its head from one to the other, the unspoken question of Gabriel and what he was to me, of the baby and whose baby it is.

I cut up the wedding bodice like she's told me and I make a start on the christening gown. There's enough lace for a bonnet too. I am slow at it. My needlework is clumsy, nothing like hers or the Tailor's, but I do it as neatly as I can and when it's done I'm proud of the work. It's important for a child to have a thing made for it by its mother.

My time is near. The Tailor has left early for the fair on Islay; he says he's seen weather like this before, there's a fog rolling in. I have a notion he wants to be out of the way in case the baby should come. I don't think the Tailor would be of much use at the birthing of a child. He has taken old Susie the horse and dropped Ginny at a gathering in Maddygalla near the Rue, but he mustn't have tied the horse securely because from inside the cottage I hear the jangle of her harness and when I go out, I see that the horse has come back on her own. I tie her to the thatch-hook at the gable end and scatter a forkful of hay for her. Ginny, I am thinking, will have to stay the night in the lower end, or find some other way home.

I am running the iron over the things I've made, have the lace protected with a piece of muslin, am standing at the table, my back to the fire when a shadow passes the window to my left and I hear a foot on the step. I am thinking the Tailor must have turned for some reason – maybe he's come back for Susie – but it's not the Tailor that pushes open the door. It is Tam Casey who steps in.

Time has not improved his sneering look. 'How're you, Nuala Byrne?' he says. I do not speak to him. I am eyeing the cottage door and now he turns and pushes it and the bottom half swings closed behind him. The table is between me and him and he's between the table and the door. The room door behind me has no lock. The bed is big on the other side of the wall at my back. 'Not that I've any call to ask,' he says, and nods at my stomach. 'I can see fine well how you're doing.' His words are slurred and overloud, a glassy look in his eyes. He moves towards the table, unsteady on his feet. 'You're expecting more than me. You're a nice one,

Nuala,' he says. 'Three men that we know of, maybe more, and one child between them. Whose is it, do you know? A cuckoo in the nest? Or did the Tailor finally manage to pin you?'

I feel the words like a rope tugging up my throat and out my mouth. 'Get out, Tam Casey,' I say.

'What sort of a welcome is that?'

'You've no business in this house.'

'My business is with you.'

'The Tailor will be in.'

'I don't think so, Nuala. He stepped into Johnny Boyle's boat at Ushet when I stepped out of it. I watched them leave the pier.'

'Ginny . . .'

'. . . is in Maddygalla, wetting the head of Quierys' baby, along with half the island. I called in there on my way. She looks powerful comfortable. I can't see her making a move anytime soon.' He looks out the window, to where the horse is chewing on the straw. 'And it looks to me like if she took the notion, she's lost the means of getting home.' He is at the corner of the table now and he picks up the bonnet, runs his thumb over the lace edge. I can smell the drink off his breath, off his clothes. 'What's this you're at, now? A garment for the baby? Sure you're the picture of Mother Ireland herself.'

'What are you doing here?'

'I thought we could get reacquainted, now that things have settled down. It was sad – about Mr Donati. I'm sure you miss him.'

'I know what you did.'

He puts the bonnet down, almost tenderly on the table. The tick of the clock is loud on the wall.

'What are you talking about?'

'I saw the note. It was in Gabriel's pocket when they found him.' He turns his head, glances back through the open top half of the door, the evening light seeping in, clear after the rain showers early in the day, a light breeze creaking the hinge.

'What note are you talking about, now?'

'The one that you wrote, the one that sent him down to Dan's Cave.'

He shakes his head and grits his teeth and takes a step towards me. I move back into the corner. 'Was it signed, this note? Was the handwriting clear?'

'You know it was written in code.'

'Then who's to say it wasn't you that wrote it, Nuala? What proof do you have?'

'I know it was you. I wasn't in Dan's Cave. I didn't send him there.'

'Oh, I know where you were, Nuala. I remember it well.' He moves around the table in front of the fire, leans his hand against the wall, blocking my way. His eyes are bleary, blood-shot with drink. 'The memory of it has kept me warm all through the winter. Are you ready for me, Nuala, like you were the last time?'

'Stay back from me.'

'Easy now, girl. You know what's going to happen.'

I step back against the hearth wall. He takes another lurch towards me. 'There's a little something more between us now, but no matter,' he says, and he grabs me by the hair and thumps my forehead down hard on to the wood of the table. 'There's more than one way to skin a cat.' I feel him shift behind me, the heel of his hand on the back of my head, his other hand tugging up my skirts. He flings them up over my shoulders, grappling to loosen his britches, pulling at the buttons to free himself. I can feel his foul stomach, pressed against my back, then he lets go with his left hand. I turn my head to the side and see where the iron sits on its heel and I slide my arm up under the cover of my skirts and I reach over and grip the handle, and then I swing the blunt end of it up over my shoulder as hard as I can. There is a sizzle and a scream and the smell of scorched hair and burned skin like there was outside in the yard the day the Tailor slaughtered the pig. Tam Casey staggers and I back away from the table and face him. He grabs at his ear and, with his other hand, swings round to reach for me again but I still have the iron and this time I aim the sharp end straight at his eye and he roars and doubles over in pain and then runs at me again, still roaring, with his head down like a sticking bull. My back is against the settle bed but I still have the iron in my hand. There is nothing else for it then but to bash him as hard as I can on the side of his head. He catches me by the hair before I hit him, bounces my head off the end of the settle, but there's enough swing in my arm to strike him still and I do, as hard as I can. He makes a grab for the table and leans on it and looks at me, the blood pishing down his pitted face. And he gives another roar and calls me a whore's melt and makes to swipe at me, but as soon as he takes his hand off the table he loses his balance and falls. He crumples like a sack over the edge of the table and slides off onto the floor and groans, and then stops groaning and lies still on his back, his leg twisted up over his body, the blood puddling thick under his head, blackening on the clay floor. I stumble around him to the door and pull it open and lean against the jamb and look back at him to see if he will move again but he does not. After a minute, I chance it back in, careful to keep the open door at my back, and I poke him with the toe of my boot. I threaten him with the iron again and when he doesn't budge I drop it on his head and he doesn't flinch, his twisted body still lying where it fell. So I pick the iron up and drop it again and I stand over him, dropping it and picking it up until there's nothing left of his face but mashed up skin and blood.

My head aches. I lift a rag and go out and dip it in the rain barrel by the door and hold it to my head. Old Susie shakes her harness at me and then goes back to munching hay. I go in and sit down on the settle bed and look at what's left of Tam Casey, my heart pumping in my chest. I'd no idea it could be that easy to be rid of a bad thing. It's as well I didn't know that sooner. The fog rolls in from the sea, thick as the smoke from the kelp kilns when they're lit. I sit by the fire and watch the flames catch the soot at the back of the chimney, a constellation of sparks, as bright as any clear night sky.

* * *

There is no sleep on a night with fog. Up at the Light, the eighteen-pounder goes off every eight minutes and the sound runs around the compound and up the walls, and rattles the windows and shakes the floors, and echoes all the way down to Portavoolin and over the sea and beyond. The smell of cordite hangs in the air, sweet and thick. The puffs of smoke thin and disappear into the fog as the beam from the lighthouse slices the air. I sit on the settle bed in the Tailor's house and count the seconds between each pass: ten in the dark, fifty in the light; the unchanging character of the Light. In the morning, the balcony round the tower will be heaped with birds and moths bewildered by the fog and the lantern. I can almost hear the dull thud of their small bodies as they hit the glass. Mr Kernohan's boys will go out and gather them into flour bags: wheatears and starlings, thrushes and robins. They'll sweep the moths up with a bisim, a harvesting of small deaths.

When darkness thickens the fog to black and shadows creep over the floor, I hear the jingle of Susie's bridle, a step on the threshold, and then Dougal fills the frame of the door. He looks at me, sitting on the settle bed, no lamp lit, the room dim, the fire low in the grate.

'Ginny's the worse for wear,' he says. 'She'll not make it back the night. I saw that the horse had slipped her moorings. I just called to see you were—' and there he stops as his eyes find the mound and the mess on the floor that is the remains of Tam Casey. 'Jesus, Mary and Joseph,' he says. 'Who the . . . ? What . . . ? Nuala?' He takes a step into the room.

'Tam Casey,' I say, and get up then.

'What happened? Are you all right?'

'I'm grand,' I say. I take the still damp rag away from my head and bend to pick the iron off the floor. I wipe the toe and the handle and the heel and set the iron back down on the hearth. I step over Tam Casey and go out past Dougal to the rain barrel and wash my hands and splash my face and dry my hands on my apron and come back in to put the baby things away. There's a spot of blood on the bonnet. I set it to soak in a basin of water and salt. I wipe the table and throw the rag on the fire where it spits and sizzles in the dying coals. Dougal hasn't moved. He's still standing where he was at the door, staring at Tam Casey's head.

'Will you give me a hand with this?' I say to him, like Tam Casey is a bag of turf that has split and spilled over the floor. Dougal opens his mouth and closes it and looks at me with no sound coming out. I go out to the barn past Susie and lift a pitchfork and a spade from the wall. Then I go back into Dougal again. 'Will you?' I say to him and for all that Dougal seems simple at times I know he understands what I'm asking him.

Slowly, he nods his head. He walks to the basket by the fire and picks up a rag. He drapes the rag over Tam Casey's face and knots it at the back of the head. He picks him up, flings him over his shoulder and walks out the cottage door.

In the darkness behind the barn at the Tailor's house, where the fog is still as thick as broth and every sound bar the firing of the fog-gun is muffled by the air, Dougal scrapes a hole in the midden with the pitchfork and the spade and plants Tam Casey in it. He plants him as far down as he'll go, the way you'd plant a seed potato in a rig. God only knows what badness will sprout out of him – nothing good, that's for sure. I do what I can to help Dougal but my belly is big and it is awkward to lean over it. But for the firing of the gun, it is quiet work with the fog rolling in round us and the light from Altacorry sweeping out over the island and the moon dark as a griddle pan, doing its best to break through. Together we level the ground over

Tam Casey's head, scrape the ashes back over him, dampen them down with water from the barrel. You wouldn't know that a thing had changed. I scoop up a shovelful of clay from the rise and scatter the fresh earth on the bloody floor inside and grind it in hard with my boot. I take Susie by the harness and lead her into the barn. Such a biddable animal, old Susie, and never tells a tale. When I come back in, Dougal is at the door.

'I could sit by the fire till it gets light?' he says.

'I'll be grand,' I tell him.

'I don't like to leave you on your own.'

'Good night, Dougal,' I say.

Dougal sighs. 'Good night, Nuala,' he says.

In the early morning, I hear the rattle of Jamesie's cart and in rolls Ginny and collapses into the settle bed. It's no time before the snoring starts, her wheezing like an old cat you'd hear sneezing in the ditch. The Tailor isn't due back for a day or two. When she comes round she asks what happened to my head, a purpling bruise at the temple. I tell her the cow kicked me when I sat down to milk her.

'She's never done that before,' she says.

'She's getting old and crabbit,' I tell her, and she knows it's not the cow I'm talking about and that stops her enquiring any more.

I walk out to the midden with the ash bucket in the one hand and the slops bucket in the other. Every day the same thing from Ginny, like I've never heard it before: 'Empty the ashes first, the slops'll keep the dust down.' But this morning I hardly hear her. I empty the slops over Tam Casey's head and watch the cloud of ashes rise and drift away. Then I walk to the shore and fill my apron with stones and carry them up and dump them on the midden.

'What are you at?' says Ginny.

'The hens have been stratching at the ash heap,' I tell her. Every day I walk the earth, I swear, I'll drop another stone on his head.

At first Tam Casey isn't missed. I don't think he had anyone belonging to him that would miss him, and the people of the island who'd seen him that night would have assumed he'd left again. A day or two after, when me and Ginny and Dougal are sitting by the fire, who arrives in over the door the whole cut from Ballynoe only the sergeant himself.

'How are you doing?' he says, nodding at each of us: 'Ginny, Nuala, Dougal.'

Says Ginny, 'How are you Sergeant Brennan? It's not often we see yourself.'

'Not bad,' he says, sitting down on a stool, taking off his pillbox hat, his old bones creaking as he moves.

'You'll take a drop of tay?' says Ginny.

'I wouldn't say no,' he says.

I get up to wet the tea, wondering what's brought him nosying around here when I hear him say: 'Did any of you hear any word of Tam Casey?' and I have to hold my hand steady so as not to pour the water into the coals of the fire.

'Tam Casey?' says Ginny, and she leans forward on the settle bed. 'I haven't seen hide nor hair of him this long time. Wait now. Was he at Maddygalla the other night, at the christening of the Quierys' new bairn?'

'He was,' says the sergeant, stretching out his legs, warming his hands at the fire. 'And he hasn't been seen since.'

'He's likely away back to Dublin,' says Ginny. 'Isn't that where his own people's from?'

'They haven't seen him either. He's been working for the new man, Preece,' says the sergeant. 'He was to survey the land from the Rue to the Light. But he hasn't reported back to him these two days or more.' I hand him the bowl of tea and he takes a sup. 'He never made it back up to the Light the night of the Quierys' do.'

'That's a mystery all right,' says Ginny, scratching her chin.

The sergeant takes another sup of his tea. 'Randal Smith says he saw him on the lower road that night,' he says, 'heading in this direction.'

Ginny laughs. 'Sure Randal Smith hasn't a straight eye in his head he's that full of drink. You couldn't trust a word he says.'

'True enough,' says the sergeant. 'But whatever's happened to him, it's happened on the island. I've spoken to every boat. No one has taken him off.'

'Do you think he came over the moss?' says Dougal, speaking for the first time.

'It's possible,' the sergeant says.

'That was a shocking night,' says Dougal, and the sergeant gives him a quizzical look. 'The night the Quierys' child was christened. You couldn't see your finger in front of you. I remember the fog-gun going off.'

'That's right,' says the sergeant. 'Well remembered, Dougal.'

'He was the devil for a short cut,' Dougal says.

Ginny shivers, despite the fire. 'The pad over Craigmacagan is very tempting when you're coming from the lower end. Many's the one that's struck out for Coolnagrock, instead of going round by the road. It's the Light that does it, blinking over the moss at you and you know if you follow it, you'll be in Altacorry in half the time.'

'It was a bad night for taking that pad,' says Dougal, 'the fog was as thick as butter.'

'He's maybe missed his footing and is lost under the rushes and the water lilies with the cattle lowing over him,' Ginny says.

'They say he'd a fair bit of drink in him before he left Maddygalla. Who knows, he could be lying in a ditch, sleeping it off yet. He'll maybe turn up,' says the sergeant, draining his bowl of tea and rising. 'But if he turns up dead, I hope I'm long retired. I could do without the bother.' And he heads for the door and takes his leave of us.

When he's gone I chance a look at Dougal. He's staring at the floor, at the patch of newly trodden earth.

'God bless us,' says Ginny, 'not another one surely?' And she crosses herself and looks over at me.

'He's no big loss,' I say, putting my hand to my back to get up. Both Dougal and Ginny look at me and then look back into the fire. I go out to throw the dregs of the tea on the rhubarb at the side of the house, and I look over at the midden and then down on to the shore where not a being stirs. It occurs to me then that I haven't heard Tam Casey's dead voice in my head and I don't know what this means. Maybe he's planted too far down in hell for anyone living to hear him.

The weather holds fine and all hands are early at the kelp, gathering the weed in off the shoreline, spreading it out on the low walls to dry. The men begin to stoke up the fires. From the Tailor's house I can smell the briny smoke as it rises in the air, the sharp tang of iodine as the kelp starts to melt. In the evening, I can see them moving about in front of the kiln over at Portcam in the dark, the shouts and the jeers of them with their poles stoking the kelp, trying to shorten the night with stories and punch, like imps at the fires of hell.

The child is coming. The Tailor is still on Islay. Ginny, out of design or out of luck, is nowhere to be found. I walk about the house bent double, from the half-door to the dresser to the settle bed with the balls of my fists on my back. With every jab of pain I think it's me the kelp workers are stoking with the red-hot crowbars in their hands, think it's my insides that are churning, slowly, into a molten mass of weed.

I struggle up to the well at Glackaharan and send one of the young Harrisons over to Glacklugh for Grainne Weir. She comes with Ginny in tow, wherever she found her, and brings a handful of dry tangles to disinfect the house, and the smell of it burning and the smell of the kelp is enough to put you out if you were fit to move one foot past the other. She lays saved newspapers over the bed-tick and when the pain gets too much to walk about I lie down on the bed with all that old news rustling under me. The ironwork on the Tailor's bed has a pattern I've never seen anywhere else, a six-pointed star at the head and the foot, more like a cobweb than a design. There is a face I do not recognise looking back at me from the tilted mirror on the dressing table. I slip in and out of a waking sleep, the slow-burning pain moving lower down my back, the only thing that is real. The handywoman dampens my forehead with a rag, gives me raspberry-leaf tea to sip. Ginny flits in and out of the room like a bad spirit. I'm afraid to push the baby out, without the Tailor there. I'm afraid of what she'll do. I lie under the shallow surface of sleep and pain, fighting to stay awake. I dream I am standing on Cantruan looking out over the Moyle. I dream that a river runs out of the yellowing bruise on my head, over my shoulders and down my back, eddies round my ankles and pools on the rocks at my feet. And when I look down at my reflection, the girl by the fire with the tongs in her hand is looking back up at me with something like love in her gaze. And then the water at my feet darkens with blood and the reflection clouds and disappears. And then there is nothing but dull slippery pain. I hear the handywoman's voice in my ear saying, 'Push, Nuala Byrne, you have to push. You can't rear a child in your belly.' I think then that the pushing will kill me. I think there is no saving me now. I will die and there is no one here to protect my baby. But I know he cannot thrive where he is and there is nothing else I can do so I push. There is an end to the worst of the pain at last and a silence and then muffled talk and a flurry of movement and a baby's cry, and after that, all is dark.

I wake with pale light seeping in through the sash, rain hitting the window as hard as hail, the steady gurgle of water draining off the thatch, gushing and spitting into the water barrel at the eaves. I can hear the clock tick in the kitchen, the ashes falling through the grate of the fire on the other side of the wall behind my head. I cannot tell if the light is fading or growing or how long I have lain there – minutes, or hours, or days. There is a pain in my head and a dull throb between my legs, a sticky wetness under me. The bed is empty but for me. I put my hand on my stomach, feel a tenderness there, the skin slack and wrinkled as a pig's bladder. The handywoman is asleep in the wooden armed chair, her two big feet up on the milking stool, the patchwork quilt across her knees. Even from the bed I can smell the stale drink off her breath in the room. There is no sign of Ginny.

I roll myself over, feel my stomach cramp. I can see a tight little mound of clothes in the crib at the foot of the bed and I haul myself out, weak as water, feeling like my insides are in tatters, and walk in my bare feet and my stained nightgown towards it. I pull back the clothes, my heart thumping in my chest, but there is nothing there, only a rolled-up pair of the Tailor's britches, and I let a roar out of me would rise the devil out of hell. The handywoman leaps up and overturns the stool. She has that much drink on her she hardly knows where she is, but she grabs me by the wrist and shouts, 'Nuala Byrne, you put the life out of me. What in God's name is wrong with you, roaring like that?'

'What have you done with it?' I say to her through my teeth. 'What have you done with my baby?'

She looks into the crib and around the room, at the bed, back over to where she was sitting. 'Sure, it's—' she says, and stops, 'It's only—' and then, 'Ginny'll have it.' She heads for the door but I'm there before her. The settle bed is shut up and empty. The door to the lower room is closed. When I push it there is no sign of Ginny or the baby, the loom standing silent in the room. I go back to the bedroom and look under the crib and crawl in under the bed. I search the big press and empty the drawers of the dresser into the middle of the floor. In the kitchen I pull open the settle bed and drag all the old coats out. I empty the coal scuttle into the floor. I knock every plate off the dresser. I overturn the table and pull the lid off the pot, Grainne Weir staggering behind me the whole time pleading with me to 'Stop, Nuala Byrne, stop!' but I can find no trace of the baby. I sink down onto the creepie stool and stare at the lower room door.

'You're not fit, Nuala Byrne, don't fret yourself. Ginny will have the bairn. Get back into bed, for the love of God. You'll do yourself harm with this.'

I lift the tongs out of the fire and I point them at her head. 'What have you done to my child?' I say to her. 'Tell me what you've done.'

'Jesus, Mary and Joseph, put the tongs down, Nuala Byrne, I haven't done anything, I swear to you. The bairn was in the crib where I left it. You've been shocking bad, not fit to move your head. We had to feed it ourselves. Ginny said for me to rest; she said she'd take it for a while. She must have gone to get . . . it was a bit sickly . . . I . . . God, it's not clear in my head.'

'She's taken it,' I say to her through gritted teeth, 'she's taken it and you've let her. You're murderers, the pair of you.'

'Good God!' she says. 'What's got into your head? Don't be saying things like that. You weren't fit to nurse it. The child wasn't thriving. She talked about the priest, she's maybe taken it to him.'

I look again at the lower room door, which has swung shut after me. In my head there is something not right about this and it's something to do with Ginny and the child. In the fourteen months I've slept under this roof that door has never been closed. Why would Ginny close it now? I walk to it and push it open. There's a small hollow in the clay of the floor.

'Where's the loom stone?' I say to Grainne Weir.

'What are you talking about?' she says.

'The old cracked loom stone that props open the lower room door?'

'I don't know. What does that matter now? Look, Nuala, come with me, get back into your bed.'

A loom stone is a heavy thing, even with a crack in it. Heavy enough to dent a small head, to weigh a small body down, in a hole in the moss, or in the swirl of the sea. Such small bones. Hardly formed. They'd never be seen or heard tell of again.

'Where's Ginny?' I say to Grainne Weir, the bile rising in my throat.

'Nuala, I'm sorry, I don't know where she is. It's all mixed up in my head. Get into bed now, there's a good girl. We'll sort it out. We'll find them. Just get back into bed.'

I stand up, quiet, and nod my head and then I make a run for the outer door but Grainne Weir gets in front of me. She's not a big woman but in my present state she is more than a match for me. 'Get out of my way, you drunken bitch!' I shout at her, but she doesn't budge an inch.

'The bairn may be lost,' she says to me, 'but I've never lost a mother yet,' and she stands firm in front of the door with her two arms stretched across the jamb. Her words are like a hot poker in my heart.

'What do you mean it's lost?' I scream at her. 'Get out of my way or, God help me, I'll be took up for finishing you, Grainne Weir,' and I make a swing at her with the tongs. But Grainne Weir is fit for me and she ducks her head and I lose my footing. My stomach cramps and I have to grab the door jamb to stop from doubling over. She coaxes the fire tongs out of my hands, puts an arm around me, turns me into the room.

'You'll kill yourself, Nuala Byrne, if you don't get back in that bed.'

My head is light and the room has tipped up so that the floor is where the wall should be and the window is in the roof. Through it I can see that the sea is dark and high and tipped with white. I have no strength to fight her. I am dizzy with fear at what Ginny has done. I can feel the bile rising in my throat again and I start to retch and cough. Grainne Weir grabs the coal scuttle and holds it under my nose and I empty my stomach into it.

Something inside me gives way. She oxters me back to the bed. The last I remember is the bolster cool against my burning cheek, the newspaper darkening with blood under me. I close my eyes and dream that I am lying in the marshy ground of the rise behind the Tailor's house with the millrace running down over my head.

I open my eyes and the Tailor is there, sitting in his wooden armed chair by the side of the bed, looking at me with his dog-sad eyes, and Ginny is standing behind him. I raise myself up on an elbow but the effort of it is almost too much for me. I look over the Tailor's head at Ginny.

'Where's my baby?' I say to her, and the Tailor shakes his head.

'The bairn's lost,' Ginny says.

'He is not lost,' I tell her straight into her eyes. 'I know you took him. What did you do to him? Tell me where he is.'

'You weren't fit to feed it, Nuala Byrne,' she says, 'you were too sickly yourself. We did our best, me and Grainne Weir, but it didn't do. It wasn't strong. It's in the killeen, up at Kilbride,' she says. 'I buried it myself.'

The way she says it, the way she speaks of my child,

like he was a boast potato or a shot leek, something useless to be forgotten, not worth mentioning again. I cannot summon the energy to do what I want to do to her. I fill my gaze with my loathing for her and I fire it at her head.

The Tailor has his eyes lowered, his chin resting on his chest, two bright spots of colour high on his cheeks, the white hair standing on his head. He has his hands folded in his lap, his thin legs tucked under the seat of the chair. He looks like a painted wooden puppet whose strings have all been cut. He looks like all the movement and voice have left him.

'The priest had a wedding in Ballycastle,' Ginny is saying. 'We couldn't get him in time.'

'You're lying,' I say to her, straight to her face. 'Are you going to let her lie to me?' I say to the Tailor and he looks at me, startled, like a dog that doesn't know why it's been kicked.

'The child's with the angels,' he says to me, gentle. 'There's nothing can be done.'

'Where's the loom stone?' I ask him.

'The what?' He leans in to me, and makes to take my hand.

I pull it away. 'The loom stone,' I say with my eyes

on Ginny, and I see her flinch and frown.

The Tailor turns to look up at her and her expression changes, in time, to pity. 'Is she raving still?' he says. Ginny shakes her head. To me he says, 'The loom stone's where it always is, woman, on the loom in the lower room.'

'The old one,' I say to him, holding his eye now. 'The one that cracked the day the loom was moved in. The one that was propping open the lower room door.'

Again he turns to Ginny. 'What's this about?' he says.

'She's all muddled up,' says Ginny to the Tailor. 'God knows what's going through her head. She's been talking all sorts of nonsense. She's been through a lot,' looking directly at me.

'It's not there,' I say, again looking at the Tailor. 'She took it when she took the baby. Ask her why she did that. Ask her why she never woke Grainne Weir. Ask her what she's done.'

'Ach, Nuala,' the Tailor says. He scrapes back the chair and goes out of the room. I stare Ginny in the eye. She is looking at me with a pitying smile on her face, like I'm no match for her, like she's got the better of me. There's the sound of a door swinging shut and the Tailor comes back into the room and drops a stone on the bed. 'Here it is, if you're looking for it, though what good it'll do you I don't know,' and he slumps back down into the chair. Ginny puts her hand on the Tailor's arm, like butter wouldn't melt in her hot lying mouth. I run my hand along the stone. It's the same one with the same crack in the same place as before. So she took it and brought it back again. Wherever my baby is, he's not in the cold water. But where is he? What has she done to him? My heart is screaming but that is no help to me. I have to try and think with my head.

'She'll be all right, in a day or two,' Ginny is saying to the Tailor. 'I've heard tell of women being affected in this way before. But she's young and strong. She'll get over it. Sleep is the best cure.' The Tailor shakes his head, looks down at the floor. 'There'll be other babies,' says Ginny, and looks straight at me, 'stronger babies, not sickly ones, not—' And there she stops herself from saying whatever it is she is going to say. 'Let her sleep now,' she says to the Tailor, and the pair of them leave the room.

I don't know what Ginny's done. I don't know why she moved the stone and brought it back again. My baby is lost and there is no one to help me. No one will tell me the truth. The Tailor will believe every word Ginny tells him. I am entirely alone in the house. Ginny leaves a bowl of broth on the chair by the bed but I won't touch it. When it's cold she takes it away and says I can starve myself if I like. I think if she could she would poison me, though that would be harder to explain away than the tiny bundle in the crib. Sometimes when I wake, the Tailor's in the chair, snoring through his nose. One time it's Mrs Davey there, with soup she's brought herself. She feeds it to me from the spoon and smiles and pats my hand.

'My baby,' I say to her, but, 'Shush now, Nuala,' she says. 'Don't try to talk. Eat and rest. Time will heal the pain.'

One time I open my eyes and it's Dougal sitting there. I can hear Ginny rattling about in the kitchen. There's no sign of the Tailor.

'Dougal,' I say to him. 'You have to listen. You have to help me now. Tell Dorothy to come. Tell her I need her. Tell her there's no one will help me here.'

'It's all right, Nuala,' Dougal says to me. 'You can be quiet now.'

'You're not listening to me, Dougal. You have to get

Dorothy. I need her help. You don't understand what's happened.'

'I do,' Dougal says. 'I do understand. Honestly, Nuala. I do.' And he raises his eyes towards the door to where Ginny's steps grow louder, and then Ginny walks in.

'What's she raving about now?' says Ginny, standing over him, looking down at me.

I want to grab Dougal by his two big ears and shake him till he rattles. What does he mean, 'You can be quiet now'? He knows nothing at all. He's as thick as the Tailor; he'll swallow everything Ginny feeds him. I can't get through to him. I want to scream at him to get up now and run for Dorothy, but his eyes are pleading with me to be quiet, and Ginny is still standing there. I look at the two of them: Dougal, who's utterly useless; Ginny, who wishes me nothing but harm. I turn my face away from them both and bite my lip as the tears sting my eyes.

'She's looking for Dorothy,' I hear Dougal say. 'She'd be easier if Dorothy was here.'

'She can look,' says Ginny, nodding to the window, beyond which I can hear the sea roar. 'I'd like to see anyone take a boat out in that. Come on, Dougal, it's time you were away. You've kept vigil long enough.'

* * *

Three days now, they tell me, I've been slipping in and out of sleep, the whole time bleeding like a stuck pig. I am still too weak to rise out of bed. Ginny walks in and out of the room with her two hands turned out as if she has nothing to hide, the old shawl tucked into her apron and the knitted hat tied under her chin and the face of her, like her mouth would split if she smiled. Whistling through her teeth at the rosary, the old heathen, her that never bothered praying before. What's she scared of now, I'm thinking? What's she sullied her soul with that she needs prayers to undo what she's done?

This morning a shadow passes the window, there's a knock at the cottage door. I hear a woman's voice and I'm praying that it's Dorothy, come to help me at last, but in a moment or two, the room door opens and in walks Grainne Weir, Ginny behind her like a shadow.

'I just stopped to look in on you,' Grainne Weir says. 'To see how you're getting on.'

'She's doing grand,' says Ginny. 'Come in and take a drop of tay by the fire, Grainne Weir.'

'I will, so,' says the handywoman. 'Thank you kindly, Ginny, but I'll just sit here with Nuala a minute,' and she sits down in the chair beside the bed.

Ginny hovers at her back, unwilling to leave us alone. 'How're they getting on with the kelp?' she says.

'Grand. They have a load of it into the store.'

'That's good,' says Ginny, still standing. 'The storm will have set them back a bit.'

'It did,' says Grainne Weir, shuffling about in her seat. 'But they're making good headway now.'

She looks at me and Ginny looks at her and then because she can do nothing else Ginny says: 'I'll just go and wet the tay, so,' and she sidles out of the room. I hear her clattering at the fire behind the bed head, making a day's work out of it. Grainne Weir twists her hands in her lap.

'I'm very sorry for your loss, Nuala,' she says. 'You had a far worse time of it than I thought you would, but then you can never tell with a first. I've seen wee slips of girls push out babies with heads the size of turnips and it hardly take a puff out of them. But you seemed to want to keep it in your belly. I thought we were going to lose you too.'

I don't say anything to Grainne Weir. There's no point in trying to get her on my side. I wouldn't trust her as far as I can throw her. For all I know, she was in on it too, her and Ginny scheming together. She starts to fiddle with her apron pocket, slips out a brown paper parcel, rests it on her lap. Whatever it is she's brought as a peace offering, I'm thinking, I don't want it from her.

'I put this away in the whole flurry,' she says to me. 'And forgot all about it till I lifted my apron to wash it the other day. I didn't know what to do with it but it's not mine to keep.'

'What is it?' I say to her, and she puts the parcel down on the bed cover. The clattering has stopped in the other room and Ginny appears at the door. Grainne Weir looks towards Ginny, stopped with the kettle in her hand, and then looks back at me.

'The bairn was born in a caul,' she says.

I take the parcel, light as air in my hands. Inside there's a thing like a thick web, like a blister of skin that's been burst. I put my hand on it and my stomach lurches and my sore and still-swollen breasts prickle and a rush of milk runs down my front. My eyes sting with unshed tears, my heart feels like it has been ripped out of my chest. When I find my voice to speak again I look at Ginny, still standing in the door and I say to her, 'Why didn't you bury it with the child?'

Ginny makes a puckered shape with her mouth like the pulling of the neck of a drawstring bag and she shakes her head and says, 'I minded nothing about it. It went clean out of my head.' I know for certain that she is lying. If Ginny had put the child in the ground at Kilbride she'd have seen that the caul was buried with him.

'Whereabouts did you bury him?' I say to her, keeping my voice as level as I can.

'Sure, I don't know exactly where.'

'You must have a notion. Was it this side, near the march wall? Or further over towards the well?'

'I tell you, I don't remember,' says Ginny, 'and what does it matter anyway? The place is not marked. You know that the child was never christened.'

'I'll go up myself. I'll find it. The child should not be separated from the caul. I'll bury it myself.'

'You can't do that!' she says. 'You're not fit,' and she reaches out her hand. 'Give it to me and I'll do it.'

I grip the parcel to my chest. It's all I have of him. 'I'd like to know where you buried him. I'd like to see for myself.'

Grainne Weir looks from one to the other of us and Ginny turns on me. 'Go on then,' she says. 'Go on up and look for yourself and good luck to what you find.' She ducks back out through the door again and I hear her drop the kettle with another clatter on the stones before the hearth.

Grainne Weir stands up. 'I'll not bother with the tay,' she says, and makes for the door like there's a bull at her heels, and slams it shut behind her.

Little by little, my strength returns to me. Dorothy hasn't come and Dougal stays away. What have I done to deserve the loss of my friends? I walk a little further every day and when I'm fit for it, I climb up the high road through Ballycarry and Ballyconaghan, into the hill of the houses at Crockanagh. I walk past the stone with the devil's hoof print, past the barn with the horse turning the thresher, over the mound where the monastery stood. I don't look towards Cantruan; I keep my eyes on the heather and the stony ground. I march through Fallta, past the Mass rock, cross over the potato and barley rigs, climb the famine wall into Kilpatrick. I can hear the smith at work at the forge at Carravanankey, the clang of the hammer against the anvil, the pump of the bellows in between. It's a day of low cloud, strange light, the rain never far off. I stand on the rise and look down on the ground at Kilbride and there is no patch of freshly turned earth as I knew there would not be. I know my baby's not there. If he was in the ground I would hear him. I would hear my own child keening, and I would follow the sound and dig him up with my hands and strap him tight to me, under my shawl, so he would not be alone. There is a pain at my centre that no salve can heal. There is a fat round tear on the red rim of each eye, ready to drop in grief for him but I can't drop them yet for I know he's not dead. He's not dead because I won't let him be.

They say on the island that if you tell your troubles to the same stone long enough it will speak back to you. What a sorry tale I'd have to tell. I can't speak to any living thing about what I suspect Ginny of doing without casting suspicion on myself. What possible reason could Ginny have for doing away with the Tailor's child, when all on the island knows it's the news that she's been hoping for? Such a thing would make no sense, the talk of a mad woman, unless, of course, there was reason to believe that the child was not the Tailor's? And that's not a notion I want to plant in anybody's head. Ginny has me caught but I have her caught too. She's a woman who likes to talk plenty but the last thing she wants is to be talked about. She won't let me loose unless she has no choice. But as for, 'There'll be other babies,' what does she take me for, a cow or a pig to be covered at will till she gets the breed she wants? There's no place on the island for a woman who has left her husband's house. And where else would I go? Dorothy does not want a disgraced cousin on her hands, and I don't have the passage for Newfoundland. Me and Ginny are like two women facing each other on a collapsing bridge, swinging above a drop, both scared of moving or seeing the other one move, for fear that the ropes will snap. It's a question of which of us makes the move first. I keep my eye on her. I slip the little brown paper parcel in between the leaves of Gabriel's book and I push it back in above the lathes in the tatch in the big room. There must be some answer to this. I will find a way.

I turn to the island for succour and to the stories Granda Frank used to tell us. I walk the whole length and breadth of it from the Bull to the Light to the Rue. I'm up at Cooraghy this day, passing the well when I remember the story Granda told us about the herdboy who tried to trick the fairies there by buttering the stone at their drinking well but who slipped and was drowned himself. I look into the dark of the well to see if I can see him or hear any sound of him, and there's something sticking in my head, something about Grainne Weir and the morning the child disappeared, something to do with the fairies. And then I remember: the Tailor's britches in the empty crib, rolled up into a ball. It's the custom to swaddle a newborn in his father's trousers to protect him from the fairies. Grainne Weir would have seen to that – she knew all the old ways. But Ginny didn't believe my child to be the Tailor's so she'd have known that that was no protection. He is not in the water. He is not in the killeen. Ginny has let the fairies take him, and now I know what I must do.

I hunt for the child in the fairy hiding places. I call for him in the white caves at Oweyberne and at Killeany, in the dark caves at Kinkeel. In Kinramer I stare into the faces of the sheep and ask them if they've seen him. I sit on the wall at Castle-na-feesugh, round the brae at the Park where the fairies are known to gather at dusk, and I call and call and call for them till my throat aches with the sound. I search for him under the whitethorns and under the fairy stones at Coolnagrock. I walk to where they're known to pull the docken rods out of the marshy ground to ride as horses, but the fairies do not show themselves to me. I follow a light that could be theirs, over the moss at Cleggan, but it disappears into the ground before I can catch up with them, and I can't see where they've entered the moss though I dig and dig and dig. I walk further and further every day, and every day I end up back at the Tailor's house, footsore and weary, with nothing to show but dirt on my hands and thistle burrs in my hair.

I'm up at the Two Wolves near Craigmacagan this day when Mrs Davey finds me. 'Nuala, dear,' she says to me, 'you can't go on like this. Come home?'

'I can't find my baby,' I say to her, and she takes my two soil-covered hands and looks into my face.

'This is not the way,' she says. 'Come home to the fire and warm yourself. There'll be another baby in time.'

'But I want the one that's lost,' I say to her. 'If I don't look for him, who will?' And the tears roll down her face for the poor lost child and she goes away, wringing her hands, sobbing to herself.

Ginny tells everyone that I'm mad with grief and full of nonsense-talk; that I cannot get above what has happened. She says that I'm to stop walking about, digging holes and talking to the seals on the shore, that I'm to leave off eating cuckoo leaves, sucking the honeysuckle out of the hedge. I'm become a bag of bones, she says. If I am then she's to blame. She says I'm not the first woman to have lost a child. She says I need to put it out of my head. I'm to go to the priest to be churched, she says, I'm the talk of the whole island. I can be mad enough for Ginny, I can be mad enough for the island, and for the big world too. But I have a glimmer of hope in my heart that I will fan and feed so it won't go out, however long it takes. I can wait. No one can wait like me. I know my child will be returned to me, and when he is, I'll be here and he will have a home.

The day Dorothy comes, I'm down on my hands and knees near the shore at Portavoolin with the Tailor's shears, cutting a path in the grass for the fairies. It's occurred to me that they may not be able to find their way back to the Tailor's house. Ginny stands at the door of the cottage, with her arms folded, watching me. Dorothy kneels in the grass beside me, her brow furrowed like a potato rig.

'My baby's not dead,' I say to her, first, before she can utter any words of comfort. I have no time for Ginny's lies or for those who believe in them. Gently, she takes the shears out of my hands, all the colour falling from her face.

'What are you saying, Nuala?'

'My baby's not dead. I know he's not. Ginny took

him from me. She's hidden him somewhere. I don't know where. I think the fairies have him.'

Dorothy puts the shears down in the grass and takes my hands in hers. She looks up towards the Tailor's house and leans in to my face. 'You have to get yourself better, Nuala. You have to stop behaving this way.'

'I have to find him, Dorothy. Will you help me? Will you help me to find him, please? One day of ours is like a hundred with the fairies. The longer he stays, the older he gets and the harder it will be to get him back again.'

'I'll help you, Nuala, but you have to get better. You have to look after yourself.'

'The seals lie up in the sea caves at night. They know where the fairies are. I think I'll get it from them if I keep on asking. I think I will, Dorothy.'

The tears are brimming in Dorothy's eyes with sadness for the stolen baby. 'Nuala, do you hear me? This is going to kill you. You have to stop talking like this.'

'He's not dead, Dorothy.'

'This won't bring your baby back. You have to get the better of it.'

I stare at my cousin, my friend, and I feel the loneliest

I've ever felt. 'But what can I do?' I say to her. 'Dorothy, what else can I do?'

'Do you trust me, Nuala?'

'Of course I trust you. You're my best and only friend.'

'Come with me,' she says. 'I have the water heating for a bath. Wouldn't you like me to wash your hair the way I used to? Come with me now, won't you?'

'Do you know where he is, Dorothy?'

'Come with me now, Nuala,' she says.

## Dorothy

## Rathlin Island, July 1924

For weeks now Dougal has been fiddling about with what he calls his 'cat's whisker' set. He says that now the Belfast station is running, we're in with a better chance of a signal. He's gathered up bits and pieces from the Light and he has a wire rigged up from the chimney to a post on the rise behind the house at Portavoolin. He's like a child with a toy. He says these are exciting times. I've heard that before. Hours he's spent putting the whole thing together. He set the headphones on me and all I could hear was a sizzle the like of what you'd hear when the fat hits the heat of the pan. He has picked up a concert and a play, he says. He's heard part of a news broadcast. I've warned him not to put the headphones near Nuala. She's muddled enough as it is, without music and voices coming through into her head. I'm not convinced that Dougal heeds me, though. He has notions, I think, that the wireless will be a comfort to her, that it will bring her back to herself.

Nuala fooled us all: Ginny, the Tailor, Dougal and me. For all I know, she may be fooling us still, though it would be a strange kind of pleasure she would get from that since it acts against herself. Who knows what really happened between her and the Italian; who knows the truth of it all? She spends most of her day in the Tailor's old armed chair, sitting in the light of the window, looking out over the sea, her lips moving wordlessly, turning old stories over in her head, improving on them, maybe, remembering a version of events in which she can bear to believe. You can see the jolt in her when me or Dougal speaks, how long it takes her to travel back, to the now and who of us. She doesn't always make it. There are times she looks at me with suspicion, at Dougal with something like impatience, or pity, and I think then that it's not us she sees, but Ginny, maybe, and the Tailor. She's back over twenty-five years ago, hearing the sounds from that time, seeing who she saw then. When Rose comes, she acts like she hardly sees her at all. Something broke in her, finally, after the baby was born. Something in her gave way. There was always a weakness in her, a sort of living inside her head that made her unreachable. Even from the time she was young she had it. There were occasions when you spoke to her that she didn't hear or answer you at all. You could see her journeying back from some far-off place, see the wrench it was for her to return. Maybe that's where she is now. Maybe that's where she's gone to live. There's not much of her left here, not any more.

And now Rose is here, come at last, sweet Rose Corcoran, although we all know that not to be her name. She's older than the century, and wiser, by the looks of things. Her hair is as dark and shiny as was Nuala's at a time, pinned back off her face, rolled up at the back. She's dressed nearly always in her Land Girl gear: britches and boots, a long tunic over them. It's practical clothing for a trip to the island, she says, for herding the animals, for helping Dougal in the fields. I think she likes to scandalise the islanders. The apple didn't fall far from the tree there. She walks behind the plough like she was made for it, the gulls squawking after her and the horse. Sun-touched skin, blue eyes the shape of plum-stones, two little marks behind her ears. She's not given much to smiling, or talking either – a serious sort, a quiet girl. She looks a little like the photo of Nuala that the Englishman, Lewis, took of her and Granny and Granda, standing outside the old house at Crockanagh, bare-headed and bare-foot, a frown on her face. We have told her that her mother wasn't able to look after her, that she had a kind of failing at her birth, that she has never regained herself. We have told her only that. Nuala says so little these days, she has hardly spoken to her at all. It's hard to know what she makes of Rose, how much she understands. She is watchful of the girl, fearful even. She looks at her like only she can see her, like she's a ghost in her head. We've put Rose up in the settle bed, where Ginny used to sleep. She has been happy. The Corcorans have been kind. They have raised her well; she's such a shy, helpful girl, at my elbow every turn, asking what she can do to help. Still, I can't help but think how different life would have been for her, growing up on the island, if Ginny hadn't been so suspicious, if she hadn't behaved the way she did.

We've tried to tell Nuala, Dougal and me, but I don't think she's taken it in. There are nights when she wakes with a jump in the room behind the fire, her eyes wild and staring when we go in, frantically searching through the bedclothes, calling for her baby, and her terror is a fearful thing to witness. She's trapped in a nightmare she can't escape, and on those nights there's nobody but Dougal can settle her. Dougal, sitting on the chair by her bedside, holding her hands, talking low into her ear, telling her it's all right, that she can be quiet, that the baby is safe, that nothing can harm it now. There's something between the two of them that I know nothing about. Every day Dougal walks to the shore and picks up a stone and brings it up and drops it on the midden at the back of the house. I don't know what that's about and I won't ask. There's been enough trouble. We should all be allowed our secrets, our silent rituals. Dougal has always loved her; I believe he married me to be near her. I can live with that.

I don't suppose we'll ever unravel the tangle of threads in Nuala's head. The best we can do is mind her. She's always needed minding. I can't remember a time when I did not feel responsible for her. The madness of her marrying the Tailor, and him nearly twice her age. But she wouldn't be turned. There was no turning Nuala when the notion was on her, no more than you could turn a dog from a bone. Even as a child she couldn't be contained. She danced almost before she could walk. She heard melodies everywhere, in the chink of a spoon on a bowl, in the crackle and spit of a damp log on the fire, in the steam escaping from the lid of a pot. You could see her listening for them, her head cocked to one side, a look of concentration on her face. She was like a whirligig at the ceilidhs. You could see the music take over her, crawl up through the boards into her feet and into her knees and her hips and her arms and off she went. She swung till she was dizzy at 'The Waves of Tory', her hair flying, her feet thrumming off the floor. Granda doted on her, of course. She could have bought and sold him from the time she was five years old. In his eyes, she could do no wrong. I don't wonder at him passing the cure to her, but there was more to it than that. Those strange trances she'd go into, like she was there and not there, like she was always listening for something that the rest of us couldn't hear. She learned to disguise it – I watched her do it – but every now and then, when she was caught off guard, I saw her, tuning in to some other world that none of the rest of us had access to. I think that may be where she is now. I think that's where she's gone.

We pieced together the story between us, Dougal and me, with all the colour and the texture of a patchwork quilt and with all of the pain stitched in. We did what we thought was best at the time. But neither of us has given birth to a child and had it wrenched away from us. How could we know if what we did was for the best or not? How do we know that we didn't make things worse for her? There's no way of telling now.

I could have seen Dougal far enough the day he arrived to say I was to go up to the White Lodge 'to witness an experiment'. Though it's nearly a quarter of a century ago, it's as clear in my mind as if it was yesterday. The shop was busy. I'd no notion of going. Whatever it was, I said to Dougal, could wait till another day. But Dougal said for me to go. He said Sadie could mind the shop for an hour and he would stand by, in case she needed help. I must admit, I had to hide a smile at the thought of Dougal with his big shovels for hands helping to costume one of my ladies, but it was a fine August morning and the sun was shining and in the end

I was persuaded to put on my straw bonnet and go.

I walked up under the bowed branches on Quay Road and as I turned into North Street I could see the jib of the crane rising from the Pier Yard, wires running to the cliff top to a window in the White Lodge. The boats were all hauled up at Port Brittas, what looked like a shooting party preparing to board, the bathing huts further down the beach busy with visitors crossing to Glass Island. The hill fairly took it out of me. By the time I got to the top I was panting for a drink of water.

Mrs Walker, I remember, turned her nose up at me at the door. Mrs Walker used to walk about the town like she was the only person who wasn't naked under her clothes. She never bought from me but went to Alexander's in Ballymena for her wares. I explained that I had business with Mr Kemp. 'I'll let him know you're here,' she said, but at that there was a shout from upstairs and a man's voice bellowed, 'Show the lady up!'

'Into the bedroom?' said Mrs Walker, like he'd suggested I take my bloomers off and wear them on my head. 'I don't think that's appropriate.'

'In the interests of scientific experiment,' bellowed Mr Kemp again, 'come up, come up, come up!'

'Follow me,' said Mrs Walker with a face on her like a velvet crab, and up the stairs I went behind her ample rear.

Mr Kemp was standing by a small table at a window on the north side of the house, a length of the hat wire he'd bought from me running in through the open pane. I could see Rathlin clearly in the distance, lying low and grey, the white cliffs picked out in the sun. A small narrow bed draped in a pink counterpane was pushed into a corner of the room. The table held a collection of wooden boxes, coiled wire and wheels. Two large rectangular metal parts were painted with the words 'Reliable in all Climates'. He reached out his hand. 'Miss Reilly, you're welcome. Please – take a seat,' and then looked to Mrs Walker, standing sentry in the door. 'At ease, Mrs Walker,' he said. 'Miss Reilly is quite safe. We shall keep the door open at all times. If anything untoward were to occur, you would hear it straight away.' She gave one final twitch of disapproval and turned on her heel and left.

'I got a message from the island to come,' I said to him, sitting. 'I don't really know why I'm here.'

'Mr Donati's orders. A request from one of the new recruits.' He glanced at a clock on the wall that showed almost eleven, fiddled about with some wires at the back of the boxes, then picked up a set of earphones and placed them on his head. He took the only other chair.

'And now we wait,' he said.

There was a pause and a wheel began to whirr and a tape spooled out, dashes and dots. The Englishman glanced at it, more fiddling about with wires, then put his finger on a little metal hammer and began to tap.

'Are you sending a signal?'

'Just letting them know we're here.'

Another pause and the wheel whirred again, more tapping, more silence. 'Mrs McQuaid is there,' he said to me. 'She has a message for you.' I got up from the chair to look out the window to the Light at Altacorry, seven or more miles away, as if I would see some movement there that I could identify as Nuala, but there was nothing, of course, but the blink of the Light and the slow movement of the sea. Then the wheel started to whirr again and Mr Kemp frowned, picked up a pencil, began to write on a sheet of paper on the tabletop. When the machine fell silent, he looked at the words on the page, handed it to me.

'Does this mean anything to you?' he said.

I stared at the words he had written. 'You speak Gaelic?' I said to him.

'Not a word of it.'

'But you wrote this!'

'I transcribed it,' he said. 'The message is Mrs McQuaid's.'

'So you don't know what it means?'

'No more than I understood the message sent by the Italian Ambassador to King Umberto. I am but a conduit.'

'And Mr Donati?'

'I doubt very much that he knows either, unless Mrs McQuaid has translated. Now, madam, what is your reply?'

I stared at the words that Nuala had sent, a profoundly intimate message from her to me that had travelled the length of the Sound under the uncomprehending gaze of two strangers: '*Tá mé ag iompar linbh*,' she had messaged: 'I am carrying a child.' And then, incredibly, 'You're the first to know.' I was the first to know? She hadn't told the Tailor, or Ginny? I thought of her sitting there in the watch house beside the Italian, Donati, who wouldn't know what message she was sending me, unless she had told him, of course, and why would she do that? I thought of the way he'd held her, that night at the ceilidh in the big barn, of the way he had looked at her the day we came out of the sweat house with Ginny. I thought of the way she'd talked about him, about their work together. And I was sure then, what message she was sending me, although neither of us could ever say it out loud for fear of what could happen. She believed that it was his child she was carrying, I was certain of that. Mr Kemp was looking at me, sitting there, waiting for my reply.

'Not bad news, I hope?' he said, and although I thought it very bad, I shook my head at him. I sent her back the only reply I could. '*Bail ó Dhia ort, a chailín*,' I said to him.

'You'll have to write that down for me,' he said.

I walked back down North Street, along Quay Road and up to the Diamond, thinking about the message that Nuala had sent, wondering what it would mean for her, for the Italian, for the Tailor, for Ginny, wondering what she meant to do, or what she meant me to do with the news. I couldn't get her out of my head. I would have to go over to see her, to talk to her. I'd have to hear the truth of it for myself. I walked about the shop in a daze, not knowing what to do or how I was to respond to this. Then a few days later, the news came from the island that the Italian was missing, and after that the news that he had been found. And I didn't know what to say to Nuala then, or what she would say back to me, and so, like a coward, I stayed away. The Lammas Fair came round; Mr Marconi arrived in the town. The weather turned rough; there were no crossings to the island. My father took ill and needed nursing. I put off the trip, week after week, until September turned to October and November, and a crossing wasn't possible. I wrote to her as though all were normal. I sent my congratulations, hoped all was well with her. I stayed away when she needed someone to confide in. I stayed away until staying away seemed the only thing to do. I was a bad friend to her at that time. She wrote to me finally in March and asked me to come. She was going to see Grainne Weir, she said, she'd like some company for the visit. And all seemed grand between us, if grand is when neither of you says what's on your mind, if grand is a veil over what you both believe to be the truth. I wondered if she would say something, if she might mention the Italian. I tried to leave room for her to speak, while fearing what she would say. But she did not tell me anything then, and I took my leave of her with, I must admit, some relief. What would I have done with the news I believed she had for me? What good would have come of confirming my fears?

The morning of the Easter Fair following my visit, I was up early, standing at the window above the shop. The Diamond was thronged with traders, the rattle of the stalls going up all around the new memorial, the shouts of the vendors, cattle and horses being driven through the middle of it, the smell wafting in through the open sash of dried fish and dung and dulse. The Rathlin boat was in. I could see Henry James's cart pulled up at the Antrim Arms. I was keeping an eye out for Ginny to hear if there was any news of Nuala. Ginny never missed the Easter Fair. Her first stop was usually into McDonnell's for a glass of stout, but I could see no sign of her passing under the pub door and it was getting late so I headed on down to the kitchen to throw some coal in the range. I was turning the sodas on the griddle when there came a sharp rap at the Clare Street door, and when I opened it, who was standing there only Dougal, with the oddest-looking bundle in his arms, and the smallest face I've ever seen looking out of it.

'Dougal? What in . . . ?'

'I didn't know what else to do with it,' he said. 'I found it on the chapel steps.'

I stood back to let him in, then took the child from him, loosened the flour bag around its head. Its eyes were tight shut, a wrinkle for a nose, a little twitch of a mouth. The small chest rose and fell, taking in air, one tiny breath at a time. There were two little nicks of blood at the ears, a lick of black hair on its forehead.

'Poor wee mite,' I said. 'God knows how long it's been lying there.'

'Not long,' Dougal said, and I looked at him. 'Ginny left it there.'

I sat down on a chair in front of the range, my legs going weak from under me and tried to gather my thoughts. 'It's Nuala's?' I said up to Dougal, and Dougal nodded. 'Why would Ginny leave it at the chapel?' Dougal didn't speak and I didn't need him to. We both knew the answer to that. 'Tell me everything,' I said to Dougal. 'Tell me what you know.'

He had gone that morning early to pick Ginny up for the Fair. She had come stooping up the road from the house with the basket on her arm. 'How is she doing?' he asked Ginny.

Ginny shook her head. 'The child came,' she said to

him, 'but it didn't do. Grainne Weir's with her in the big room.' He made to take the basket from Ginny so she could climb up into the cart. 'I can manage,' was all she said.

She told him what she wanted him to believe, the story she was preparing for the entire island, but Dougal had thought it odd of Ginny to go the whole cut to the killeen herself. And he'd thought it cold of her too, to leave Nuala alone with Grainne Weir at such a time, even if it was the Easter Fair when she'd a good chance of selling well. But Ginny had always been a no-nonsense sort, and there was never much love lost between her and Nuala. He dropped Ginny off at the harbour, unhooked the horse from the cart, took it over to the Pound Garden to graze. The men from the upper end were boating a cow. When he got back, Ginny was sitting on a bolt of plaid in the lighthouse boat and Mrs Davey, the Rector's wife, was sitting in beside her, the cow lying on scattered straw at their feet. Dougal sat in to the other side of Ginny, who didn't look best pleased. She was shaking her head at Mrs Davey.

'Ach, no,' the Rector's wife was saying.

'She went on for too long,' Ginny said.

'The poor girl,' said Mrs Davey. 'She'll be in all our prayers. Be sure to tell her I was asking for her. I'll bring her up some broth when I'm back, get her strength back up.'

'Thank you, kindly, Mrs Davey,' said Ginny.

'She's young and strong. There'll be other children.'

'Please God,' Ginny said to her. 'Please God,' she said again.

There wasn't a wrinkle on the water, hardly a breath of air. The crew had to row the whole way across. Even at Slough-na-Mara, he said, there was barely a rock of the boat. The Rector's wife kept Ginny chatting the whole cut over about what sort of price would she expect for her napkins and would she take a stand in the Diamond? Ginny was not much in the way of talking, looking round the whole time, shifting in her seat.

'I'll go up on Henry James's cart,' she said, and, 'I'll not take a stand. I'll walk about with the basket to where the ladies are and hope to empty it before the day's out.'

The next thing they knew, they were pulling in to Brittas Pier and there was Henry James's cart waiting. In they all climbed and headed up Quay Road, the sunlight slanting in through the trees on the avenue. In the Diamond, Dougal helped Mrs Davey down off the cart, then took the basket from Ginny and handed it to the Rector's wife, and the way Ginny snatched it back, he said, you'd have thought it contained the lost sacred vessels from the monastery itself.

'What a weight!' said Mrs Davey, laughing. 'What have you in the basket, Ginny, the milk churn?'

'I'll take a turn up to the chapel,' Ginny said, 'and light a candle for Nuala Byrne.' And that got rid of the Rector's wife at last.

Dougal knew Ginny was up to something. She wasn't much of a one for praying for anybody, never mind for Nuala. She was struggling with the weight of the basket; he'd never seen her so stooped before. She stopped at the corner of Clare Street and looked up and down the road, then lifted the corner of the old bit of sail she had thrown over the basket to save the contents from the sea, and peeked in and then walked on. Dougal followed her at a distance up past Naylor's Row towards the spire and saw her pull the shawl up over her head and look all around her before she turned in at the chapel gates. He stepped in at the Forge, in under the shadow of the horse-shoe door, and waited to see if she would appear back down the road again. She passed him in minutes, looking back over her shoulder, the basket still in her hand, but stepping more lightly now. As soon as she was gone, he walked up to the chapel. What did he see, at the top of the steps by the door? Only a little tight-wrapped bundle.

'She had it in the basket the whole time?'

Dougal nodded. We were both thinking the same thing: Ginny didn't believe the child to be the Tailor's, and while she believed that, it was never going to be safe in the Tailor's house. I was sitting on the chair, the child still in my arms, when I heard my father stirring up the stairs.

'Who're you talking to, Dorothy?' he shouted down to me.

'It's only Dougal,' I shouted back. 'He needs a hand with something. I'll be back in a minute,' I said. 'Come on, Dougal,' I said to him. 'There's only one thing we can do.'

Miss Glackin, the priest's housekeeper, gave us both a quare look standing there on the kitchen step, me, white-faced, with a bundle in my arms, Dougal awkward beside me. Father Diamond was at his breakfast in the parlour, she said; she'd go in and speak to him. Then she came back out and herded us in.

'That's a strange kind of bundle you've brought me, Dorothy,' said Father Diamond from over the top of a boiled duck egg. He got up from his chair. 'Let's have a look at it. Is it male or female, do you know?'

'I don't,' I said to him. 'I never thought to look.'

'You never thought to look?' He turned to the housekeeper. 'Miss Glackin, would you do us the honours?'

Miss Glackin took the child over to a red armchair by the fire. She put it down and loosened the wrapping. As she did, a smell rose up: the child had soiled itself. It was naked but for the bit of flour bag it was wrapped in; that dark knot at its navel, its two small knees drawing up, fists clenching, feet treading air. It began to whimper and then to cry in earnest.

'It's a girl, Father,' she said. 'God knows when it suckled last. I'll have to see about making something up.'

'First things first, Miss Glackin,' said Father Diamond. 'We must safeguard its soul. Bring it into the font. I'll baptise it straight away.'

We walked, the four of us, around to the chapel. 'God knows who owns it,' said Father Diamond, scratching his chin, considering.

'God knows,' I said, in agreement, though both Dougal and I knew fine well and neither of us opened our mouths to say it. Something of this must have translated to the priest, for he stopped at the entrance to the side chapel and turned to us again. 'A huckster, maybe,' he said, peering at us both, 'coming to the fair?'

'Like as not,' said Dougal, and Father Diamond seemed satisfied with this agreed version of events, and walked ahead of us into the chapel.

Early as it was, the mosaic man was there in the apse preparing for a day's work. He was mixing up a putty of lime and boiled oil, plastering it on to the wall. He had almost finished the design, by the looks of things, was adding a few gold tiles to the border. He left off what he was doing when he saw us, came over to speak to the priest.

'Almost done, John?' said Father Diamond.

'Last few pieces,' the Corcoran man said.

'I wonder . . . ?' said Father Diamond, and then, 'John?' he said, 'we're in a very particular situation here, as you can see. A child has been found on the chapel steps. Would you be willing to stand up for it?'

Mr Corcoran said he would, gladly, and then Father

Diamond said, 'And perhaps Mrs Corcoran?' So the man went off to fetch his wife. We all stood around the baptismal font looking at the little white face of the child, squirming and twisting, and waited for the couple to return.

'I'm thinking,' said Father Diamond while we were waiting, 'the less said about this the better. The mother, God help her, will be long gone by now. There's no good will come of talking. Would you agree, Dorothy?'

I nodded. 'If you think that's for the best, Father.'

'Dougal?' he said. Dougal nodded too. 'Miss Glackin?' Father Diamond said.

'Whatever you say,' said Miss Glackin, and stole a look at us.

'She's a lucky child that you *found* her,' said Father Diamond, putting an odd stress on the word. 'And since she doesn't have a family name we'll make up for it with a first. We're not far off the feast day of St Anastasia; St Felicia's is this month as well, but they seem like big names for such a little mite.' He looked at me and then at Dougal. 'Any thoughts?' he said, but a name for Nuala's child was not something I'd considered I'd have to conjure, and Dougal looked affronted at the question.

Father Diamond turned to Miss Glackin. 'Miss Glackin, what was your mother's name?'

I believe Miss Glackin actually blushed. 'Rose, Father,' she said.

'Perfect,' said Father Diamond. 'Rose it is.'

There was a step at the door and in walked the Corcoran couple, the wife all a-fluster. 'Will you stand up for the child?' Father Diamond asked. 'Be godparents, to the little girl?' The husband and wife nodded and said that they would. 'Miss Glackin,' Father Diamond said, 'pass the child to Mrs Corcoran, please.'

The wife took the little bundle into her arms, and tugged the rough blanket down off its head. She held the child over the font as Father Diamond poured water on its skull, and right away the child began to yell, drowning out the priest's words. Mrs Corcoran smiled and smiled. When the ceremony was over, she said, 'She must be hungry.'

'Yes,' said Father Diamond, 'she must. Do you think . . . ?'

'Of course,' said Mrs Corcoran, and she and her husband disappeared down the chapel aisle with the child.

I walked back down the road with Dougal, into the

hustle and bustle of the Diamond, and who did we bump into first, only Ginny herself. I could hardly bear to look at her.

'I was just coming to give you the news,' she said, 'only I see Dougal has got here before me.'

'He did,' I managed to say, thinking of the bundle that the Corcorans had just spirited away. 'And heavy news it is. How's Nuala?'

'She had a rough time of it, but Grainne Weir'll mend her.'

She paused and looked at me, hoping, I suppose, for an invitation to come in and rest herself, take a cup of tea, but I couldn't bring myself to do it. 'I suppose you'll be opening the shop?' she said, and I nodded, and before she could ask me any more I turned and walked away.

'I've my father to see to now,' I said to her over my shoulder. 'I'll come over to Nuala as soon as I can.'

The cheek of her, standing there, after what she'd done, and neither me nor Dougal able to say a word to her for fear of what would happen to Nuala. I let myself back into the house in a tizzy and climbed the stairs to my father.

The sea got up; the boat couldn't go. The day that had begun so still and calm ended with rain lashing against the windows, mud and water pouring down the street like a river in full flood. The islanders who'd crossed for the Fair spent the night on McDonnells' floor. There was no way of getting word to the island. The weather kept the Tailor on Islay. Nuala was alone with Grainne Weir. Ginny must have wondered that there was no mention of the baby that had been found on the steps up at the chapel. The priest wanted no talk about it and neither Dougal nor I were likely to start it, knowing what we knew. Every penny that Ginny had earned at the fair disappeared over the counter in McDonnells' and still she held fast to the basket. The next day, the wind died down enough to try for a crossing and off they headed into the Sound with a hungover skipper and a cargo of sore-headed passengers. Jamesie had stabled the horse for Dougal. He harnessed her up to the cart and met the boat coming in. Dougal loaded Ginny in and up the road to Portavoolin they rattled.

When Ginny lifted the latch on the door of the Tailor's house, the door wouldn't budge an inch. 'Put your shoulder against it, Dougal,' she said. 'It must have swollen up with the rain.' But there was something heavy behind it, something that scraped across the floor as he pushed. There was a shout inside from Grainne Weir and then she was in the door.

'I had to push the settle bed against it,' she said, 'for fear of her running out. She's been like a mad woman since you left. I've tried to talk sense into her but you might as well talk to the rain. What happened to the child, Ginny McQuaid? Why did you leave me here?'

Ginny shook her head, gave Grainne Weir the same story she'd given to Dougal, to Mrs Davey, to anyone who'd asked.

The handywoman picked her apron up off the chair, tied it round her waist. 'You shouldn't have left me alone with her,' she said. 'I'm going, I've had enough,' and out the door she went.

'You'll have to stay until the Tailor comes,' said Ginny. 'I can't contain her on my own. Go in there to see how she is.' A sorry sight, she was, Dougal said, with her hair all matted and her face as white as the moon. He felt a cruel sort of friend to her, then, he said, but it was all he knew to do. When he went back in to the fire, Ginny was scuffling about at the door of the lower room, the basket beside her on the floor. He swears that she took the loom stone out of it, the one that he dropped and cracked the day they moved Ginny in; that she'd brought it the whole cut to Ballycastle and back, and why would a woman do that? What had she intended? To throw the child in the Sound? Dougal was convinced that if it hadn't been for the stillness of the day, and the Rector's wife chattering on the boat and himself keeping a tight eye on her, she would have thrown it in the sea. It was clear that the child couldn't return to the Tailor's house while Ginny was under its roof. There was nothing for it but to bide our time and try and figure out what to do.

Once the boat had gone, and Ginny was safely away, I called in to Father Diamond. The Corcorans were preparing to leave, he said. The husband had work in the glens, in the church out by Cushendun, near to where their own people were. Mrs Corcoran had taken to the child, he said, and he was wondering to himself if the best course for the youngster was for them to take her with them. He could sort it all out through the Church, he said. What did I think? he wanted to know. 'What would Dougal say?'

'Dougal?' I said to him, shocked. What did Dougal have to do with it? And he gave me that odd sort of look again, the way he had the morning we found the baby, and it occurred to me then that Father Diamond, who was a kind man, had got it into his head that the child was ours, however unlikely an idea that was. 'It's not . . .' I started to say to him, and then I didn't know what to say. He knew there was something odd in our behaviour. I couldn't tell him the truth, and my denials would make me look all the more guilty. I began to see that there might be some merit in going along with his notion. 'I would hate to think of the child going to the workhouse,' I said to him at last.

'Certainly not,' said Father Diamond. 'That will never happen.'

'And they seem like kind people, the Corcorans. I think they would be good to her.'

'They're the best,' said Father Diamond, kindly. 'I can vouch for that. Honest, and hard-working, and – well – between me and you, Dorothy, desperate for a child of their own.'

'And would they – since we found her – me and Dougal, I mean – would they allow me to keep in touch with her, to see how she does?'

'Certainly, Dorothy, certainly. There would be no difficulty at all.'

And with that, it was agreed, him believing one thing, me knowing another and not at liberty to say it.

And so the Corcorans took Nuala's baby. It seemed like the only thing to do. I don't know what notion Nuala took that the child was a boy, but it served our purposes well enough. It made Rose easier to hide.

My father failed and passed away at the end of the summer. I was alone in the house. Dougal called with me every time he crossed to get news of the Corcorans and of Rose. People thought me and him must be courting, such was the contact between us, and after a while, it didn't seem like such a mad idea. We married the year after. I moved to the island, to Dougal's house in Ballycarry. Between us we kept Nuala safe. We brought her back from her wanderings, we washed her and fed her and put her to bed in his mother's old room. And before too long, she settled down with us. Ginny didn't want the bother of her. The Tailor felt sorry for her, I think, though he was too much under Ginny's thumb to express it. He never said much at all, the Tailor. I often wondered what was going on in his head. Nuala's like our own child. We keep her safe between us.

My back is not as straight as it was; Dougal's hair has turned as white as the chalk road. The Tailor is gone these thirteen years but Ginny took a long time to die.

I've never known a woman take so long. What was it she was lingering for? I have it in my head she didn't want Nuala to have the house but in the end there was nothing she could do about that. The Tailor left the lease to Dougal. I think he knew that Dougal would look after Nuala. He never stood up to Ginny in life but he did something decent in the end. When Ginny died, we had the roof re-thatched, and the whole place whitewashed and we moved in together. All three of us at Portavoolin. A strange little family we make. There are two more Lights on the island now, at the Bull and at the Rue. There's a new pier built at the Manor House. The general is long dead, the Benson estate broken up, most of the islanders hold a freehold on the land their families have tenanted for years. The barracks is closed at Ballynoe; there's not a policeman left on the island.

It's over twenty years since Mr Marconi sent a message from Cornwall to Newfoundland, across the wide span of the Atlantic, five years since the first telephone conversation between Nova Scotia and Kerry. I tell Nuala these things in the hope that they will mean something to her but though she sometimes smiles and nods her head I've no way of knowing if they do. At times it feels like she grasps it and then I watch it slip away again. It must be like being reborn every day to live a life like this, to not remember what's gone before, to live each pain, each joy afresh. And now here is Rose, like a reprieve. What will she make of us, me and Dougal and her mother? What will she have to say?

What she said to me, shy, yesterday when she came in off the fields, was that she'd heard there was to be a dance in the Parish Hall and she loves to dance and would I help her wash her hair? Her mother usually does it for her, she said, she can't get the tangles out of it herself. She meant Mrs Corcoran, of course – we both know who she meant – but she glanced at Nuala, sitting by the window as she said it. Of course I'll wash it, I told her. I'm great at washing hair.

'Are you going in your britches?' said Dougal, and she laughed and said she would if she could. We set up a basin on top of the rain barrel outside and heated a big pan of rainwater on the fire. When it was warm enough Rose unpinned her hair and leaned over the basin while I poured jugfuls of water over her head. We got a good lather going with the lye soap. She has a great head of hair, thick and curly like Nuala's used to be. I was rinsing it all out with vinegar and hot water when the shoulder of her shirt slid down her arm and I saw a thing I didn't expect: a little mark on her shoulder, the exact shape of a tadpole, the exact colour of tea, and the jug fell out of my hand on to the ground and smashed into smithereens.

'Are you all right?' said Rose.

'Buttery fingers,' I said to her, and bent to pick up the pieces of the jug.

'I think it's rinsed well enough now.'

'I think it is,' I said. I gathered the pieces of delft into my apron and brought them into the house.

A mark like that would be a tiny thing on a newborn child, not something you'd see unless you were looking for it, and Ginny wasn't looking. It's the same mark we saw on Ginny the day we went into the lake at the sweat house. Rose is the Tailor's child, she must be. Rose is a McQuaid after all.

And now I know what to do with the book I found the time we re-thatched the house, the one that fell out from above the lathes in the big room: the book that the Italian had kept, full of measurements and times and code, the colours of the rainbow, weather reports, words in a language I don't understand. The book that Nuala had scribbled in, in the pocket in the back of which I found a lock of dark hair and a strange brown parcel and a little christening bonnet, trimmed with Carrickmacross lace, marked with one dark stain. I had thought that one day I would give it to Rose, that I would tell her what we knew. But now I know I can put it on the fire and burn that whole story up. I will take pleasure in watching it turn to ash, in raking it out and dumping it, cold, among the tea leaves and the eggshells on the midden. It will be as if none of it ever happened at all.

## Nuala

### July 1924

I am between two ticks of the clock, between one swing of the pendulum and the next, between the last thing that happened and the thing that is yet to come. I am in a gap in time where it might be possible to go forward or go back, or to stay in between and do both. I have lived, it feels, for a long time, if living is what this is, if searching and yearning for what is lost can be called a living; if waiting is any kind of life. Was it a good or a bad day, the day I stood on Crocknascreidlin and watched the boat carry Gabriel in? It's hard for me to say. What I learned from him made me think that there might be a way of going back again, back to the beginning and that knowing what you know, that you might be able to change things. You might know that there could be something better coming. You might know why that face when you see it, or that voice when you hear it, unsettles you so. How different it would be, I said to myself, if we could look down the wrong end of the telescope of time, see what was ahead of us, as if it were behind. I know now that if you do that the telescope becomes a mirror and it's only yourself you see. We are who we are, we go on making the same mistakes over and over. Except that now and then, there's the smallest scratch in the silvering of the glass of time and instead of seeing ourselves reflected, we see clear through to what's on the other side. There's a flutter in the belly, a hand over the heart, a jolt of memory, or not memory, maybe a half-glimpse of what's to come, of what's already there. Do I regret anything? I can't tell. The sight grows hazy, the hearing muffled, touch is not what it was. Every day my grip loosens. Words repeat themselves in my head. But I am getting closer to something, whatever it is: the scrape of a foot across the threshold, the lifting of a latch, the return of something precious; lost, unrecognisable, maybe, but a homecoming none the less.

I'm coming down along the low road near the Big Garden where the plum and the apple and the greengages grow, my hair wet from its dip in the rain barrel, my shawl tied round my waist for a pocket, the yarrow tucked into the folds, my skirts skimming the tops of my boots. Morning on a day in early June, still and clear, the island stretching out green to the lower end in the east, rock and heather to the west. The red bow of Jamesie Duffin's boat rounds the gap in the Bo reef and makes for the pier. Below by the Waterguards' houses, the Tailor has the cart backed into the water, alongside Dougal's boat and old Susie the horse is standing steady as she's bid between the two shafts. Such a biddable animal, old Susie, and never tells a tale. Gabriel climbs out of Jamesie's boat and stands on the slipway and looks around as if he's expecting something. He looks across the bay towards Mallacht, takes in Ballynagard and Church Quarter, the stone belfry of St Thomas's, the graveyard with its crooked white stones. If he looks up now he will see me, watching him. But he doesn't look up. He turns his head and sees Tam Casey on the lighthouse cart rolling along the limestone road like a black fly moving over a white stone in the sun.

I sit back into the Tailor's old chair by the window

and a finger of sun closes my eyes. I don't know how long I've been here, whether I've been asleep or awake, whether the people and things I've seen and heard are shadows or remembered things or whether they are here with me now. There's a thing that's hard for me, a thing I know that keeps slipping away. It's a hard thing to hold. It's to do with Dougal, and Dorothy, and the baby, and Ginny and the Tailor, too. It's something they had to keep from me, or keep from Ginny, or the Tailor, something that used to be a secret but that isn't one any more. It's a sad thing and it was a hard thing to keep, but they had to keep it, they said they did. And now that I have it, that they've given it to me, I know why it was hard for them, for it runs away from me even as I try to catch it, like the water from the holy well at Brackens runs out of a cupped hand. It's to do with the mosaic man, and his wife, and her smile, and the music in the priest's gramophone, and the notes of the piano drifting over from the Light, and the Madonna, and the child. I open my eyes, and after all this time, here's the girl again. She sits down on the edge of the settle bed, and bows her head and combs her wet hair through with her fingers and lets it drop like a curtain to be dried by the heat of the fire. The light from the window falls on her slender hands, on her wrists, on her neck, on the white of her shirt. Then I see a thing I know I've seen before and seeing it is like opening and walking through a door into a room you'd forgotten was there. I see a little scar behind her ear where once there was a nick of some kind, the kind that would be left by a caul pulled away, the kind that would have its match behind the other ear. She cocks her head to one side at a noise from outside the window, a shearwater screeching like a banshee overhead, and then she does a thing she's never done before. She sits up straight and she smiles at me. And I know who she is then, who she belongs to, and knowing that is like a hand opening and closing again over my heart.

All this time I've been looking for a son when it's a daughter that I had. And now I see that she is mine, through years and years of fairy time, but mine all the same. I reach out to her and she takes my hand. I don't know what journey she's been on, I don't know how she's come to be here, but I do know that she's found her way back to me again. I have gotten what I wished for: to stay on the earth, to keep going round, to wait. I've been listening and watching out too long for the dead and all this time not hearing what she had to say to me. That we are together at last in the Tailor's house. I close my eyes. I hear Dougal speak and the girl laughs, a fine and hearty laugh and then I hear Dorothy, close to me.

'What are you smiling at?' Dorothy says.

'I hear the child,' I say to her, with the sun still on my face. 'It feels like summer.'

Acknowledgements

For the resources as well as for the physical space to write this book thank you to: the Arts Council of Northern Ireland; the Society of Authors and the Authors' Foundation; the Bodleian Library, Oxford; the History of Science Museum in Oxford; Libraries NI; the Library of the Ulster Folk & Transport Museum at Cultra, and the Tyrone Guthrie Centre at Annaghmakerrig.

Thank you to all the people, friends and strangers, of whom I've asked questions: Bill MacAfee, Bill McBride, Frank Rogers, James Meredith, Mary Boyle, Gráinne Daly, Philip Watson, Liz McCormick, Roy Toner, Jane Millar, Frankie Sewell, Colin Breen, Lesley Wishart, Andrea Spencer, Scott Benefield, Alison Lowry. The story didn't always go in the direction in which I had intended, but your answers helped me get there nonetheless.

Thank you to the islanders, in particular to Angela Green, Richard Green, Julie Staines, Jim McFaul,

Jessica Bates, Stephen Ryan, Noel McCurdy, Margaret McQuilkin, Jennifer McCurdy, Hilary Curry and Alan Curry. Thank you too to the Commissioners of Irish Lights.

Thank you to Flowerfield and to Ballycastle Writers (where this story began) and in particular to early readers Debbie (DJ) McCune, Julie Agnew and Mandy Taggart.

Thank you to my agent Clare Alexander, and my editor Mary-Anne Harrington and to all at Tinder Press. Thank you to Averill Buchanan and Gillian Stern for early editorial help.

And, finally, thank you to Kevin, Mary and Rosie for understanding when the door was closed.

There are a number of books and articles that have been invaluable to me in the writing of this one. They are:

*Rathlin Reminiscences: its People, its Stories, its Places* by Loughie McQuilkin (Ballycastle, 2013)

*The Guttering Candle or Life on Rathlin 1920–1922* by Letitia Stevenson (original documents held in the Ulster Folk & Transport Museum Library, Cultra, Co. Down)

*Island of Blood and Enchantment: the Folklore of Rathlin* by Michael J. Murphy (Dundalk, 1987)

*Rathlin: Nature & Folklore* by Philip Watson (Glasgow, 2011)

*Rathlin's Rugged Story* by Augustine McCurdy (Coleraine & Ballycastle, 2000)

*Stories and Legends of Rathlin* by Augustine McCurdy (Ballycastle, 2006)

*Rathlin: its island Story* by Wallace Clark (Coleraine, 1993)

*Rathlin Island: An Archaeological Survey of a Maritime Landscape* by Wes Forsythe & Rosemary McConkey (Antrim, 2012)

*Moyle Memories – 50 years and Beyond*, written by Danny McGill, edited by Tommy McDonald (Ballycastle, 2008)

*The Harsh Winds of Rathlin, Stories of Rathlin Shipwrecks* by Tommy Cecil (Ballycastle, 1990)

*Sea Wrack, or Long-ago Tales of Rathlin* by Mary Cecil (Ballycastle, 1952)

*Forgetting Frolic: Marriage Traditions in Ireland* by Linda May Ballard (Belfast & London, 1988)

*Marconi: the Irish Connection* by Michael Sexton (Dublin, 2005)

*My Father Marconi* by Degna Marconi (London, 1962)

*Signor Marconi's Magic Box* by Gavin Weightman (London, 2004)

*The Early History of Radio* by GRM Garratt (London, 1994)

'Traffic Island' by Philip Watson in *Archipelago*, Issue 7, 2012

'Seal Stories and Belief on Rathlin Island' by Linda May Ballard in *Ulster Folklife*, Vol. 29, 1983

'Traditional Houses of Rathlin Island' by E. Estyn Evans in *Ulster Folklife*, Vol. 19, 1973

'Wireless Telegraphy and Journalism: Accounts of the Reporting of the Kingstown Yacht Race by the Dublin "Daily Express" ' published by the *Daily Express*, Dublin

'Old Ballycastle, and Marconi and Ballycastle, two lectures delivered on the occasion of the town's civic week 17th–24th August 1968' by Hugh Alexander Boyd (copy in Ballycastle Library)

'Marconi/Kemp in Ballycastle & Rathlin Island 1898: Locations used in Ballycastle' source and author unknown, Ballycastle Library

'Wireless Experiments, Rathlin Island: the evolution of communications' by G.H. Scarlett, J.P. (Local Studies, Ballymena Library)

'Marconi's Wireless Telegraph' by Cleveland Moffett, published in *McClures Magazine*, June 1899

'An ancient Irish hot-air bath, or sweat-house, on the Island of Rathlin' by Rev D. B. Mulcahy in *The Journal of the Royal Society of Antiquaries of Ireland*, Ser. 5, Vol. 1, pt. 2, pp. 589–90, 1891

For those who are interested in reading more about Marconi, there exists an invaluable online digital archive, created by Marconi plc at marconicalling.com, including typed and hand-written excerpts from the diaries of George Kemp (although not, at the moment, records of the Rathlin/Ballycastle experiments).

# Author's Note

My first encounter with Rathlin Island, off the north coast of Ireland, was in September 2002 when I went there as a participant in a writing festival organised by Ballycastle Writers' Group. It was a glorious weekend. The sun shone down as we sat around tables in the Manor House and in island homes, at picnic benches and on dry stone walls on the shoreline writing. There and then I fell in love with the place. Rathlin is an island with a proud heritage, a place that resonates with stories preserved in place names and local folklore. It is also one of the quietest and one of the darkest places I have ever been. Walking back to the hostel alone in the dark through Ouig, away from the harbour lights and the sweep of the beams from the lighthouses, it was easy to be rattled by the stories the islanders were only too ready to tell, of the *gruagach* that haunts the Manor House, of the souls of drowned seafarers turned to seals, of the shape-shifting hare that, with one glance, can put a twist in your face. When a black cow announces itself from behind a thorn hedge on such a night, it can put a fair skip in your step.

Marconi's connection with Rathlin is well-documented. In the summer of 1898 the island found itself at the forefront of technological advances in communication when the engineers of the Wireless Telegraph and Signalling Company arrived there to conduct their experiments across the narrow channel to the mainland. This is the setting for *The Watch House*. I wanted to write a story about the impact this visit might have had on the islanders at the time. My interest was in exploring the phenomenon that radio was in the late nineteenth century: the extraordinary idea that your words could travel beyond you, specifically in the context of a community that knew all too well what it was to be cut off from the rest of the world. In my head, Marconi's engineers must have looked, to some of the older island dwellers at least, like conjurers engaged in some brand of devilish magic. But I was also interested in the idea that some of the islanders would have been fascinated by the experiments, by the future potential of this extraordinary technology.

George Kemp was Marconi's first assistant, an ex-naval instructor who was released by the Post Office to work with Marconi's company in July 1896. The Bodleian Library in Oxford holds photographic copies of Kemp's original diaries as well as his hand-traced maps. A couple of years ago I was given permission to view the collection. It was a privilege to sit in the hushed atmosphere of the library, and to read Kemp's words in his distinctive cursive hand. I got to know the idiosyncrasies of his writing: the floating 't' strokes; the looped descenders, as well as a little of his personality. His writing is not expansive; it is detailed regarding the difficult and often physically demanding work he was there to do, and he is largely uncomplaining. But every now and then there is a glimpse into his thinking. On one of his first crossings to the island a short note reads: 'strong breeze, boat taking in water'. On another occasion, the one-hour journey took four times that length. Having made that crossing on a few occasions now, I can sympathise. Even a short journey on a large boat on a rocky sea can feel like a very long time.

Around 1930, Kemp created a typed manuscript of the diaries, but from what I have seen, these are not an exact copy but a sometimes synopsised, sometimes expanded version. There is some disparity in content between the hand-written and the typed material. It is also clear that Kemp didn't always write his diary entries on a daily basis but sometimes wrote them up some days later and this, combined with the variants in the two versions, interested me greatly. As a fiction writer, I am always looking for the gaps between recorded events, the spaces in between. The tales I had heard of the island, the unique and mystical atmosphere of the place, weaved themselves in and out through Kemp's somewhat terse, often prosaic notes, and a story began to emerge.

By the time Kemp arrived in Ballycastle in the summer of 1898, Marconi's wireless station at the Royal Needles Hotel on the Isle of Wight was fully operational. The purpose of the Rathlin/Ballycastle experiments was to prove the commercial worth of the new technology. Lloyd's of London had commissioned Marconi's company to report on the passage of ships and their cargoes (many of which were insured by Lloyd's underwriters) through the North Channel between Ireland and Scotland. The vessels passed close to Rathlin on their return journey across the Atlantic to dock in Belfast, the Mersey or the Clyde. Although they could be seen from the lighthouse at Altacorry on the island, the difficulty was in conveying the message to the coast guard station on the mainland at Torr Head. In conditions of poor visibility, the semaphore flags could not be seen from Torr, and carrier pigeons were often prey to the hawks that inhabited the island.

On Wednesday 8 June 1898 Kemp reports that he took the boat to Rathlin where he inspected the lighthouse. At that time the only lighthouse on the island was the one at Altacorry, now known as the East Lighthouse. He also mentions that he inspected Lloyd's hut which became, for me, the watch house of the novel. From the diaries we know that he instructed the Lloyd's agent Mr Byrne and his sons to run the mainland station at the Coalyard. In other sources, the Rathlin lighthouse keeper Mr Dunovan, along with his sons and an islander named John Cecil are reported as assisting with operating the station on Rathlin. In July 1898, Kemp broke off the experiments under orders from Marconi to travel to Kingstown, near Dublin, where the company had been commissioned by the *Daily Express* to report on the yacht races. In my version of events, I have Kemp leave the Italian engineer, Gabriel Donati, behind on Rathlin, assisted by Nuala Byrne, with Tam Casey appointed to temporarily operate the station on the mainland.

In the last few years I have become interested in the stories and images of the women codebreakers that have emerged from Bletchley Park in World War Two. I knew that women had worked as operators since the early days of telegraphy in the 1840s, and the idea of creating a character, a woman who would live on the island and who would become a wireless operator, began to take shape. Nuala's was one of the first voices that came to me in the book and right from the start she had that ability to 'tune in' to different frequencies of sound and of time. The early drafts of *The Watch House* had chapters written from the point of view of the character that would eventually become Rose. In those versions, Nuala and Rose, existing in two different time frames, in the same place but decades apart, would catch unexplainable glimpses of each other. In the end, though, it was Nuala's voice that grew stronger, her story, tied as it is to the rhythms of island life and to the richness of those traditions, that gathered momentum and took over the book.

On his return to Ballycastle after Kingstown, Kemp was accompanied by a young Irish engineer and graduate of Trinity College Dublin called Edwin Glanville, who had been in Marconi's employ for around eighteen months. Glanville was stationed on Rathlin on 30 July and in the first weeks of August, Kemp reports receiving signals from him at a number of sites on the mainland. On 21 August, Kemp received word that Glanville was missing. Tragically, the young engineer's body was found at the foot of a steep cliff the following day. His remains were transported to Dublin where he was buried on 26 August and where Marconi, returning from the royal wireless experiments at Osborne House, attended his funeral. Glanville makes no appearance in *The Watch House*, but Gabriel in the story dies in a fall from the cliffs to the north of the island.

There has been some contention over the years as to the exact location of the site at which the first commercially sponsored wireless signals were received from Rathlin in Ballycastle. I read several accounts of the history of the experiments, some of them anecdotal, many of them conflicting. In the end I followed as closely as I could Kemp's original hand-written diaries and hand-traced maps and used those as a guide to time-frame and location. Many local people are familiar with 'Marconi's Cottage', a building to the east of Ballycastle near Carrickmore, beyond the Salt Pans colliery, and now a private residence. I believe that this building, formerly known as the weighmaster's house, marked on Kemp's map as station 'Y', and referred to by him as 'the coal yard station' was one of the first sites used. The diaries list a number of other mainland sites that were later tried with varying success including Lloyd's Station on Torr Head; a site on the McGildowney estate at Clare Park to the west of the town; and the spire of the Roman Catholic Church in Clare Street. The most successful of the sites tried appears to have been The White Lodge (now Kenmara House) on the cliff top at Quay Hill on North Street, used by Kemp in August 1898. His hand-written diary entry for 26 August reads: 'Sent and received from 10 to 6.30 and got mostly red each way. Reported 10 ships to Lloyd's and Mr Byrne sent on a report concerning the work.'

Marconi arrived in Ballycastle on Monday 29 August, on the eve of the Lammas Fair. Both he and Kemp put up at the Antrim Arms in the town. The following day they packed up the equipment on the mainland, the weather being too rough to cross to Rathlin. It was 1 September before they were able to reach the island where they visited the lighthouse and the cliff top from which Glanville had fallen. Marconi left for London on

2 September; Kemp followed on the 8th. Kemp continued to work as Marconi's chief assistant for a further thirty-five years. He was by his side on 12 December 1901 at St John's in Newfoundland when the first transatlantic signal was sent from Poldhu in England. Kemp died in 1933, Marconi in 1937.

Both Kemp and Marconi appear fleetingly in *The Watch House.* All the other characters are completely fictional. What I have tried to stay true to is the island itself. For a number of years, the Ordnance Survey map of Rathlin and Ballycastle has hung above my writing desk. I have recited the litany of the island's place names like a poem or a prayer: Sloaknacalliagh, the chasm of the old women; Kilvoruan, the church of Saint Ruan; Crocknascreidlin, the hill of the screaming; Lagavistevoir, the hollow of the great defeat. Every name tells a story of its own. Each time a character has moved to make a journey, on foot, by boat, by cart, I have plotted their progress across the map as they navigated those dark historics. The tailor's house at Portavoolin is a fabrication of mine – to my knowledge there has been no dwelling place there since the mill fell into disuse well before the nineteenth century.

The technology that Marconi pioneered at the turn

of the twentieth century is the same technology that is used in text messaging today. What would the islanders of 1898 have made of the idea that words and images could be shared in real time, across continents, and using devices that could be held in the palm of a hand? The trials on Rathlin have ramifications in today's world of fast messaging and information sharing, of the debate around privacy and the potential loss of it, of the natural suspicion that inevitably accompanies advances in technology. But when I think about the historical wireless experiments on Rathlin, I think first of all about the people there and the abiding impact that that early visit from strangers must have made on all their lives.

When I was writing THE WATCH HOUSE, I had a very keen sense of the legacy of the story for Nuala's future, fictional descendants. The early drafts included an additional narrative around the arrival on the island of a girl who has been left a cottage in her mother's will. In the end, I moved away from that storyline, but the presence of that contemporary figure stayed with me and after I'd finished the novel, I began to write a short story. GLASS GIRL is the story of Ella. In my head she is the great-great-granddaughter of Nuala Byrne. The story was originally published in FEMALE LINES: NEW WRITING BY WOMEN FROM NORTHERN IRELAND (New Island Books, Dublin, 2017).

# Glass Girl

There is something wrong with my sister, Evangeline. She is thin and light for a ten-year-old, and her toes turn in when she walks; she carries the wrist of one hand in the other, as if it is not a part of her, as if she is taking care of it for someone else. Her elbows stick out either side of her body and her ears stick out either side of her head. Her fingers and toes are long and bony, her legs look like they are not fit to support her, could not be capable of lifting and moving the thick-soled black shoes she needs to wear, that fix her to the ground like weights. Her pale green eyes are over-sensitive to light. She has a sensation, she says, from time to time, of something feathery brushing over her skin. I cannot prevent the thought that these could be wings that have never grown. I find it hard to shake the idea that my sister is a creature tethered to the earth, who was originally designed for flight.

The doctors have said that Evangeline needs to strengthen the muscles of her legs, that walking on sand in bare feet is good for this. With sand, they say, there is the correct balance of support and give. This does not sound like a medical treatment to me, but every dry day since I have come to the coast to stay with my father, I have taken my sister to walk on the strand. We set out from the house and make our way along the cliff path past the high smell of salt and drying seaweed and down the graffitied concrete steps that lead to the beach.

My father is Evangeline's father, and Catherine is her mother. My mother is dead. Evangeline is my half-sister, but I won't say 'half' about Evangeline. She is completely whole to me. Ours is a complicated story but that is just the way of things.

Evangeline knows the names of all the wild flowers and on our walk she tries to teach them to me: birdsfoot trefoil, marsh marigold, forget-me-nots, wild thyme. She won't allow me to pick them to use them in my work. She says they are where they ought to be and I must learn to leave them alone. If the tide is out when we reach the strand head, we take off our shoes and go searching in the rock pools for shrimp and limpets and hermit crabs and I photograph them for her. This is the only form of capture she will allow. If the tide is in, we climb into the dunes and lie on our backs with the roar of the sea behind us and listen for the rattle of magpies and make shapes out of the clouds overhead.

On the days when it's too wet to walk to the beach, when the rain bounces off the tarmac on the road and drums a steady rhythm on the roof of the house, Evangeline sits, cross-legged on the living room floor with her headphones pinning flat her ears and cuts photographs out of magazines and sticks them into scrapbooks. Mostly, these are pictures of plants and flowers and sea life and she asks me to pronounce the names for her and repeats them over and over until she has memorised every one. At night when she asks for a story, I tell her one of my mother's, the ones that she used to carry about in her head, that she got from her mother and grandmother; legends of treasure sunken in moss holes, of children stolen by fairies, stories from the island.

'You're so good with Evangeline,' Catherine says, but the truth is that Evangeline is good with me. Since my mother's funeral, the world has been blurred at the edges, altered in a way I can't explain. I am unsure, when I speak, of the right order of words. My voice sounds overloud in my head. I cannot find the language to talk to my father.

'You've had a shock,' Catherine says. 'It will take time to get over it.' But Evangeline seems to understand, Evangeline who said when I came here: 'Don't worry, my Ella, we'll look after you now.'

Today, Evangeline has an appointment at the hospital and I have the day to myself. 'Take the bike,' Catherine says. 'See a bit of the coast.'

Outside, my father unclamps the child's seat from behind the saddle of the old yellow bicycle, pumps up the tyres, says, 'Good as new. But I could drop you somewhere, pick you up, if you want?' He looks to the west, to the grey bank of mist that has hung for hours over the Barmouth, the flattened stretch of water beginning to silver and stir in the bay, a trace of damp in the air. I toy with the raindrop of green glass in my pocket, polish it under my thumb, check that the key is still attached. I remember the soft orange bulb the glass made in the gas flame when I worked it, the molten possibilities of it before it hardened and cooled. And still I cannot speak to him.

'There's a mist coming in,' my father says, not looking at me.

Evangeline trips out of the house, followed by Catherine, takes hold of my father's hand and lowers herself into the bicycle seat balanced on the ground. She sits in with her bony knees up either side of her ears, intent on braiding the safety straps. Without looking up she says, 'Bring me back a picture, my Ella.' I reach down, run the dark ponytail of her hair through my hand.

'We won't be long,' my father is saying. 'I'll phone you when we're done.' My phone is in my raincoat pocket. I don't tell him that I've switched it off.

'Will you cross to the island?' says Catherine.

He shoots her a look of alarm. 'It's too far, surely?' he says. He avoids all talk of my mother, as if mentioning her will crack me in two. And I can tell that he's still angry with me, about Liam, about everything that happened.

'I'll see how I go,' I say to Catherine, and heft my

rucksack on my back and straddle the bike, and blow a kiss to Evangeline. When I push off all three of them wave to me from the drive of the house.

It feels strange to cycle away without Evangeline's thin arms around my middle, without the slight weight and wobble of her in the seat behind. All summer we've toured the cycle paths, into the swimming pool in town for her water exercises, over to the amusements in Portrush where she is transfixed by the 2p machines. 'Just one more, my Ella,' she says each time we drop a coin through the slot, and she holds her breath as the tray sweeps forward, and squeals at the anticipated cascade of metal into the scoop below.

It's the tail end of August and already the colours are starting to turn. I follow the tourist route, past the golf links and serried caravans that nose the road around the coast. At Dunluce the limestone is streaked with the green and black of old watercourses; a marker in the sea beyond the ruined castle surfaces like the spire of a drowned church. Beyond Dunseverick I have to dismount when the climb proves too much for the old bike's gears, my thighs and rear beginning to ache. At Portnareevy the sun breaks through and I pull in to the viewing point. The fields around are dotted with black-bound rolls of silage. Across the water I can just see the chalk cliffs of the island picked out in the sun, green uplands above, the dark hollow of the bay, the northern side cloaked in mist. It's too far for me to see the tower of the church, the crooked white headstones where my mother is buried along with her mother and father. I take my camera from the rucksack, aim it at the white tip of the lighthouse in the east, the blue peak of Kintyre beyond.

My father moved here when he married Catherine, a year or two before Evangeline was born but until this summer, I've only ever spent weekends here. When I was younger he travelled to see me in Belfast, fitted visits in around site meetings and client appointments, collected and dropped me at the door. After he left, my mother and father spoke rarely. They texted when they needed to make arrangements about me. When he asked after her, I said she was fine. I am guilty, I know, of years of deceit, of the show I kept up to hide her drinking from him, from everyone. We were a good team. She went out to work every weekday; I never missed a day at school. Monday to Friday she was a model citizen. She'd wave me off on Saturday morning and be nearly sober when I got home on Sunday night. By the time my father figured things out I was old enough to choose where to live for myself.

'You have to leave, Ella,' he said. 'You're not responsible for her. You have to think of yourself.'

'Like you did?' I said and that ended the discussion. That was unfair, I know. She didn't drink when he lived with us. It had gotten worse over the years. The truth is, it was easier for me to stay and to worry than it was to worry and go. At least if I was there, I thought, I could keep an eye on her, monitor the level of intake. In the end I failed even to do that.

My father bought me this camera for my twenty-first birthday, turned up at the glass workshop in the College on the day, too tall and tidy in his suit. It had been weeks since I'd seen him, since the last argument about my mother, about what should be done. I'd stopped answering his calls. He walked in at the point when Liam had been helping me remove some pieces from the annealing oven. Liam moved away too quickly when my father appeared, busied himself with another group of students. I saw my father note it. I did not introduce them.

'Where have you been?' he said.

'Here,' I said. 'Working.' He glanced at Liam. He didn't seem to like what he saw.

'I've booked us a table,' he said, 'for tonight.' I didn't speak. 'That is, if you're free?'

'I'm not.'

'Tomorrow then?'

'You're not supposed to be in here,' I said, running my hands over the glass pieces, checking for fissures, for flaws.

'Okay,' he said. 'If that's the way you want it. Happy Birthday, Ella,' and he slid a gift bag under the work-bench and left.

I couldn't believe it when I saw the camera; I hadn't known how much I'd wanted one. I was sorry I'd been hard on him. It wasn't all his fault; most of it was my mother's, I knew that. It was just easier to blame him since he wasn't there.

He has been talking lately about my plans for the future. He says there's a job in his office, junior draughtsperson; he could teach me the ropes.

'Give her some time,' Catherine says when he starts to talk about this, but time is not going to make his offer any more attractive to me. We have had to let the Belfast house go. The landlord found a new tenant; all my materials are packed into boxes in my father's house. But as I look out from Portnareevy, I am thinking of a shingle shore and a bay of purple kelp; of a gravel path by a dry stone wall overgrown with fuchsia. I am thinking of a red tin roof and a whitewashed chimney. I am thinking of a gable that is rendered with shells and rounded pieces of bottle glass, brown and blue, that glint when they catch the sun. I am thinking of a blackened hearth and the smell of old soot and a byre that could be a workshop: my mother's home on the island.

When I first tried my hand at glass-making, I was mesmerised by the process, the movement of the glass rod in the flame, the change in the colour through blue, white, yellow, green. The rod that, moments earlier, would have shattered had it been dropped on the ground became a molten rope which could be manipulated, balled, drawn out thin as a thread. I learned how to blow glass tubing until it ballooned into a globe; learned how to turn and shape it in the flame, hollow it out with a knife. I watched, entranced, as gravity did the work of modeller. I pinched the ends with tweezers, nipped off the unwanted stalk, my favourite part, closing off the glass. I attempted snow globes but as I experimented, the glass vessels grew narrower so that they began to resemble not made but grown things. After that, nothing I created had a base. None of my work stood up by itself.

Liam became my tutor in final year. When he saw what I'd made, he directed me towards the work of Stankard. I studied the flameworker's exquisite paperweights: lifelike glass honeycombs with hovering bees; pink-petalled tea roses complete with stamen; haws and blueberries, their stems intact. But I was surprised to find that in his work there was too much artifice for me. I did not want the solid. Weight was the opposite of what I was striving for.

'There is no point in making a thing,' Liam said to us, 'if there is no emotional risk to it. You need to be prepared to make yourself fragile. You need to be afraid to expose some breakable part of yourself.' I knew he was married but when he said that I didn't care. I'd have risked anything to have him.

I began to use the glass as a thin-walled cell to house the things I found. In one elongated piece I inserted a dried mimosa bud, fused the organic stem into the closure with a molten string of glass. In another I placed a pine cone, then a chestnut burr, a dead beetle, a dried moth from my windowsill. My heart fluttered when I reheated and squeezed the openings shut, attaching glass tendrils, colouring the glass, until it was impossible to tell where the natural ended and the made began. The pieces I created for my final exhibition I had to suspend by wires from a frame. They looked like unopened shells, seedpods, egg sacs, discarded skins.

'What are they for?' my father said the night of the final exhibition. I wanted to say that 'use' didn't come into it, but I knew what his response would be to that. I don't know how to tell him that this is something I need to do; that it may help me to find what I can no longer find in language, that finding it might make the world bearable again.

'They're beautiful,' Catherine said when she saw them. 'They look like they've grown there. Like they were meant to be.'

'They're sad,' Evangeline said. 'Why are they sad?'

'How do you know stuff?' I said to her, taking her small hand.

'I see through you, my Ella,' she said.

My mother didn't make it to the exhibition opening. 'It's there for a few weeks, isn't it darling? I'll go when it's quieter, when I can take it all in.' She'd started drinking before I left the house.

After the reception, when the guests had all gone, Liam joined the final year students in the pub. He stayed apart from me most of the night but I was aware of his every move, the lowering of his mouth to the glass when he drank, his hand reaching for the phone in his back pocket, his eyes on me when I rose. I knew where this was headed. I could afford to wait. The others drifted off, some to a nightclub, some to another bar. Liam's flat was a ten minute walk away. 'I've got it to myself tonight,' he said.

His work was scattered on high shelves throughout the rooms, bizarrely shaped glass objects, comic strip characters welded to glass lava, experimental forms. We kissed on the living room sofa, abandoned our coffee cups and climbed the carpeted stairs. It was hard not to feel a pang of guilt at the toys strewn around the living room, the small pile of shoes inside the front door. In the bedroom he took a towel from a linen basket, laid it out on the quilt over the bed. There wasn't much spontaneity about it: the sex, through a fug of beer and shots, was joyless in the end. In the kitchen afterwards, pouring myself a glass of water, I uncurled the dog-eared corner of a crayoned drawing taped to the fridge door.

'Don't touch anything,' Liam said from behind me and slipped his arms around my waist. 'Come back to bed.' I stayed the night; thought I'd give my mother something to worry about, supposing she was conscious enough for that. In the morning Liam woke me, said he was sorry: I'd have to leave; he wasn't sure what time his wife would be back.

I walked through the city in the thin light before the buses had begun to run, past the still-shuttered shops and the littered pavements, the spoils of the night before. I'd never been out that early, had never seen the city in that light. I followed the street sweepers brushing the kerbs from City Hall up to Bradbury Place. On Botanic, a train rumbled under the road. I turned into our own car-lined street, twisted the key in the lock of the front door: my mother's heeled shoes in the hall, her bag on the ground beside them. I climbed the stairs, headed for my bedroom, but the door to her room was open, the smell of stale alcohol seeping out, the smell of vomit too. I pushed the door wide. She was lying, face-down on a dried pool of sick on top of the bed, still wearing the spaghetti-strap dress from the night before, open-mouthed, shut-eyed, blue-tinged, cold to the touch.

At Portnareevy I take the phone out of my pocket and switch it on. There are three missed calls from my father and a text that reads, 'Whereabouts are you? We'll pick you up?' I slip the phone back into my pocket. As I climb back on the bicycle, I see a white line stretch across the grey water: the wake of the car ferry crossing the Sound, almost at the mainland now. I have twenty minutes to make the harbour.

From here, the journey is easier; I can feel the gradual descent into the ferry town. The road winds through conifers. Past the slender trunks of the trees I can see the boat nearing the shore: glimpses of the vehicles on board, the mist closing in behind. The air dampens. Further on I hear the rattle of chains as the boat moors, the scrape of metal on concrete when the ridged ramp is lowered onto the quay, the sound of engines moving off. I freewheel down the steep hill towards the town.

I am rounding a bend on the sloping road when a white pick-up truck speeds towards me, a man at the wheel in a baseball cap, music blaring from the wound-down window. I brake and put my feet to the ground, pull in to the verge but as it passes, the truck hits a pothole, there is a rattle in the back, a jolt towards the tailgate, and the gate bursts open, landing two wooden crates with a crash on the tarmac a few feet behind me. I turn in the saddle to shout after the driver but he is hurtling along oblivious to what he's left behind on the road. In seconds the truck is out of sight, the engine whining into the distance. The road grows quiet; there is no other traffic; the mist rolls in.

I angle the bike into the hedge, ease the pack off my shoulders and walk back up the road. The crates have fallen right before the bend, will be invisible to drivers from the town side until they are on top of them. Closer, I can see that they've both burst open; that their dark contents are spilling over the road. I can't make out what it is at first: coal, maybe, or turf, but as I near the spill, I see that the dark mass is moving of its own accord; the crates are heaving with something alive. The road is crawling with crabs. The brown creatures scuttle out sideways and spread across the highway, legs scissoring, blue pincers raised, their red eyes shuttling from side to side: velvet swimmers from the island, the most vicious kind there are. I shiver in the cool air. The crabs make for the hedges on both sides of the road. I watch as the first of them scurries into the grass and then I remember my camera. Evangeline will love this: escapee sea creatures, her kind of story. I am standing on the verge in the fog, wondering if they will make it back down the cliffs to the sea, photographing the strange retreat, when I feel my phone buzz in my pocket. I know who it is without looking at the screen.

'Ella?' my father says. 'Where are you?' I look through the trees towards the sea and down the hill to the town, but everything has been swallowed up by fog. I could be marooned on a cloud, or on an island the size of what I can see. I feel the panic begin to rise in me. 'Ella?' he says again. 'Ella? Are you okay? Just tell me where you are.' The air around shimmers, the earth makes a fractional shift. I have the sudden conviction that I have stood here before, looking down at the sloping road, at the smashed crates, the circling fog, the escaping crabs, impossible though that is. Then I hear another voice behind my father's, Evangeline's, quiet, distracted by something, only half-engaged: cutting out or pasting in or colouring at the table.

The moment passes, the world realigns.

'Ask my Ella if she got me a picture,' she says. 'Tell her I'm waiting for her.'

'Ella?' my father's voice again, walking away from my sister now, trying to disguise his concern. 'Ella, please, tell me what's happening.'

A sound escapes me, a laugh or a cry; I can't be certain which. 'You wouldn't believe it,' I hear myself say, surprised at the sound of my own voice. 'Tell Evangeline I've got her a picture. Tell her I'll see her soon.'

I slip the phone into my pocket; pack the camera back in my bag. I cross the road to where the crates lie and drag them into the verge. There isn't a single creature left. The mist is beginning to thin. Through the trees I can see the ferry back out of the harbour and turn around in the bay. I feel for the key in my pocket, the fob of smooth polished glass. It's too late now to go to the island. I will go another day. I pick up the bike and climb back on and I cycle through the thinning mist in the direction from which I came.

# THE BUTTERFLY CABINET

## BERNIE McGILL

'Utterly compelling . . . a haunted tale, pitch-perfect in tone'
*Marie Claire*

On a remote estate in the north of Ireland, a little girl dies and the community is quick to condemn her mother, Harriet Ormond. Now, after seventy years, Maddie McGlade, a former nanny at the house, knows the time has come to reveal her own role in the events of that day.

From Maddie's reminiscences and Harriet's long-concealed diaries emerges an unforgettable story of motherhood and betrayal, and of two women, mistress and servant, inextricably connected by an extraordinary secret.

'McGill has the ability to enter the brain and heart of her characters' Julian Fellowes, *Guardian* Books of the Year

'Dramatic . . . enthralling and beautifully written'
*Good Housekeeping*

'An absorbing story of marriage, motherhood and murder'
*Woman and Home*

ISBN 978 1 4722 4021 7

TINDER
PRESS